BELLY THROUGH THE BRUSH

By
Omar Z. Shareef

Copyright © 2021 by Omar Z. Shareef

All rights reserved.
This book is protected under the copyright laws.

Copyright Registration Number/Date:
TXu002237219 / 2021-01-02

Chapter 1:
The Train is Coming!

"No, don't put that over there," Mr. Sun Wong said, gesturing to the stagecoach with a gloved hand and sighing in exasperation. He pulled his hat off and wiped his head as he looked at the whirlwind of activity all around him.

"Mr. Wong, where should I—"

Sun Wong interrupted the man, one of the many Chinese laborers en route to Rattlefort, Arizona, pointing straight at the train without looking. "What do you think?" he replied in Cantonese. "Get it loaded already, we need to leave now!"

"Yes, Mr. Wong," the laborer replied, looking down at the crate and frowning. It shifted in his hands as if something was inside it. The laborer hurried off, navigating past busy railroad workers and stacks of luggage, building supplies and tools. The train's chief engineer was making his way through, a ruddy-faced man with a thick beard, passing by a couple immigrant workers moving a heavy chest inside. The train station in San Francisco echoed from the sounds of voices and the bangs and clatter of freight being loaded.

"We need to be off soon," the engineer said to Mr. Wong, scratching at his salt-and-pepper beard nervously.

"We're just about ready, Mr. Wilkins," Sun Wong replied, switching back to English, and set his hat back on his head. "Within the hour, I expect."

"Very good," Mr. Wilkins muttered, rubbing his leather gloves together. "It's just, I heard tell of the Wolfe Gang prowling around along the railroads. The sooner the better, if we aim to avoid—"

"Never you mind them, Mr. Wilkins," Sun Wong replied. "This is the era of progress, is it not? I wouldn't trouble myself over a few bandits if I were you. It's a straight shot to Rattlefort, after all, and that's as peaceful a town as you'll ever find."

***

Jake Mullens wiped his bare head in the noonday sun, hefting the bundle on his shoulder, and tossed it into his family's wooden wagon. He took a long breath and stood still for a moment. It was a pitiful sight, to see just how few crops they had left after the raid by the Wolfe Gang, but there wasn't much else the family could do besides take what they had to market.

Belly Through the Brush

At least it's just me, Jake thought, spitting on the ground. *Ma and Pa can get by alright.* He turned back, scanning the horizon, an expanse of yellowed grass and dirt. A light breeze blew, but it did little against the baking sun. To his surprise, his mother and father were approaching, having made the trek outside their simple house and down the road. Jake approached his horse and ruffled his mane as he waited.

"I told you I had it taken care of," Jake said sullenly as his parents approached. He straightened, wishing he hadn't said it quite like that. *But I'm nineteen now! I can handle selling our goods in town.*

"We just wanted to see you off," his mother, Dorothy Mullens, said first. Her lined face crinkled as she smiled, but Jake noticed she was worried. "With the Wolfe Gang around, you know... well, a mother gets to worrying."

"It's fine," he said. "Rattlefort's just down the way. It ain't like I'm riding for New York City."

His father, Lawrence Mullens, chuckled. He came in close, clapping Jake on the back affectionately. "Like we'd let you go to a den of thieves like that! Oh, I know you'll be fine, you just know how your mother gets."

"You see any sign of trouble, you just go riding away," she said in a tone that brooked no opposition. "You hear?"

"Yes, Ma."

"And give Ulysses here a sugar cube when you're done," she added, patting the flank of their stolid horse. "It's going to be a lean winter, what with the Wolfe Gang burning half our crops down, but we still need to take care of Ulysses. He's a good horse, and he'll see us through."

"Yes, Ma."

***

"And lo, the angels did sing," Percy "Preacher" McGowan called out with a cackle, twisting off his horse to spit tobacco juice into the dusty Utah plains. Jimmy Wolfe grunted, hearing the twisted clanking of metal and steady rocking sounds of a train coming down the line. Dashing toward them was another horseman, waving his black hat in the air. Jimmy's little brother Billy Wolfe.

"The train is coming!" he shouted out.

"Ah, shut your piehole," Rawhide Cooper said, inching his dappled horse forward, gloved hand resting on the nearest of his revolvers. "We can all hear it, Billy."

The horseman slowed, pulling up beside the others, and looked over at Jimmy Wolfe. "So, what do you think, Boss?"

The gang leader squinted into the distance as his hands fell to the two pistols at his sides: Agatha and Delilah. Those two had never failed him yet. "What do I think?" Jimmy asked emotionlessly, and then a slow smile spread across his broad features. "I think we're

Belly Through the Brush

about to make a killing. Grab your guns, boys, that train is ours!"

He spurred his horse forward, galloping down the dusty ridge, and the rest of the Wolfe Gang hollered as they joined along with him. Percy slid on a blue, spotted handkerchief he'd been using as a mask—Billy and Rawhide doing the same—but Jimmy Wolfe kept his face unmasked. It was a clean face, by bandit standards, with bushy black eyebrows and a somewhat contemplative expression covered with stubble. Jimmy looked just like he did on the wanted posters and took more than a little pride in that, too.

He bounced up in down in the saddle, taking his slate gray hat off and waving over to the fifth member of their gang, sheltering under a tree beside the tracks. Doc Otis rose to his feet, acknowledging Jimmy Wolfe's signal, and tossed a burning torch from his campfire onto the bundle of wood and debris blocking the railroad. Soaked in oil, the debris erupted into flames, black smoke rising high. Doc turned and kicked an unmoving form, shouting something unheard over the distance.

Rawhide snorted. "Is Sam drunk again?"

"When is he not?" Billy asked, as Doc hauled Sam Reeves to his feet. Drunk as he might be, he was a hell of a shot, and followed the older man as they got into position right above a boulder that overlooked the train.

The steady chugging of the engine turned into a squeal now, the engineer doubtless spotting the obstruction up ahead, and the train slowed as it came near. Jimmy Wolfe's party of outlaws had reared up beside the railroad, and Jimmy whipped around, brandishing his two pistols.

"We'll stick 'em up here as they stop," he said, "and give 'em chase if they look to keep going! Ride alongside and board the train if it comes to that!"

The others nodded, aside from Percy McGowan. "Ah, Jimmy, my train leaping days are behind me now. I'll cover you from my horse, but—"

Jimmy spat. "So what good are you to me, then?"

Percy frowned. "Ah, now don't say that. The good book says—"

"Get your guns ready!" Jimmy Wolfe shouted, levelling his pistols at the oncoming train. It was slowing now, the chief engineer leaning out to look at them, eyes widened as he spotted the bandits. "You'll want to stop that, sir!"

The man nodded, ducking back inside, but instead of slowing down, the engine began to speed up. Jimmy swore, jerking the reins of his horse, now riding alongside the train. Sam and Doc Otis fired from their position on the boulder, bullets smashing into the glass and plinking off the metal of the train, but the slowly moving train just barreled through the burning obstacles.

"I'll cover you, Jimmy!" Percy called out, firing away with his revolver. Jimmy saw a few surprised faces peering out, Chinese laborers by the look of them, and then reeling back as they saw the bandits riding alongside. Rawhide was darting ahead, spurring his horse faster and faster, already rising in his saddle. *That's the spirit, Rawhide,* Jimmy thought as his horse came alongside. *Get on in!*

With a sudden leap, Rawhide Cooper flung himself onto the ground, his horse slowing. Jimmy hauled his horse in close, gripping the saddle horn while he raised his right foot free, turning awkwardly as he faced the open train car. Gritting his teeth, he leaped forward, landing heavily on the metal floor. He rose to his feet, whipping his guns up, and stepped into the engine room.

"Stop the train!" Rawhide was shouting, already sticking his shotgun in the face of the stammering chief engineer. The man hauled down on a brake, then shuffled to the side, eyes darting to the ground.

"What's your name?" Jimmy Wolfe demanded.

"Wilkins, sir," the chief engineer replied, looking to be on the verge of sobbing. The wheels of the train were squealing under them, and Jimmy had to shout just to be heard.

"You're an idiot, Mr. Wilkins, but no one needs to die here. Just stop the train and keep everyone nice and peaceful. We'll take what we want and let you go on to wherever it is you're heading."

"Yes, sir. It's just about stopped, sir."

Jimmy Wolfe grunted, feeling the truth of his words as the carriage slowed under him, and turned to leave the engine room. From the gap between the engine car and the first carriage he could make out a vast expanse of reddish dirt dotted with the occasional cactus. Then his little brother Billy Wolfe, awkwardly clambering aboard. Jimmy stooped over, offering a hand, and yanked him to his feet.

"Well ain't you the acrobat," Jimmy said. "Preacher getting the horses?"

"Soon as he's done shooting out the windows," Cooper said, rising to his feet, sporadic pistol shots breaking the silence.

Jimmy Wolfe hefted his two guns, Agatha and Delilah, bracing for the moment he'd burst through. "You two boys ready? Back me up."

"You got it, Boss."

"I'm with you."

Jimmy Wolfe strode forward, sliding the first door open and whipping his pistols up. He stared into rows of seated Chinese laborers.

"No one make a move," he said, striding forward, his two henchmen close behind. "Just keep put. Ah, if you can even understand me," he muttered, already moving through and on to the second car. Agatha covered the left and Delilah the right as he stomped his way through the passenger cars. Finally, he passed the last compartment—a dead laborer slumped by the broken window—and then opened up the next door. Jimmy grinned. They had reached the train cars where the building supplies were stored. He waved the others through, then shut the door behind him. *They're not fighting back, but you never really know how it goes. Some folk might get stupid ideas.* Already the rest of the gang had arrived, ransacking the supplies as they moved on. Percy rummaged around, opening luggage and grimacing, moving on to another chest.

"You know, you killed a few of the laborers," Billy pointed out after a moment, rummaging through the supplies. "Didn't have to."

"It's the nature of the business," Percy grunted.

"It ain't like they were armed," Billy said, examining a pocket watch, and tossing it into his satchel.

"They ain't Christian neither," Percy said, "so don't worry yourself." He grinned as he opened another chest. "Gold! Hey Jimmy, take a look!"

Jimmy Wolfe moved over, bending down to look, and smiling at the gleam of the metal. "We're loading this one up for sure." He turned and looked at the rest of the compartment. Luggage chests, a dozen crates, and an assortment of tools and railroad equipment. A horse whinnied from outside the train—Doc with his two horses and empty stagecoach, Sam stepping into the open compartment and smelling like a brewery.

"H-how's the h-haul, Boss?" he asked with a belch.

"It's good. In fact..." Jimmy glanced over the compartment, "let's just load all the crates, and some of the tools if we have room. It's about time we left, and you never really know what might be in these crates."

Chapter 2:
Rattlefort

"Hey Boss, how about we have the workers here load everything up?" Doc Otis asked, gesturing a thumb back at the passenger compartment behind them. "That's what they're here for, anyway."

"You're a wise man, Doc," Jimmy replied, his gruff voice giving way to genuine amusement.

"I'll get 'em for you, Jimmy," Billy said, eagerly rising to his feet. "Slam my pistol in their face if I have to."

"Sure thing," Jimmy replied, eyeing his younger brother and Doc. They were a strange combination, those two. Jimmy could always rely on Doc for good advice, but his little brother Billy was another thing entirely. A bit of a coward, if Jimmy was being honest, but the younger man loved to throw around the Wolfe name and wasn't at all lacking in enthusiasm. Jimmy jerked his head over. "Well, get 'em over here."

He paced over to the chests, ignoring the shouting in the passenger compartment as Doc and Billy marshalled the laborers together, and stepped out to look at the stagecoach maneuvering in beside the train. Sam Reeves had the chief engineer kneeling in the dirt and mumbling a prayer. Sam belched and nodded as Jim approached, greeting him with his usual stutter.

"Doc said to k-keep an eye on h-him. D-don't want any t-t-trouble."

"Good thinking," Jimmy replied. "Mr. Wilkins, was it? Sit tight here while we get loaded and then beat it once we're gone. Think you can do that?"

"Yes, sir," Mr. Wilkins mumbled. Jimmy turned to see a dozen press-ganged Chinese laborers, one wiping away a bloody nose, hauling chests onto the stagecoach.

"Squeeze it in nice and tight there," Jimmy said, gesturing with Agatha. They worked fast, cramming the stagecoach with chests, luggage, and even a few tools. Billy kept watch, grinning merrily, swiveling his gun from one to the other.

Finally they stepped back, eyes downcast, the stagecoach just about full to bursting. Sam clambered on to the coach, looking over, the reins of the coach's two sturdy horses loose in his hands.

"Let's go!" Jimmy shouted, waving for the others to mount up. He climbed on his own horse, keeping

Belly Through the Brush

pace with the rattling stagecoach, then speeding off ahead of it. He glanced back after a while. The train's engine was already puffing away once again. Percy spurred his horse over and looked up at Jimmy.

"Let's head home to Rattlefort, Jimmy."

"What, all the way back to Arizona?" He whistled. "That's a hard bit of riding, especially after a long day's work."

"Gets us clear of the law, Jimmy, and Madam Josephine has the finest cathouse in all the West."

Jimmy grunted. "Well, it's up there with the best of them." He squinted up at the noonday sun. "Ah… they won't be expecting our return so soon after our farm raids, I suppose. And we can lie low a while." He nodded; the decision made. "Let's do it, then! No time like the present, gentlemen," he said, wheeling his horse around.

***

Jake Mullens hunched forward in his family's wagon, the outline of Rattlefort seeming to appear out of nowhere, a patchwork settlement of wood and adobe. Still, it was home—or close to it, anyway. Jake straightened in a moment as he saw a flash of motion, unconsciously beaming as he saw an angel step out of the nearby shop. She glanced over, her golden curls bouncing.

"Lucille!" Jake said, grinning over. "I haven't seen you in a while."

"Oh, hello Jake," she replied, seeming distracted.

"Would you like to share a pie with me?" he babbled. "Mrs. Orren makes the most wonderful blueberry pie, and whenever I'm in town I like to—"

"I'm not hungry," Lucille replied. "Besides, I've got errands to finish. I'll see you around, Jake," she said, moving past.

"I hope so," Jake said, "maybe another time we could... well, alright," he concluded lamely, as she sped through town.

Lucille herself hurried along back to her mother's establishment, thoughts swirling in her head. *The Wolfe Gang is in town! And after what they did to the Mullens...* she shook her head, fixing a smile to her face as she pushed the door open. The Wolfe Gang was lounging inside, a few prostitutes laughing at their idiotic jokes, and Lucille hurried up to the counter.

"Here's the soap and lye," she said, uncomfortably aware of Rawhide Cooper staring at her lecherously from a few paces away. Her mother nodded, glancing over at Rawhide, her disapproval masked by her professionalism.

"Let's get you sorted, Rawhide. Will Goldie be to your liking this evening?"

"No, ma'am," Rawhide replied, glancing over at the room, his voice dropping huskily. "Least, not yet. Is Pearl around?"

"Oh, she's just upstairs," Madam Josephine said, then glanced over to her daughter as Rawhide stamped up the stairs. "Clean out the washbasin up there, Lucille."

Lucille grimaced but began trailing Rawhide as he walked up the stairs.

"Remember, Rawhide," Jimmy called out from the main room. He put a finger to his lips as Rawhide looked back.

"Yeah, yeah, of course, Boss," Rawhide said, turning and half-running up the stairs. Lucille hurried to catch up. "Pearl, you in there!"

"Why, a gentleman caller!" a voice rang out from one of the rooms. "And at so late an hour!" She tittered, and Rawhide chuckled, making his way into the room. Lucille rolled her eyes as she moved past. *I'll just get this cleaned as quickly as I can,* Lucille thought, scrubbing away at the washbasin in the upstairs restroom.

"What have you been up to, Rawhide?" Pearl asked from the nearby room.

"Robbed a train!"

Lucille paused mid-scrub, blinking in surprise. *I know they're crooks and bandits but admitting to a crime like that...* she shook her head, scrubbing away once again.

"Oh..." Pearl managed.

"Ah! Shouldn't have told you that. Should not have told you that," Rawhide muttered. "Don't tell anyone, you hear?"

"Of course," Pearl said. Lucille splashed a bucket of water, scrubbing away as the grime washed away. "I won't tell."

"Good," Rawhide's gruff voice could barely be heard. "Cause if you do…"

"Never mind that," Pearl cooed. "How long will you be staying here?"

"Jimmy's given us a couple hours," Rawhide said, "and I aim to use them!"

***

"And one sugar cube," Jake Mullens said, finishing his business with the shopkeeper. The crops didn't sell for much, but he supposed they'd make it work. Somehow.

"Awful sorry to hear about the raid a few days back," the shopkeeper said, adjusting his eyeglasses. "Please convey my warmest wishes to your family."

"I will," Jake replied, stepping out into Rattlefort. Dusk had settled, and there wasn't much traffic about, just a young woman walking down the street in a bit of a hurry. Jake blinked. *Is that…*

"Jake! I hoped to see you still here."

Jake grinned. "Lucille! So did you want to—"

"Listen, I know your family farm got raided by the Wolfe Gang a while back," she said, all in a rush, "and they're in town! Not only that, but I heard they robbed a train, and they must have everything they've taken back at their hideout. I know where it is, too!" She paused, brushing her hair back. "It's just, there's no law here really, and... and I thought you'd want to know."

Jake blinked, his joy at seeing Lucille shifting into a cold, seething rage. He had vowed revenge on the Wolfe Gang but never really expected much to come of it. But now?

"Show me where it is," he said in a cold voice.

***

"I can't go any farther," Lucille had whispered at the turnpike just outside Rattlefort, a few miles away from the hideout. "Just follow that trail until you see three huge boulders resting together. They'll be expecting me back," she had said, clambering off the wagon.

Jake had mumbled something to her, though his thoughts were a blur, as he steered Ulysses down the trail. *What am I going to do, exactly? Lucille said they were all at the cathouse for a couple hours... but what if they come back?* Jake gritted his teeth. *It doesn't matter. They came after my family's stuff, so I'll go after theirs.*

The three boulders came into view before too long, Jake gently steering Ulysses off the road and dropping down. "Here you go, boy," he said, offering up the sugar cube. Despite the tension and the cool of the night, Jake smiled as he felt the horse's soft warmth on his palm.

Then he turned and made his way into the night. The flickering of a torch caught his attention, and Jake slowed, crouching low as he paced through the sand. The boulders were on a gently sloping hill, and now that he was up close he could see a rusted tin roof at the top, with a crude wood wall covering the gaps.

Aside from the entrance, just up ahead.

Jake crept forward, looking to his left and right. It looked like the train had disgorged its most valuable contents all in one piece; it was a mess of chests and crates and shovels and half-opened liquor bottles. Jake strode past a few, not bothering to be silent now, picking up a bottle of whiskey and examining it a moment. He whistled, then set it down, sloshing against a small crate. There was a soft, faint mewling sound from within, and Jake stepped back in astonishment.

The sound was followed by a snort in the distance and then a burst of coughing. *There's someone in here!* Instinctively, Jake took cover behind the crate. Up close, he definitely sensed a creature was inside… but more importantly, who else was here? Jake risked a peek up.

A man lumbered up from his sleeping pad, rubbing his mussed-up hair, the gleam of a crucifix on his neck. He looked to be about forty, by Jake's reckoning. The man groaned as he hauled himself to his feet. After a moment, he spat to clear his throat, and then staggered over to the gap in the wooden wall. He whistled, the cheery noise startling as it broke the silence, and stepped out into the night.

Belly Through the Brush

Jake lost no time in sliding open the crate and stared as the creature seemed to unfurl itself. *Is that... a snake?* A winding, reptilian head peeked up at him, and then two tiny wings fluttered behind him. *A dragon? No way!* Jake slid the crate back on. His decision was made.

Grabbing the crate under his arm, he hurried toward where he'd entered, away from the unsuspecting bandit. He slowed as he passed a bottle of whiskey, yanking it up, then snuck through the entrance. Jake jogged away, then began running along the sandy ground, the black shape of Ulysses and the wagon in the distance. Rather than tossing the crate in the back, he slid it up where a passenger might sit and clambered up into position.

Softly, quietly, he spurred Ulysses away and rumbled off into the night. Jake could barely breathe for the first couple of minutes and then he slowly relaxed. His left hand tapped the crate, and he gulped, hesitating. Then he slid the crate open and gazed down. The moonlight reflected off the creature's reptilian form.

"A dragon," Jake breathed, "a real-life dragon!"

The creature made some soft chirruping sound.

"A baby dragon," Jake added. "Ah, aren't you a cutie?" He grinned down at the dragon. "You need a name, don't you, buddy? Hmm..."

Jake thought to himself as the wagon trundled onward. His family wouldn't approve, no doubt, as they were simple folk not looking to get involved with bandits and mythical creatures. His grandfather Henry would have helped him, for sure. He'd always loved adventures and animals, and he had even picked out Ulysses back when the sturdy horse was a foal.

"That's it," Jake said with a snap of his fingers. "I'll name you Henry. And… I'll find a place in the barn to put you for now."

The dragon tilted his head. "Mew?"

"Don't worry," Jake said reassuringly. "It won't be for long. And there's plenty of rats. Do you eat rats, Henry?"

Chapter 3:
Henry

"Where are the rats?" Mr. Sun Wong asked, nervous about the upcoming performance. With mechanical motions, he smoothed down his garish red and white circus performer outfit. "Feilong loves his rats."

"They're right here," Lifun Chen replied in brisk Cantonese, pointing to the barrel beside the stage.

"Good, good," Sun Wong replied to himself, smoothing his hair back and setting his red velvet hat on. The show was about to start, and he had a thousand tasks to worry about. It wasn't easy, being San Francisco's leading circus performer, but it could be quite profitable. His gymnasts were stretching in the corner, his knife thrower was tossing a few practice throws, and already the hubbub and clamor of the crowd was echoing all around them. Sun Wong smiled for a moment, enjoying the anticipation, feeling the excitement and energy all around them.

"Sir, there's been a telegraph!" Lifun Chen said, breaking his thoughts. She seemed uncharacteristically bothered by something. "You should read this."

"No time," he snapped back in Cantonese, then switched to English as he gestured at the stagehand. "Get ready to raise the curtains when I say 'bewildered!'"

The man nodded and Sun Wong slipped on his white gloves to complete the outfit. "My baton," he said, holding his right hand out. To his surprise, Lifun Chen just stood there.

"I really think you should read this telegraph, sir," she said in Cantonese, still scanning the unfurled telegraph. The two of them were fluent in English, though Lifun still had a strong accent, and Sun Wong raised an eyebrow. Usually they stuck to English when the show was about to start. After a moment she passed over the baton and he whirled it in a flourish.

Fixing a grin on his face, Sun Wong brushed through the curtains, raising a hand as polite applause broke out, the audience settling into their seats. "Ladies and gentlemen, I welcome you to my circus! We have all sorts of amazing feats to perform for you, but I know what drew most of you here. Oh yes! Our main act! Captured in the mountains of distant Tibet,

Belly Through the Brush

an amazing specimen of dragon, and it is yours to see! Prepare to be shocked, amazed, bewildered!"

Sun Wong paced to the left, the stagehand raising the curtains at the mention of the word 'bewildered,' and Sun Wong turned as the curtains began to rise. He whipped his baton toward the cage beginning to emerge under the curtains. Lifun Chen darted close.

"Terrible news. The train was raided. The Wolfe Gang, they call it. Most of our goods were stolen."

Sun Wong remained stock still. As if that was bad enough, the longer he stared, the less it made sense. The cage was empty. He stared at it for a long moment as the audience began to titter, a few boos ringing out from the confused audience. He squeezed his head, blinking as if trying to make sense of it.

"Ah, and also," Lifun Chen continued whispering. "I believe your dragon was taken as well."

"Unbelievable," he muttered, putting aside the rage, and turning to the audience with a smile somehow plastered on. "Ah... haha. How about that, folks? Our dragon is feeling a bit sick today. Well, as they say, the show must go on! Acrobrats! Let's bring out the acrobats!" Sun Wong turned and strode for the exit, rage smoldering inside him, as Lifun Chen struggled to keep up.

"All the way from Tibet and now this?" he hissed. "Lifun, book me passage aboard the next steamer to China. You're in charge of the circus now! I need to retrieve the dragon's mother..."

***

"How are you doing, buddy?" Jake asked early the next morning. He adjusted the crate from its position in the corner of the barn, illuminating the haystack near Henry's crate, along with several milk cows. Henry craned his long neck up at him. With the lantern hanging in the barn, Jake got a better look at the baby dragon. It had a leather muzzle attached to his mouth, although it seemed to breathe easy enough. *There's no fire, either. Is that just an old story?*

Jack carefully untied the muzzle and set it aside. Henry tilted his head in curiosity as Jake dropped a potato inside the crate. "That's all I can spare for now." The dragon sniffed it, then stretched his wings, and Jake stood back in concern. He glanced over, to the cows rustling inside the barn. The barn door was shut, and there weren't any windows, but still…

"Don't leave the barn, alright?" Jake asked, stepping back.

Henry chirped, flapping through the air with surprising speed, darting from one end to the other as the cows mooed in surprise. The baby dragon soared upward—and then it dove down, pouncing on a mouse as it darted away from under a hay bale. The baby dragon crunched away as it ate its captured mouse. The cows continued their mooing, their bells jangling as they lurched away, and Jake cursed at the noise.

"Easy, easy," he said, one hand on a cow's flank.

Belly Through the Brush

"What's going on in there?" came his father's voice from outside. Jake turned, swiftly muzzling Henry as he finished gobbling down the mouse, then carried the light dragon over to the haystack.

"In here," Jake hissed, stuffing the baby dragon in the haystack, brushing it over him. He stepped over to the grain, grabbing a handful, and raised it to the mouth of one of the mooing cows just as the barn door creaked open. His father, Lawrence, looked on in surprise.

"You're up early," he commented after a moment, as the cow began eating.

"Yeah... just thought I'd feed the cows."

"Huh." Lawrence tilted his head. "Usually it's a pain to get you to do that."

"Well... you know... with the Wolfe Gang burning our crops, I kinda figured we all had to help out a bit more."

Lawrence scratched his head. Finally, he shrugged. "Glad to hear it, son. Glad to hear it."

***

Lucille bustled about on her own morning chores, hauling fresh linens from the house she shared with her mother to the cathouse, just a little ways down the street. Even that short distance was enough to hear the gossiping chatter of the folks of Rattlefort spreading like wildfire.

"You see the newspaper?" someone was asking. "There was a train heist in Utah just yesterday!"

"A train robbery? You don't say."

Lucille hurried over to the cathouse, pushing the door in, nodding at Olive. The young prostitute looked fresh-faced as she picked up a few empty beer bottles sitting in the common room.

"Morning, Lucille."

"Was it a late night?" Lucille asked, pausing at the foot of the stairs.

"Late enough. We entertained those Wolfe boys until the early hours. I think Pearl is still asleep."

"I'll wake her, then," Lucille said, stepping up the stairs. It was quiet on the second story, in the daytime at least, but that was how she liked it. She did most of the cleaning up in the morning and tried to keep her distance once business got going in the evenings. "Morning, Pearl," she called out, pushing the door open. "I've got some fresh…" she fell silent, lowering the linens. "Oh no."

Pearl was lying in bed, partly uncovered, rope burn visible around her neck. Slowly, Lucille set the linens down in the corner of the room, then approached her. She felt Pearl's leg—it was ice cold. "Pearl…" she said quietly, then turned to the door. "Pearl's been killed!" she shouted. "Ma! Someone!"

Lucille gritted her teeth and looked back. The poor woman had clearly been strangled to death. *I'd only just seen her last night. Back when she and Rawhide…* Lucille clenched her fists together. *It had to have been him!*

Her mother strode into the room, holding her skirts up, frowning at Lucille. "What did you say about... oh, Pearl. Oh, oh, my poor darling." Josephine leaned in close, as footsteps echoed around them, the other women coming over to check on her. Josephine straightened, her expression grim, as the others crowded around and muttered to each other in shock.

"Raw... Rawhide," Lucille managed, her voice feeling dry, looking up at her mother. "It must have been him."

Madam Josephine nodded once.

"The Wolfe Gang is probably at Silver Springs Saloon, if they've stirred themselves out of their hideout," Olive said. "They usually go there after a big score to play poker."

"Oh, Pearl..." Goldie said, her golden curls in disarray. "I knew Rawhide was acting strangely."

"The Silver Springs Saloon," Josephine said, turning and making her way through the women. "Then that's where I'm going," she said, as she strode down the stairs. Lucille hurried after her, the other women following along as well, all chores forgotten. The Silver Springs Saloon wasn't too far away, and as the prostitutes strode through the dirt road the chatter about the train robbery died away, folks looking over in surprise at this new development. Lucille herself wouldn't normally go in the saloon, but she felt a mix of eagerness and righteous anger, and she bustled in through the doors after the others.

Josephine weaved her way past a couple of old-timers swapping jokes, ignoring the raised eyebrows of the barkeeper as he washed a mug with a filthy rag, and made a beeline for the laughing bandits ringed around a poker table.

"Jimmy Wolfe, you no-good son of a bitch," Josephine began, crossing her arms as she stood before the poker table.

Jimmy looked up in surprise. "What? What did you just say to me?"

"Your idiot cousin Rawhide here," Josephine said, nodding over to the bandit shuffling the deck of cards, surrounded by the rest of the gang, "strangled Pearl last night. That's murder—and any jury would convict." Rawhide blinked, a few cards flying loose, as his shuffle came to an uncertain halt.

Jimmy scowled and leaned back in his chair. "That's a serious accusation."

"Here's another," Madam Josephine shot back. "You lot are no-good bandits who robbed that train and are just spreading your trouble and misery down here."

Billy sputtered and half-raised himself out of his chair, a fist raised in the air, as Jimmy glared at the madam. "I'll thank you to keep your voice down, Madam Josephine. What proof do you have that Rawhide did anything to this girl?"

"She's lying dead in her bed. Strangled!" Josephine said, staring firmly down at Jimmy Wolfe. "We had a deal. 10% of our income and none of my

Belly Through the Brush

employees get hurt. What's the point of running a protection racket if you don't offer any protection?"

Jimmy glanced over at Rawhide, a look of uncertainty washing over his face for a moment. Rawhide hunched down, staring intently at the green velvet of the poker table. Jimmy shook his head, and then he glared right back up at Josephine.

"You'll want to think this through," he said in a low voice. "You don't have any protection aside from what we offer. There's no sheriff in town, no militia— there's no anything. This is my turf. And you might be down one girl, but I still have two. Agatha," he said, placing one pistol on the poker table, "and Delilah," he added, placing the second beside his stick of chips. His hands rested atop the pistols as he stared at Josephine. "I ain't afraid to use them, whether to beat some sense into that pretty little skull of yours, or to shoot you down where you stand. So... Pearl is dead." He shrugged. "It happens. Don't go spreading rumors around town."

Josephine stood stock still for a long moment. Then she whirled around, storming out of the Silver Springs Saloon, the rest of the women following behind her as she stamped back to the cathouse.

"What now?" Olive asked, hurrying to keep pace.

"Now?" Josephine snorted, but kept her voice low. "Now we go and find us some *real* protection."

Chapter 4:
Two Bulls in One Pen

Over the next few weeks, Henry grew bigger and bigger, the cows eventually growing to tolerate him as he flapped about in the barn. As he went about his daily errands, it became increasingly clear to Jake that he couldn't hide the dragon forever. Still, how to broach the subject?

One day, as he was clearing out the manure with his father, Jake paused mid-stroke with his pitchfork. "Hey, Dad? I wanted to talk to you about something."

"Ah," Lawrence Mullens replied, wiping the sweat off his forehead. It was well into autumn now, but it never really got too cold at their family farm in the plains of Arizona. "I thought you might have something to say."

Jake blinked. "You do?"

"Oh, of course! Why, just yesterday your mother and I were having a discussion about it."

"Uh…"

"You want my advice? Man to man?"

"Advice?" Jake blinked. "Well, I suppose so. You see… there's a dragon in the barn."

"Oh, I know all about that," Lawrence said. "Your mother, too. You don't need to worry about us."

"Oh…" Jake said, feeling his tension drain away. *So they know about Henry, and the barn hasn't burned down. I guess it's all worked out then?* "I was going to tell you, but…"

Lawrence nodded sagely. "Lucille is a good girl. Your mother and I approve."

Jake tilted his head. "Uh… what? I'm talking about the dragon in the barn."

"Oh, I know what you mean," his dad said, nodding sagely. "It can often feel that way. Like a dragon trapped in a barn, what a lovely way to put it. That's love, Jake. I felt that way when I first met your mother."

"What?"

"Oh, indeed! She was so beautiful in her summer dress, and when we would go for walks, oh, how her shining calves would—"

"Ew! Dad!"

"What?" Lawrence leaned back on his pitchfork, grinning over. "Your mother was quite the looker once."

"Once?" Jake grinned back. "So not anymore? Should I tell her you said that?"

Lawrence winced. "Don't do that, son. Your mother would pitch a fit. I can just hear her right now—"

A scream broke the silence from the other side of the farm. Lawrence tilted his head. "That's strange. Am I getting more imaginative in my old age?"

"I heard it too," Jake said, feeling a sinking feeling in his stomach. He turned and ran over, his father right behind, both keeping their pitchforks in their hands. *Is the Wolfe Gang raiding us again?*

He turned the corner and slowed as he saw his mother backing away in panic out of the barn. She glanced back at Jake and Lawrence as they approached.

"There's a huge bat in our barn!" Dorothy Mullens screamed, a broomstick raised in the air. "Jake, help your father chase it out."

"No, Ma," Jake said with a pained expression as he reached the barn door.

"No?"

"It's not a bat, it's... uh... it's something I should have told you about a while ago."

Jake's mother hesitated, lowering her broomstick, and glanced over at his father. "What's Lucille got to do with it?"

"Enough about Lucille," Jake snapped. "Look, I kind of... came across this baby dragon," he said, thinking he'd better not mention that he had raided the Wolfe Gang. "And I thought I'd keep it stowed in the barn. It's friendly," he added, sliding the barn door open.

From the rafters, Henry soared down, landing in the middle of the barn and looking at the baffled Dorothy and Lawrence Mullen. Henry mewled, taking a few hesitant steps closer.

"I named it Henry," Jake explained with a nervous smile.

"Like your grandfather," Dorothy said, nodding approvingly. She smiled at the dragon. "What a cutie!"

"That explains why I haven't seen any mice around lately," Lawrence muttered.

"So, uh..." Jake grinned. "Can we keep it?"

Dorothy already took a few steps closer, bending down with her fingers extended, clicking at the dragon as if trying to attract a cat. Henry hopped forward a few times, then leaned its sinuous neck forward, sniffing at Dorothy's outstretched fingertips. A red forked tongue peeked out to brush against her fingers and she giggled.

"Looks like we are," Lawrence muttered, taking his hat off and brushing back his thinning gray hair. "Look, son, you'll take care of this... of Henry, right?"

"Of course, Pa. You know I'll treat him well. And I was thinking that he could hide in the cornfields if anyone comes by. I'm sure he could hunt for coyotes and prairie dogs and any other varmints around. Our corn won't be eaten by mice anymore. Not to mention the Wolfe Gang, if they come through again."

"Well..." Lawrence smiled to see his wife stroking Henry's neck and chuckling. "Your mother likes it. Now did you want to ask me something about Lucille? How to approach her? You know, I used to—"

"Dad, enough about Lucille! I was never talking about her in the first place," Jake said, grimacing and turning away.

Lawrence smiled, patting his son on the back. "We all went together to Rattlefort the other day, or don't you remember? And there you were, staring at Lucille as she passed by, mooning over her... wouldn't even snap out."

"That..." Jake blushed. "I don't... well... look, I should go finish clearing out that manure."

***

"Did you hear?" Goldie asked, darting into the brothel. Lucille paused from mopping the floor, the sodden rag dripping into the wood bucket, and looked over at this refreshing break from the monotony. The prostitute glanced one way, then the other, her golden curls bobbing up and down as she grinned. Finally her gaze settled itself on Lucille. It was early afternoon and most of the girls were away resting, though Olive was upstairs with Percy McGowan, the old rascal the Wolfe Gang called "Preacher."

"Hear what?" Lucille asked, mop still dripping into the dirty bucket.

"The Riley Gang is in town! That means business will be picking up! You know what men are like after riding hard for days... oh," Goldie blinked, "begging your pardon, Lucille. I didn't mean to imply you're—"

"It's fine," Lucille replied, setting the damp mop on the brothel's wooden floor. "I know what it means from a business standpoint."

And I understand the basics. My mother didn't want this kind of life for me, as she's made clear to everyone. Leaving Chicago, pregnant and widowed, forced to scrap out some kind of living in the West. It's amazing she's done so well for herself.

A door creaked open, Madam Josephine stepping from her private office and looking over. "It also means trouble. Walter Riley and Jimmy Wolfe in the same town?" She shook her head. "You can't put two bulls in one pen. Lucky for us, I picked up some protection earlier today. Looks like that might have been just in time. Set that mop aside, Lucille, and both of you come into my office." Goldie and Lucille exchanged baffled glances as they entered Madam Josephine's office.

She never lets me in here, Lucille thought, glancing around the office. There were a few ounces of silver and even gold stacked on the shelves along with a few sheaves of paper and various bills and forms scattered about. Josephine grabbed a leather satchel, setting it on the table and pulling out several pistols, smaller than anything Lucille had ever seen.

"I placed a special order the day Pearl was killed, and it's finally come in. Pick one that suits your fancy."

Goldie whistled, grabbing the biggest one with four barrels. "What can I say, I like them big."

Josephine nodded. "That there is a pepperbox revolver. It'll be a bit hard to keep concealed."

"I know a few gentlemen who manage it," Goldie said, tapping it in thought, as Lucille selected one of the other small pistols.

"That's a derringer. Meant to protect a lady's virtue, or so the marketing says. You're the only one here anywhere close to virtuous, though I hope you never need it," her mother said with a faint smile.

"Me too," Lucille said faintly, holding the derringer uncertainly as Josephine put the rest away.

"We'll have to train with it later. Lucille, I know you haven't used a gun, and some of the working girls haven't either. But I've loaded every pistol here, and it's pretty simple to pull the trigger. Olive and I are armed now—I didn't want her alone with Preacher McGowan otherwise." Josephine bit her lip in worry. "You two, bring the rest of the girls in. I feel there will be dead men in town before sunset."

"Why, it's barely noon!" Goldie replied.

"You know how men get. There might be fighting or fornicating, or likely both, but either way I'll need all hands on deck. Now go! Bring my girls in."

Together, Goldie and Lucille nodded, turning around and rushing out the door. Lucille rushed outside, holding her skirts up as she passed a muddy patch, and turned to look at Goldie.

"Harriot's to the north of town—do you think you can get her? I'll go by Florence's house."

"You got it," Goldie said, turning to the north as Lucille hurried in the other direction. Already townsfolk were muttering, drifting away, though a few laughing children rushed in the direction Lucille was going. She soon found herself trailing after them into the middle of town. A few others were gathered by the side of the road as if awaiting a parade. One of them glanced over, waving at Lucille.

"Florence!" Lucille called back, glad to have found her so quickly.

"Hey, Lucille. Does your mother need me?"

"Mm-hmm," Lucille replied, scanning the collection of idle and curious townsfolk nearby. She leaned in close to Florence's ear. "She has protection for us. Let's hurry back!"

"Not just yet," Florence replied, looking over to the west. "Look!" The soft clop-clop of hooves caught Lucille's attention and she turned to see a band of newcomers arriving.

The Riley Gang!

Out in front was one of the heaviest men Lucille had ever had the misfortune to see. Pot-bellied, unshaven, and puffing away at a cigar with a wide grin on his yellowed teeth was Walter Riley.

"Looks just like the wanted poster," Florence said glumly. "Well, money is money," she said, stepping out into the road.

Lucille's arm shot forward, grabbing onto Florence's hand. "Wait! What are you doing?"

"What does it look like I'm doing?" She jerked her hand away. "I'm getting us work." The young, dark-haired prostitute boldly strode into the road, waving her hand in the air as she smiled.

Lucille grimaced, feeling rooted in place as she took in the other riders. One of them was a woman, overweight and bearing quite the resemblance to Walter Riley. A sister, maybe? Beside her was a man missing all his front teeth, staring blankly at the good citizens of Rattlefort.

The others had slowed now, looking down in curiosity at Florence as she sold them on the merits of Madam Josephine's establishment, even pointing down the street. Lucille snapped out of her stupor, rushing forward to join her.

"You ever been with twins?" one of the riders was saying, grinning down at Florence. Beside him another rider bore a matching grin. "I'm Floyd Riley, this here is Clarence," he said, then jerked a thumb back at an older man in a tattered wool coat. "And 'Uncle Riley' back there! Well, he's our dad, but he's Walter and Peggy's uncle, you know?"

"Oh, well you'll have to come by," Florence said agreeably.

"Hey." The harsh voice took Lucille by surprise, and she glanced over to see a long-haired man staring intently at her from his horse. "How much?" he rasped.

"Ah… I'm just the maid," Lucille replied.

The man stared for a while longer. "Want to make a dollar?"

"Stop lollygagging back there!" came a shout from up ahead as Walter Riley twisted in his saddle to glare back at them. "We have business to attend to," he said, yanking his cigar out, then turning back and looking at the curious citizens of Rattlefort. "With the Wolfe Gang? Where are those rascals?"

"They're in the saloon!" an onlooker shouted back.

"Well, one of you go fetch 'em for us! I mean to have words with Jimmy Wolfe."

"Come along with us," one of the twins said, waving Florence over. She followed beside their horse and Lucille hurried to keep pace. "That there's Maurice Barber," the other twin was saying, pointing at the man who was still staring down at Lucille. "He ain't a Riley by blood, but he's spilled plenty of it for us, so he's family."

Lucille patted Florence's shoulder, feeling intensely uncomfortable. "Let's go," she hissed.

"Not yet," Florence said, shrugging her off. "I want to see this! Nothing exciting ever happens in Rattlefort. Besides, we can take them directly back to the cathouse. I don't want to lose them to any other working girls."

Lucille glanced over, biting her lip as she saw Jimmy Wolfe stroll out alone into the center of town.

"Your train heist was on my territory," Walter Riley boomed, clearly unafraid of the witnesses gathered all around him. "I'll be taking back the goods you stole now."

"No you won't," Jimmy Wolfe replied, confident despite the fact that he was alone. Lucille wondered where the rest of the gang was. Likely Preacher was sleeping in the cathouse, but the others would normally be with Jimmy.

Walter snorted, twisting his cigar in his mouth. "What makes you think that?"

"Agatha and Delilah," Jimmy replied, tapping his two holsters.

"You think you can outdraw me in a duel?" Walter took a final puff, then tossed his cigar away to lie smoldering in the main street. "You're even dumber than you look."

"We'll see about that, fat man. Are you challenging me to a duel?"

"That I am," Walter replied. "Quickest gun in the West gets the loot." He glanced over to the nearby church. "That bell work? When it strikes one."

Belly Through the Brush

Lucille glanced up, surprised to see a glint of light in one of the windows. She squinted as it disappeared, keeping her eyes locked there as the two gang leaders traded insults, and then saw a half-remembered face re-emerge in the window. *Sam Reeves, was it? One of Jimmy's boys?*

Now she peered around, ignoring the crowd below and looking for good vantage points. She spotted a hint of motion, a hat emerging above a general store, and then the gleam of a pistol. The man half-turned and spat. *Rawhide Cooper. And the others?* Lucille looked around and grabbed Florence by the arm. This time she held firm.

"We need to go. Now."

"Lucille!" Florence looked back in surprise as Lucille pulled her away. "But it's just getting good."

"Oh, not going to stick around?" one of the twins asked. Florence tried to shrug her off, but Lucille pulled her away from the Riley Gang, disappearing into the midst of the excited crowd.

The clock struck one.

Chapter 5:
Presidential Pardon

Washington, D.C.

Abraham Lincoln leaned back in his chair, setting his stovepipe hat down, and ran his fingers through his tousled black hair. He let out a long sigh then looked down the table at his cabinet ministers arrayed along the table.

"Grant is giving the Confederates all he can, gentlemen, but I fear many of our generals lack the same fighting spirit. This war must be brought to a decisive conclusion."

"There is also the upcoming election to consider, Mr. President," Andrew Johnson cut in. Lincoln studied the man for a moment. *When Tennessee seceded, he stayed loyal to the Union, and he's done good service in those parts of Tennessee we've retaken from the secessionists. With him at my side I feel we can restore unity to this fractured nation.*

"The election?" Lincoln shrugged. "I feel the American people will not side with George McClellan. They understand that we must see this struggle through to the end."

"Nevertheless, you've chosen me as your running mate, and I've been keeping my ear to the ground, so to speak. There are rumblings in the West about a growing number of criminal gangs. Trains are being robbed at gunpoint more and more often. This has become a problem we can no longer simply avoid."

"These outlaws... they are skilled gunfighters, yes? Brave men willing to fight?"

Andrew Johnson paused. "Well... yes."

"Hmm. They would be better served in our army. A presidential pardon, perhaps, but only to those wanted outlaws who are willing to serve their country."

"Mr. President!" Andrew Johnson half-rose in shock. "I only meant that they should be hunted down for the murderers and robbers they are! What you propose—"

"What I propose will solve this problem and also bolster our forces. It will only apply to those willing to join the Union Army, after all. I've seen what can happen when a group of determined cavalrymen prowl about. Why, it was only a few months ago that Jubal Early raided the capital. We have very few daring horsemen willing to charge into the fray. That Colonel Custer, for example. But we need cavalry that can *fight!*"

There were a few nods around the table as the cabinet ministers took this in. Andrew Johnson twisted his mouth. "I feel the West is becoming a wild and lawless place, Mr. President."

"We can deal with the West once the South has been subdued." Lincoln paused, aware of the muted response this idea had received. He glanced over to his War Minister, who was stroking his long white beard in thought. "What do you think, Stanton?"

Secretary Edwin Stanton considered it for a long moment. "Every little bit helps, Mr. President. The Lord knows if our army was composed only of angels we could not field a single regiment. I could find a place for them in our ranks."

Lincoln nodded, decided now. "Mr. Bates, draft a blanket pardon for those gunslingers willing to offer themselves up to U.S. marshals. I wish to review it and send a telegram out West by this afternoon."

"Mr. President…" Attorney General Bates hesitated. "You've allowed Black soldiers in our ranks—against my objections I will point out—and now this?"

"By three o'clock, to be precise," Lincoln said, looking over at a ticking grandfather clock. "Or one p.m. in the West," he added with a soft chuckle.

"Yes, Mr. President," Edward Bates said after a moment.

"Very well," Lincoln said, clasping his hands and leaning forward. "The latest dispatches from General Grant suggest..."

***

Rattlefort, AZ

Lucille wrenched the protesting Florence back into the crowd, glancing back just as the clock struck one. Jimmy Wolfe whipped his guns up in a flash, the bang of his two pistols merging with the gong of the church bell, Walter Riley falling to the ground from atop his horse. There was a single exit wound between his eyes that Lucille knew both shots had passed through. The town square then erupted into a flurry of gunfire as Lucille darted behind a window in the Silver Springs Saloon, her wide eyes searching for the flashes of guns, curious despite herself.

Sam Reeves was just about leaning out the window of the church, blasting away with his lever action rifle, whipping it open and reloading faster than seemed humanly possible. The spent casings fell onto the roof of the church and trickled down into the ground like metal rain. Lucille glanced around, spotting Rawhide Cooper grinning from the top of the general store, shooting down into the crowd and likely being none too accurate.

She looked down now, to see the Riley Twins were writhing on the ground now, bullets slamming into them and all around them. Uncle Riley was staggering away, a fresh hole in his hat, and he bumped into a bystander as he raised his pistol up to Sam Reeves and fired wildly. A shot took him in the neck, and then several other gunshots punched into Uncle Riley and the startled bystander. The two fell into the street, coughing up blood, as Maurice Barber darted past the stunned Peggy Riley, still mounted on her horse.

Maurice whipped his rifle up to the general store, then staggered as a gunshot took him in the leg, falling to one knee. He somehow aimed right back up at Rawhide Cooper. The Wolfe Gang bandit shot frantically, missing Maurice but hitting another fleeing bystander, then ducked as Maurice fired.

"Move, girl!"

Lucille was shoved from the side, and cried out as she fell, looking up in annoyance as Billy Wolfe crowded the window. He slammed the butt of his shotgun into the glass, shattering it to pieces, Lucille stumbling away as shards of glass scattered along the floor. An echoing boom sounded, followed by another, and then the sharp *ch-ch* of the shotgun being reloaded. Billy laughed maniacally in the following silence.

By the time the reverberation of the single town bell faded away, the Riley Gang lay dead in the middle of Rattlefort's town square.

"No!" Florence screamed, a few startled and sympathetic faces in the crowd looking over. "Our customers..." she moaned. Lucille muttered a few oaths as she rose to her feet, glaring at Billy's back, as he laughed and laughed. She moved to the door and peeked around. The bodies of the Riley Gang were an absolute mess.

Aside from one.

Rawhide Cooper slid down from the roof of the general store, Bowie knife in his hands, and approached the almost catatonic Peggy Riley.

"Don't worry," he said, "I wouldn't harm a woman."

Billy Wolfe chuckled, exiting the Silver Springs Saloon, as the rest of the Wolfe Gang converged on Peggy like vultures.

"I like a bit of meat on my women," Rawhide Cooper said. "Or a lot of meat in this case."

"Nice shooting, boys," Jimmy Wolfe said as he approached, Agatha and Delilah still in his hands, eyeing the panicked citizens of Rattlefort around him. He paused for a moment. "Where's Preacher?"

"M-Madam J-J-Josephine's," Sam Reeves replied, joining the rest of him. He licked his dry lips. "C-c-c-cat—"

"Got it," Jimmy said. "Well, he can send these poor souls off. As for me?" His cold eyes flicked over to Lucille. She felt herself rooted in place. There was something almost demonic about his stare. It shifted an inch and she felt herself relaxing as he looked past her, at the astonished patrons of the Silver Springs Saloon. "I'll have myself a drink. On the house."

***

"Oh, aren't you a cutie? Aren't you just such a cutie?"

Jake paused on the threshold of the family kitchen, hesitating a moment. *Ma has just been smothering Henry ever since I showed him to them. I thought it would make things easier, but... this is getting ridiculous.* Jake stepped forward past the cast iron pans to see his mother scratching the dragon behind the neck. Henry's eyes were half-closed, and he let out a contented burp, a puff of smoke drifting out of his fanged mouth.

"Good morning," Jake said, taking a seat beside his father, who was grinning at Henry and Dorothy in amusement. "I was thinking about going into town today."

"Isn't he adorable?" Lawrence Mullens asked. "He's been doing those little puffs lately whenever we tickle him behind the—wait." He blinked, looking over at Jake. "What did you say?"

"Good morning."

"No, after that. Going into town? Are you crazy? With that big shootout the other day and the Wolfe Gang acting like they own the place? No, Jake, we're safe here. Besides, there's always plenty of work to be done."

"And supplies to get! You were just groaning the other day about not having any nails. Besides..." he paused, as Henry twisted around to sniff at his outstretched hand, smiling as the dragon's forked tongue flicked over it. "They're burying the bodies today. Some good people died in that shootout. Not only the Riley Gang, but a few bystanders. Thomas Oakes, you remember? Worked in Mr. Simon's warehouse?"

"Thomas Oakes... not ringing a bell... oh, Tommy." Lawrence blinked. "Why, I didn't know he got killed too. Yeah, I remember him. Played a few dozen rounds of cards together over the years." He sighed, then lurched out of his chair. "Fine, Jake, if you want to go then I'll just do your chores for you too. Give my respects to Tommy's family when you see him. Weren't like we were close, but he was an alright sort."

Jake nodded, looking across the table. His mother had a serious expression now.

"It's a shame to hear about all that. You do be careful, Jake. Don't start nothin' with these Wolfe Gang types."

Jake nodded.

"Make sure you take good care of Ulysses," she added, opening the ceramic dish in the center of the kitchen table and selecting two sugar cubes. She slid one over, then turned to Henry. "And one for you, my little sweetie!"

Jake sighed as the dragon gobbled it up, his wings half-spread, one of them banging a pan hanging on the wall. Henry had been growing a lot over these past few weeks. Pretty soon he wouldn't be able to fit in the kitchen at all.

"I'm glad you like him," Jake said, grabbing a sugar cube for Ulysses. "He hasn't been a bother, has he?"

"Oh, no! Your father and I trained him to hide in the corn fields. He loves it there, and I haven't seen any critters around for days!"

Jake nodded, rising to his feet. "I'll be back tonight to lock Henry in the barn like usual. Don't worry about me, I'll just do a few errands and pay my respects."

Henry mewled as Jake turned to the door. He smiled and gave the dragon an affectionate pat. Dorothy looked over with fondness. "So where did you find him? You were a little unclear about that."

"Oh, you know," Jake said, moving to the door, gesturing vaguely. "Around. Out in the desert."

"And what were you doing—"

"Bye, Ma!"

Jake stepped outside, moving to the stable, the sun already beating down on him. By the time he had Ulysses and the wagon readied, his dad had approached, a few wildflowers in his hand.

"Maybe you can leave these on the graves," Lawrence said, "to pay our respects."

Jake nodded, the reins tight in his hands. "Will do, Pa."

***

The ride from Rattlefort took a bit longer than Jake had expected, and by the time he took the last winding turn to the cemetery on the outskirts of town, he guessed that they were at least midway through the ceremony. Jake cursed to himself, but he tried to look some combination of mournful and handsome as he slowed his wagon and parked it beside the cemetery.

Truth be told, I feel more like a mournsome handful, Jake thought, grabbing the flowers and glancing over. *Oh Lord, there she is!* He smiled, then willed it away, shuffling over to join the gathering of mourners as Preacher McGowan's bleating voice continued.

"According to 2 Corinthians 5:8, we are confident, I say, and willing rather to be absent from the body and to be present with the Lord."

Jake, on the other hand, felt a powerful call to be present with Lucille, and made muttered apologies as he inched his way over through the crowd. Lucille sniffed, wiping a finger across one eye, her beautiful porcelain white face stained with tears.

"Quite the sermon," Jake said.

Lucille snorted. "I can't stand that man! It was even worse at Pearl's funeral. He is such a hypocrite."

"Ah, sorry for missing that," Jake whispered back. "I was busy doing chores."

"It's fine."

"Keep it down, Lucille," a woman beside her said. She glanced over at Jake. "Oh, hello. I don't believe we've met," she said in a low voice, Preacher McGowan's words carrying over her.

"Jake Mullens," he said with a nod.

"Florence." She smiled. "Come and ask for me next time you're at Madam Josephine's Cathouse."

"Uh…" Jake glanced at Lucille. "Not… interested. Not that you're, uh, ugly. It's just that…" he glanced back at Lucille and then to the baffled woman. "I'm in mourning right now."

"Oh, I understand," she said, looking back to the sermon.

"Shh!" someone whispered from behind them and Jake blushed and fell silent.

"And in the words of Jesus Christ…" Preacher McGowan looked up in annoyance, "who said… hey!" He paused, standing beside several wooden coffins, and scowled into the assembled audience outside. "Is one of you talking? How am I expected to give a speech if you're all chatting away like we're having a picnic?"

He stared at the audience for a while as the silence lingered. Finally, he sighed. "In conclusion, I commend their souls to heaven, except for the Riley Gang who are going straight to hell. Billy, help me roll them in."

Together, Preacher and Billy grabbed the arms and legs of Thomas Oakes, hauling him over to a crudely dug grave. The crowd began to disperse, a few sobbing, but Lucille stayed rooted in place. Jake stepped closer, hesitating for a moment. *Should I pat her on the back? Hold her?*

Lucille sniffed, then looked over. "How have you been, Jake Mullens? It was good of you to come. I know it's not an easy trip."

"It's not so hard, neither! You should try it sometime!" He grinned. "I've been well, just doing chores and hanging out with Henry... ah..." Jake grimaced. "I mean..."

Lucille tilted her head. "Didn't you have a grandfather named Henry?"

"Well, he... he's still with me in spirit, I feel." Jake nodded to Thomas Oakes' grave and raised his bundle of wildflowers. "I was going to pay my respects. Might you accompany me?" He stuck his arm out hopefully.

"Sure," Lucille said, putting her arm around his, and together they approached the grave as Billy Wolfe threw the last shovelful of dirt on the casket.

Billy glared over at them. "What are you smiling for, boy?"

Jake dropped his grin. "I'm not smiling."

Billy stared at him for a long moment. Then he smiled back, chuckling to himself as he set his shovel on one shoulder, walking over to the dead bodies of the Riley Gang.

"What was that all about?" Lucille asked, mystified but pleasantly close.

"Nothing good, I imagine," Jake said, stepping forward and tossing his bundle of wildflowers on the grave of Thomas Oakes. "Rest in peace."

Chapter 6:

The U.S. Marshals

"You ever been to this sorry excuse for a town before, Mr. Milton?" U.S. Marshal John Davenport asked, chewing his wad of tobacco and staring at the rough outline of Rattlefort in the distance.

"I have not yet had the displeasure, Marshal," Roger Milton replied. "Though in my experience most of these ten-shanty towns are all the same."

"*Wellll...*" Marshal Davenport dragged the word out, then followed it up by spitting the chewed-up remnants of his tobacco onto the Arizona sand. It steamed on the hot ground, as his oak brown horse patiently sniffed a wilted plant. "You come to us from the East, Mr. Milton. It's a deal different out here."

"The East?" Deputy Marshal Milton chuckled. "Oh, hardly. Bleeding Kansas is no coastal harbor, I'll have you know, sir. I've seen my fair share of bar fights and liquor runners, both before this War and plenty during. At least now the Secessionists have laid their cards out on the table and have been found wanting."

"That yet remains to be seen, Mr. Milton," the lawman said, taking his hat off and running a hand through his sweat-streaked graying hair. "To be frank, the war itself seems rather distant to us out West."

"I trust your opinion on that, Marshal. Yet if not for the war, we would not have been sent here to grant pardons."

"No, indeed we would not," Marshal Davenport said, spurring his horse forward. Together, the two lawmen cantered toward town. John Davenport had his own opinions about the idea of granting pardons to thieving, murdering lawbreakers.

But who am I to argue with President Lincoln? He has his own concerns to deal with, getting the Secessionists back in line. More than likely he'll sail through this coming election and see his way to bringing this fractured country back together over the next few years.

Marshal Davenport's thoughts were interrupted by the appearance of an attractive blonde woman in her forties. She smiled, waving them over.

"Can I help you two gentlemen? I run Madam Josephine's cathouse, if you would like to refresh yourselves after your long journey."

Belly Through the Brush

"The great outdoors suits me well enough, Ma'am, but I could use directions. Firstly, where's Sheriff Whitaker?"

"Who?"

Davenport and Milton exchanged glances.

"Ah… I was told he was the Sheriff of Rattlefort."

"Oh, Greenbacks Whitaker. Last I heard, he joined Hunter's Company of Arizona Rangers when the war broke out. Hasn't been a sheriff here since… and there wasn't much of one while he was on the job either, if you catch my drift."

"A Secessionist," Davenport grumbled.

"Wonderful. How you been managing?"

Madam Josephine paused for a long moment. "Well, that right there is a discussion best carried out indoors. Why don't you and the Deputy Marshal visit my cathouse?"

"We do not partake," Davenport replied for the both of them. *Though I don't know how they do things in Kansas. The honor of a U.S. Marshal still holds weight out here.* "I am a happily married man, Madam Josephine."

"Happily married men often visit my establishment, Marshal, but in this instance I mean only to converse in private."

Marshal Davenport grunted, his tongue searching instinctively for the tobacco he had spat out earlier. He glanced over at Deputy Milton. The Kansan had been in the area when the telegram had come through, hunting down a band of Indian horse thieves, and had gallantly offered to join on the mission out West. Davenport didn't know the man too well, but they'd ridden together a few days, and he seemed every bit the honest lawman.

"Your thoughts, Deputy Milton?"

"My thoughts, Marshal, are that the young woman waving at us bears a striking resemblance to the Madam," he replied, nodding his head a fraction. "Careful how you look."

Marshal Davenport coughed, turning his head as if to spit, and caught a glimpse of a woman with golden curls waving at them.

"That's my daughter Lucille," Josephine added, having spotted her from the corner of her eye. "There's a gang of bandits in our town, and I suspect you are being watched even now."

The marshal grunted. "What do you propose?"

Madam Josephine clapped her hands, the noise echoing around them, and loudly shouted, "Come on down to my cathouse! We'll entertain you two travelers!"

Marshal Davenport stroked his handlebar mustache. "That was lacking in subtlety."

"This is Rattlefort, Marshal," Josephine said in a much quieter voice. "Subtlety here means a bottle to the *back* of the head. I suspect you're here for the Wolfe Gang—join us and I will tell you all about them."

Belly Through the Brush

"Visiting an establishment of ill repute? I hope you take no offense, Ma'am, but that is conduct unbecoming of a U.S. Marshal," Davenport pointed out. Mr. Milton shifted uncomfortably beside him.

"Marshal, listen to the lady. We'd be getting information—it's why we're here, after all."

"Join us for the conversation only, Marshal," Josephine insisted. "You strike me as a smoker. Have a cigar, and a glass of whiskey, on the house."

"*Wellll...*" Marshal Davenport leaned back in the saddle. "I'm not a drinking man, myself, but I do fancy myself a cigar and a round of cards."

Josephine's smile twitched. "A cigar I can do," she said. "But most of the gambling goes down at the Silver Springs Saloon."

"Does it?" Davenport exchanged glances with Mr. Milton, who leaned over to Josephine.

"I'm a stranger to these parts, Ma'am, but is this Jimmy Wolfe a gambling man?"

Josephine opened her mouth, then flicked her eyes over. "I dare not say," she said in a low voice. "The cathouse then!" she said in a loud voice. "Finest place in the West!"

Marshal Davenport grunted, spurring his horse down the main road.

"It is not that way, Marshal!" Josephine said, hurrying after. "I would implore you to diverge from your route!"

"Got to be this way, Ma'am," Marshal Davenport replied, as the two lawmen rolled into town. "You're welcome to steer clear."

Josephine made no comment but continued walking alongside the two marshals. "Take a left, then, if you mean to have it out with Jimmy Wolfe," she said in a low voice. "Just down the street."

Marshal Davenport tugged his reins left at the crossroads, a few stone-faced residents of Rattlefort staring at the pair. He touched his hat, nodding down at them, but they made no response. He looked over, the saloon not far off, seated right in the middle of town.

"I'm getting a powerful sensation of being watched," Mr. Milton muttered from the side of his mouth.

"It's cause you are," Marshal Davenport replied. "Lookee up yonder at the church. Second story."

A gleam reflected off what appeared to be a double-barreled shotgun sticking out the window. *Likely wouldn't do much from this distance, but the intent is clear enough. Seems the Wolfe Gang runs this poor town.*

"Well, I'll be," Mr. Milton, sounding unsurprised. "And there, atop the general store."

Davenport idly gazed over, seeing a man in a tattered black coat with a preacher's hat trying to crouch behind cover, and not doing a good job of it.

The fading rays of light glinted off his crucifix—and the lever action rifle he bore.

"That's some man of God," Milton snorted, "training a rifle on a lawman."

"He ain't no man of God," Josephine snorted, still keeping pace with them as they neared the saloon. "Not much of a man, neither. But don't you worry yourselves about those two. It's Jimmy Wolfe who calls the shots."

"I'm hoping there won't be a need for shooting," Marshal Davenport said, dismounting as his horse approached a hitching post just outside the Silver Springs Saloon. "Today, at least," he added, as the Deputy Marshal joined him outside the saloon doors. Davenport grabbed the chest resting in one of the saddle bags, hefting it in one arm.

"Jimmy doesn't really work on a calendar," Madam Josephine said, gesturing over to the saloon. "I think I'll leave you boys to it," she said, turning away.

"Probably for the best," Marshal Davenport muttered, entering the saloon, his boots clattering on the wooden floor. The boisterous sounds from inside died down into a hush. From amidst the cluster of bedraggled men, an especially ragged group was ranged around a poker table, the man in the middle bearing a striking resemblance to the wanted poster Davenport had memorized.

"Ah, just the man I wanted to see," he said in the hushed, silence, making straight for Jimmy.

"Well, ain't this a surprise," Jimmy Wolfe said, scowling as he set his glass of whiskey down. "What the hell's the point of posting sentries if they don't raise the alarm?" He chuckled without amusement. "Just the two of you, huh. Trying to collect my bounty or are you here to play poker?"

"Texas hold 'em, actually," Marshal Davenport said, approaching the table and setting his chest down. "If you're game for it."

Jimmy Wolfe blinked, a flash of genuine surprise crossing his face. "Well... alright."

The dealer smiled, though his nervousness was clear as he cut the deck, passing out cards to Davenport and those Wolfe Gang members arranged around the table.

"I'll just watch, if you don't mind," Mr. Milton said, approaching the bar. "Whiskey, neat."

Jimmy Wolfe studied Marshal Davenport for a long moment, his curiosity soon melting away to irritation, like a kettle boiling over. *He's not much for bluffing.* "Why are you here?" he demanded, whipping up his hand of cards.

"President Lincoln sent me."

There were a few chuckles at this, a stout man beside Jimmy grinning widely, one of his teeth flashing gold. Even Jimmy seemed to crack a brief half-smile.

"He's offering a pardon to all outlaws," Davenport continued, selecting his cards and studying them with half-lidded eyes. *Nine and ten.* "Turn your weapons in and enlist in the Union Army, and your evil deeds will be forgotten."

Jimmy tilted his head, as if waiting for the punchline, but the silence just lingered as the dealer dealt out the flop. *Seven, eight, and a jack.* Finally, Jimmy snorted. "How stupid do you think we are?"

"It would be ungentlemanly of me to say," Davenport replied.

"Accepting a pardon," Jimmy snorted. "Once we give our weapons up you Marshals could just kill us and say we were resisting arrest." He gritted his teeth.

"That so. Maybe I'll pass your astute suggestion on up to old Honest Abe himself."

"You do that," Jimmy grunted. "You didn't come all this way to gamble, errand boy, so let's make this quick. I'll raise you... let's say 400 silver dollars."

One of the Wolfe Gang members furrowed his brow, then tossed his cards down in frustration. *Ace and two.* "I Fold."

The other hemmed and hawed a moment, taking a long swallow of his whiskey, but Davenport kept his focus squarely on Jimmy.

"The President himself is making you an offer. I'd say it's all the same to me, but truth be told, I got a preference."

"That so," Jimmy muttered, a flash of rage coursing through him.

Davenport hid his amusement behind a perfectly still poker face as the other man finally finished his hemming and hawing. "I-I will f-f-fold," he said, setting his cards aside and grabbing his drink once again. *King and five.*

"Well, it was a short game," Jimmy Wolfe said, as Davenport bent down and opened his chest. "I can't say it was interest…" he fell silent as Davenport set four canvas bags down.

"Courtesy of the U.S. government," he explained.

Jimmy frowned, then turned and snapped at a man leering in the corner. "Billy, get me four hundred silver dollars from my chest. Bring it here now!"

The man blinked. "But—"

"Hurry," Jimmy said, snapping his fingers. Billy ran over to the stairs, his steps echoing as he stomped his way up, echoing in the hushed saloon. Jimmy waited a second, then another, shifting in his seat. "I'm not a patient man, Marshal. Let's see the turn card."

"I *am* a patient man, Mr. Wolfe. Your coins are missing."

"They'll be here once my idiot brother gets back," Jimmy snapped back. "We'll play for honor till then."

"I see. Two things I do not see on your side of the table." Davenport shrugged, then gestured at the dealer. "The turn card, then."

"Uh, yes sirs," he said quietly, dealing the card. *King.*

Belly Through the Brush

"I did you a favor in delivering this message, Mr. Wolfe," Davenport said in the silence. "I could have stormed in guns blazing, but I did not. I paid you this courtesy."

Jimmy grunted, the stairs creaking above him, and Billy Wolfe staggered over to the table. "Four hundred silver dollars, Boss," he said, setting them down on the table.

"Good," Jimmy said. "Now get me four hundred more. I'm raising." Jimmy leaned forward, pointing at Davenport. "And listen here," he said, over Billy's whining. "I could have had my sentries shoot you two as you rode into town. But I did not." Jimmy smashed the table with a fist. "Besides, I'd rather die before turning myself in, just to serve life in prison."

"*Wellll...* is that so." Davenport smiled for the first time. "My conscience can rest easy," he said, slapping his cards face down on the table.

Jimmy cackled, pulling the canvas bags over to his side of the table, the rest of his gang joining in with him. Davenport grabbed his chest, standing up and looking over to the bar.

"Have you finished your whiskey, Mr. Milton?"

"A man never truly finishes whiskey, Marshal, but merely postpones the next drink," Mr. Milton said as he set his empty glass down on the counter. "But, yes, I suspect I shall sleep soundly tonight."

Together, they made their way to the door as Billy returned with more coins.

"Bring them back up, Billy," Jimmy shouted. "Along with the rest. Don't touch those cards," he said, leaning over. "Let's see what the lawman was packing."

Marshal Davenport paused at the doorway and watched as Jimmy studied the cards in bafflement. *My nine and ten to his pair of sevens.*

"But this…" Jimmy's eyes widened, then he looked back at Davenport. "Why did you fold a winning hand?"

"I folded because that's the last chance I'll ever give you! When our paths cross again, Jimmy Wolfe, I will be bringing you in dead or alive. I'd say it's all the same to me, but truth be told," Davenport spat on the ground. "I got a preference."

Chapter 7:
Billy is Missing

Wheels creaked and rattled, the badly oiled joints echoing through the plains like the wailing calls of damned souls. The corpses tossed inside shook with every bump, bits of dirt scattering off, leaving a thin trail of black dirt on the dusty road.

It was Henry who had noticed the sounds first, Jake looking over to see the dragon tilting his head as if to hear better. "What's the matter, boy?" Jake asked. Then he heard the echoing squeal.

"In the barn," Jake said, already tossing his pitchfork aside. "Now!"

Henry did as he was told, flapping low to the ground as Jake sprinted over, bracing himself against the door. He shoved it open and stepped aside as Henry waddled in, pausing only to lick Jake's disheveled hair with his forked tongue. Jake smiled, closing the barn door behind the dragon.

"You're getting big, Henry. Pretty soon you won't fit at all," he said to himself, dusting his hands off on his trousers.

"Jake!"

He turned to see his father approaching. "Did you—"

"Yeah, he's in there," Jake replied, as the rattle of the wagon grew louder. He stepped forward, peering around the house

"Good," Lawrence grunted, though he sounded far from relieved. "I'm not expecting visitors…"

"Just one visitor, it seems," Jake said, as the two stepped forward. His mother had emerged from the house as well, and together the Mullens family watched cautiously as a man in black clothing hopped down from his wagon and approached.

Jake felt a sinking feeling in the pit of his stomach as those piercing eyes, so very like Jimmy Wolfe's gazed at him, the man's hands close to his pistols. *Billy Wolfe. What the hell is he doing here?*

"What the hell are you doing here?" his father asked for him.

"Is that how you greet all your guests?" Billy asked, cold eyes taking in Dorothy and Lawrence. "Yeah, I remember this sorry excuse for a farm," Billy muttered, now staring at Jake. "We raided it, what, a few months back?"

Belly Through the Brush

"We don't have nothing for you," Lawrence muttered.

"You." Billy pointed straight at Jake. "I knew I seen you before." He leaned over and spat. "C'mere."

"I don't think I shall."

"Oh, you shall if you know what's good for you," Billy said, casually drawing both pistols, pointing one at Dorothy just a few paces away. His second pistol hovered somewhere in between Jake and his father. "Agnes and Deborah demand it."

Dorothy grimaced and snorted. "You really are a sorry excuse for your brother."

Billy's eyes boggled. "What did you just—"

"Alright!"

Billy looked over at Jake's abrupt shout.

"Alright." Jake worked his dry mouth. "What is it that you want from me?"

"You see that wagon back yonder? It's loaded with the corpses of the Riley Gang. I need to cash in my chips at the government's casino and I reckon you'll be the one to do it for me. The marshals couldn't have gotten far, and I figure they're headed to Yuma. I want you to take my wagon and turn the bodies in for the reward money."

There was a long silence.

"For a cut?" Jake asked.

"What? Hurry up and do it 'fore I cut up your old man here!" Billy Wolfe snapped. "This ain't the Pony Express. And I'm not hiring, I'm threatening."

"Just making sure," Jake said, taking a few wary paces back, his arm raised. "You're the boss."

Billy smiled suddenly. "Yeah, that's more like it."

Jake half-turned and nodded at the barn. "Let me grab my supplies, boss."

"You fixing to get a gun?" Billy leered, stepping close. "You think to trick me, but you're dealing with the brains of the Wolfe Gang. No, I'll be keeping my eye on you, boy."

"Come on back, then," Jake said in a defeated voice as his parents stayed rooted in place. "There's no fooling you, I suppose," he said, striding over to the barn.

"You suppose correctly."

Jake turned to wait as Billy stepped close, both pistols levelled at him. He opened the barn partway and slid inside. Billy stepped in right behind him.

"It's dark as night in here. Do you have a lantern or—"

A blossom of light grew in the darkness, Billy looking puzzled, as Jake had only stepped a few paces to the side. "How did you—"

"Get 'em, boy!" Jake shouted.

With a rumble, Henry's scaled head whipped forward, slamming into Billy's torso and flinging him back out the barn door. Billy sailed in the air, half-turning over, then bounced off a surprised cow to fall with a thud in a pile of manure. The cow bounded off, leaving the unconscious bandit in the field. Jake hurried out, then paused to fully open the barn door.

"You got him good, Henry," Jake said in wonderment as Henry lurched out on his claws and folded wings.

He made a rumbling sound, the faint mewling of his infancy having given way to a deeper rumble, and he sniffed at the fallen Billy Wolfe. Henry let out a deeper rumble, his jaw expanding as he put his fangs around the bandit's leg.

"Don't eat him," Lawrence said, nervously approaching, Dorothy trailing behind her husband. Henry retracted his head, looking over as the farmers surrounded Billy. "Oh, this will be hard to explain…" Lawrence muttered, wiping his sweaty palms on his shirt.

"Henry might have just saved us," Jake pointed out defensively as his father knelt beside the bandit, taking his pulse.

"I know that, boy," he said after a moment, brushing dirt off his trousers. "He's out cold, but not dead. Maybe cracked a few ribs, but I can't say that I feel much sorrow for him." Lawrence nodded at Henry. "Good work, Henry."

The dragon spread one of his wings open, then rumbled in contentment as Lawrence rubbed Henry's underbelly, his mouth sparking with a gentle flame as a puff of smoke drifted upward.

"Billy wasn't lying," Dorothy Mullens said, returning from the wagon. "There's a wagonload of dead criminals stinking up our farm. I think we might have to shackle Henry a few days while all this blows over."

"What do we do now?" Jake muttered.

"Now?" Jake turned to see his mother approaching, a slight smile on her face as she crossed her arms. "Now we listen to the brains of the Wolfe Gang and turn those bodies over to the U.S. government."

***

It was hours later, on the road to Yuma, when Jake caught up to the departing marshals. His wagon rattled along beside the curving dry gulch, Ulysses strapped in beside Billy's horse, the two of them having made a good pace all morning. Jake slowed as the two riders turned to look at him. Jake licked his lips.

At least, I hope those are the marshals. It would be a fine thing to explain a wagonload of bodies to a couple strangers along the road.

"Are you Marshal Davenport?" Jake called out as his wagon approached.

"I am indeed," one of the riders replied.

"Well, sirs, I have in my possession several wanted criminals," Jake replied. "The Riley Gang, to be precise."

Marshal Davenport raised his eyebrows. They were blond under his wide-brimmed hat, spotted with white, and he had a long, handlebar mustache. The rider beside him had a dark campaign hat and a star attached to his wool jacket.

"That wagon might just be enough to hold Walter, but…" he trailed off as he stared at the cargo. "Well… I'll be." He glanced from one face to another. "It sure is them. How…" the marshal fell silent.

"I ambushed 'em."

A snort echoed from the other rider. "Did you now?" The man raised his eyebrows. "Are you aware defrauding the U.S. government is a crime?"

Jake stirred. "I'm not sure that I take your meaning."

"Deputy—" Marshal Davenport began, raising a hand, but the man continued regardless.

"Even glancing at the bodies, I can see they were riddled with bullets from multiple shooters. Furthermore, their bodies are covered in dirt, suggesting they'd been exhumed from their place of final rest. And not just that, this one here clearly took a shotgun blast full to the chest. I see no firearm upon your person. Are you saying to me that—"

"Deputy Milton!" Marshal Davenport snapped, and the other rider finally fell silent. The marshal stared at Jake for a long moment, then broke into a thin smile. "Deputy Milton raises a fair point. In normal circumstances we would dig into the details of what transpired to bring the Riley Gang to their untimely, if well-deserved, end."

Jake grimaced. "The way it happened... well, through a series of certain events it ended up that the Riley Gang is dead and in my wagon, and out of loyalty to my country, I—"

"It's fine, son. We'll pay the bounty."

Relief flashed across Jake's face. "That's good, then. Are you going to Yuma? I am prepared to travel until we reach a bank."

Marshal Davenport nodded. "We've a mind to form a posse to deal with the Wolfe Gang. I see a sharpshooter like you might come in handy," he added, cracking a thin smile. "Anyway, you're in luck, young man. I happen to be in possession of some of the government's generous funds, meant to secure the West while this Civil War rages on. Hold on a moment while I count; I believe I have more than enough."

Jake waited, scarcely believing what he was seeing as a pile of coins in canvas sacks grew. Deputy Milton was frowning down at the bodies beside Jake and sighed.

"Transporting them may be somewhat difficult..."

"I tell you what," Jake said with a smile as Marshal Davenport produced the final bag. "I'll throw the wagon in for free. Just remember the poor citizens trying to scrape a living out in the West. It's a rough life out here."

"Well, 2,000 silver dollars would put a stop to that kind of life," Deputy Milton commented.

Jake stared down at the coins. "Yeah... it would," he said sadly.

***

"We could pick up stakes and move!" Jake's father had said earlier that day, the discussion breaking out above the unconscious Billy Wolfe, tied securely in a shed.

"To where?" Dorothy had replied. "Back out East? We came here to leave that kind of life. Farther west, to some miserable city like San Francisco? I'll take my chances here."

"Still, just giving the money back..."

His mother had stood tall then, putting both hands on her hips and giving Lawrence that stern look she always managed. Jake winced just as he relived the memory. "I don't want to take any chances with Jimmy Wolfe coming after us for revenge. Jake can make it clear he was just following Billy's orders. We can deal with the idiot brother later. Besides," she added, as Lawrence and Jake listened in silence, "I have everything I want with you, Lawrence Mullens, even if it will be a lean winter."

Despite himself, Lawrence had broken out into a wide smile, and Jake knew then that the argument had been won. Of course, he'd looked away as his parents had embraced, murmuring affectionate nonsense to each other while he'd saddled up Ulysses beside Billy's horse. Still, he knew they had something special.

For some reason, as Jake rode along into Rattlefort, his thoughts turned to Lucille. *No... I need to focus.* Jake blinked, catching a brief gleam of metal in the window of a second-story building as he entered town. A puff of smoke drifted out, as if the bandit on sentry duty had a cigar clenched in his teeth, though Jake could not make out who it was. Still, no one stopped Jake as he hitched Ulysses to the post at the Silver Springs Saloon, entering with heavy sacks of coins rattling in his bags.

Jake attracted attention from the moment he walked in, gritting his teeth as he approached Jimmy, pausing right as he was about to deal cards. Jake stumbled forward, dumping the coins on the table, and leaned back to breathe in heavily.

"That's everything Billy asked for," he said.

Jimmy blinked as the silence lingered.

"... What?" he finally managed.

"For the Riley Gang's bodies," Jake said in a nervous rush, which was not entirely feigned. "The ones Billy had me deliver to the marshals. There's the reward money. All of it, didn't take a single coin."

Jimmy might have been bewildered, but he played it off well enough, snapping at Sam beside him. "Search him." The man lumbered toward Jake, who grimaced even as he stood still, enduring the fumbling fingers and stench of whiskey.

"He's got nothin'," Sam Reeves announced. "B-B-But, B-B-Boss, B-Billy's b-been missin'!"

Belly Through the Brush

Jimmy fixed Sam with a long stare, then sighed. "I know that. I guess he weaseled up some sort of scheme and hasn't made it back. Still..." Jimmy clenched his fist. Beside Jimmy, an older man set his cards down and leaned over.

"I think the marshals had something to do with it," the man said, his voice more cultured than Jake would have expected. "We cannot ignore the coincidence of their arrival."

"You might be right about that, Doc," Jimmy replied, as Sam nodded in agreement. Jimmy looked over at Jake, then waved him away in dismissal. "Get on out of here, boy."

***

Lucille paused from dusting the corner of the cathouse's general room as she heard her mother's office door creak open. Madam Josephine looked over at her, one hand partly stained with ink. "Ah, Lucille. How's Peggy getting on?"

Lucille winced, recalled how Rawhide Cooper had stormed in, declaring that Peggy would replace Pearl. It had not been the best of beginnings. "Well, you know... she's still not taking it too well."

Madam Josephine nodded. "No doubt. Does she harbor thoughts of revenge?"

"How could she not?"

"Good. I think that it's time you brought her to my office. She's been getting along with the rest of the girls fine, and I feel we can trust her."

"Yes, Ma," Lucille said, setting down her duster and hurrying up the creaking wooden stairs. Olive had her hands on Peggy's shoulder, whispering something reassuring to her as the woman sniffed and looked up, tears breaking through her powdered face.

"Peggy Riley? My mother—I mean, Madam Josephine wants to see her."

Peggy lurched to her feet, Olive patting her one last time on the back. "It gets better!" she shouted, as Peggy and Lucille silently made their way down the stairs and to Madam Josephine's office.

"Ah," Josephine began, barely glancing up from her desk, polishing a derringer with a white cloth. "Peggy Riley. I appreciate the work you've done for us over the past few days."

"Didn't have a choice," she muttered.

"We so rarely do," Josephine said, setting the derringer down on the desk, the grip facing Peggy. "But, sometimes... we can change our destinies."

Peggy watched in silence as Madam Josephine leaned forward earnestly.

"I'll cut to the chase. We mean to have our revenge on Rawhide Cooper and kill that loathsome scoundrel like the scum that he is. Will you be with us when the time comes?"

Peggy reached over, grabbing the derringer, and pulled it close. "I'm with you," Peggy whispered.

Chapter 8:
Lucille Knows

Lucille turned her borrowed horse down the dusty road and smiled as she smelled the warm scent of Mrs. Orren's blueberry pie. *He's going to love it,* Lucille thought to herself. Lucille had borrowed the Clemson family's horse, finished a few errands early, and still had plenty of time to visit with Jake. Jake had been right on one thing; it was an easy enough ride, and her mother had even suggested it after the kindness Jake had shown at Pearl's funeral.

She squinted in the distance, seeing Lawrence Mullens working in the fields, and then spotted Jake walking toward the barn with a bundle in his arms. Lucille grinned, spurring the horse forward.

When he sees this pie, he's going to lose his mind!

Still grinning, Lucille rounded the family home, spotting Dorothy Mullens through the open window. She was humming to herself as she swept and didn't notice Lucille's arrival. With smooth, careful motions, Lucille guided her borrowed horse to the stable where Ulysses was looking over in curiosity. She slid down, tying her horse's reins to the hitching post, and hurried over to the barn with the blueberry pie in hand.

"Jake Mullens," she announced, stepping into the barn. "Look what I got for you…"

She trailed off, her eyes widening. Jake was kneeling down, prodding a leg of mutton into the smoldering mouth of a demon. It snapped down, biting into the flesh, bones cracking—and then it tossed the mutton away to smack into the barn wall. Cold, reptilian eyes flicked over to look at her. The demon was huge, encircled with metal chains, and rumbled as it glanced over.

Lucille shrieked, dropping her blueberry pie, which collapsed on her shoes and speckled her dress. Jake rose, his hands extended, trying to calm Lucille down.

"Lucille! Uh, I wasn't expecting you. Look, I guess this might be a shock to you, but—"

"You're communing with Satan!" Lucille said, taking a step back. "A winged serpent! Jake, how could I have been so wrong about you?"

"What?" He blinked. "No, this is Henry!"

Belly Through the Brush

Lucille took a few long breaths. The beast was chained up at least, lying its head down and snuffling like a tired dog. Up close, it even looked kind of cute. *Is this how heresy spreads?*

Lucille had never been the most religious of girls, especially after Rattlefort's pastor and his mistress had left to join the Confederate army a couple years back, but there was something deeply unsettling about seeing a demon in a barn. She looked at Jake, silently begging for him to explain.

"I found him a few months ago, and we've been taking care of him. Well, he won't eat since we shackled him up... I think he's depressed. Normally he loves meat, but not human meat! Henry's a dragon, and you don't need to worry about him one bit!" Jake paused, blinking at Lucille's feet. "Is that... was that blueberry pie?"

"Jake, he may have come to you as your grandfather," Lucille said, finally finding her voice. "But Beelzebub can take many forms."

"No, Henry is just his name," Jake said, shaking his head. "Look... let him sniff your hand."

Lucille gritted her teeth, unwilling to approach. Yet Henry had finished eating, and produced a very human-sounding burp, causing Jake to laugh. Despite herself, Lucille smiled. Then she inched closer, extending a wavering hand. Henry looked at it for a moment, and then favored it with a few sniffs, his forked tongue then flicking out to touch her shaking knuckles.

Lucille laughed nervously, then lowered her hand.

"Aw, he likes you!" Jake exclaimed.

"Where…" Lucille fell silent once again. She had a million questions and was still not entirely convinced Henry wasn't Satan.

"The Wolfe Gang took him from the train they robbed. Do you remember back when you told me about that? Well, I snuck in, and saw this little baby dragon in a cage. Then I took him out of there!" He paused. "I don't think they even noticed. They must have just been busy spending the gold and silver they stole."

"Oh, Jake…" Lucille bit her lip. She couldn't exactly say what he had done was dangerous, when she had all but incited him. Besides, she had no love lost for the Wolfe Gang. "It's better that you have him," she blurted out.

As if in agreement, Henry rumbled, extending his sinuous head toward Jake. He scratched the dragon behind its scaly ears as if this was a common occurrence. "But you can't tell anyone," he said. "Even your mother. You promise?"

"I promise," she said seriously. "On my father's grave."

"Well, after all this… come on over, I should show you something else," Jake said, hesitating a moment before taking her hand. Lucille smiled as she

Belly Through the Brush

followed him over to a smaller outbuilding. They'd known each other for years, but his hand felt somehow welcoming. Especially after all she'd been through. He let go a few moments later, unlatching the lock on the outbuilding.

"I guess you could say it's another surprise."

Lucille laughed. "I must say, Jake Mullens, you've surprised me a great deal today. To think that you're growing dragons in this farm? What next, I wonder, are you growing…" she trailed off. Somehow this seemed even more surprising.

A flurry of muffled cursing greeted her as Jake turned on a kerosene lamp. It illuminated the snarling, twisted features of Billy Wolfe, who had a rag stuffed in his mouth. Jake stepped behind Billy, who was strapped in a chair, and delicately pulled the gag loose.

Billy spat and sputtered. "It is downright unconscionable, what you are doing to me. Have I not rights as an American citizen?"

Jake smiled and tapped on Billy's shoulder. "He's met Henry too."

Billy grimaced. "What is that thing? I ain't seen nothing like it before!"

Lucille licked her lips nervously. "Uh, Jake… what are you doing with Billy?"

"Oh, I'm treating him well," Jake replied. "You just had oatmeal this morning," he added, patting Billy's shoulder.

"A pox on your oats," Billy sputtered. "When I get out of here, I'm going to have Jimmy and the gang kill it before your beast gets any bigger."

Jake stuffed the gag back in the bandit's mouth, tying it tight, then shrugged apologetically to Lucille. "You can see why we keep him tied up like this. Well, thanks for stopping by to visit me. Shall we continue the tour?"

***

Marshal Davenport shuffled through the written correspondence that had stacked up since he'd left Yuma. He picked one up at random, scanned the letter about a property dispute, and set it aside. He sighed to himself.

Across the office, Deputy Milton chuckled quietly. "A problem, Marshal?"

"My problem, Deputy, is with the proliferation of the English language. Any halfway-educated person in this vast territory who possesses a dip pen and a complaint is able to write to me about their petty squabbles. Just wait until every little town has a telegram in their post office. Lord, I'm glad to be getting old. This is a strange new world we're living in."

Deputy Milton grinned. "I can see it vexes you mighty fierce. How about we stroll down to the train station for that inmate pickup? It is not yet nine, but a walk would do you some good."

Marshal Davenport grumbled as he rose to his feet, picking up his hat and setting it on his thinning hair. "I do appreciate you sticking with me awhile, Deputy Milton. I want you to know that your revolver and your good advice are both valued here."

Deputy Milton laughed as he fell into line with Davenport, the two exiting Yuma's little police station. "I figure my case has already grown cold, and this takes priority. Why, the President himself has made his views known. I'm sticking with you, Marshal."

Together, they strode through the dusty streets of Yuma, Arizona, waiting at the train station. Before long, they could hear the soft *chug-chug-chug* of the approaching train, which squealed on the rails as it slowed to a stop. A tall Black woman stepped out, wearing men's clothes, and hauled a prisoner behind her in one hand. The other held a shotgun.

"What in blazes..." Deputy Milton muttered.

She looked over as Marshal Davenport approached. "Are you the local marshal?"

"I am indeed," he replied. "I believe I've heard tell of you. Oh yes, 'Stagecoach Mary.' You're escorting prisoners now?"

"The star route asked for volunteers, and I accepted," she said, hauling the man along with her. Albert Crosby, wanted in three states. "I find *paying* work suits me just fine."

"Albert Crosby," Marshal Davenport stated. "I'm taking you in for murder, rape, and robbery. Your crime spree ends here. Mary, if you would, I'll show you the way to the jail." He stepped off from the train station and the group made their way back into Yuma, attracting more than their fair share of staring.

"Davenport, was it?" Al tried to jerk away from Mary, who kept a tight grip on him. "This ain't right, being paraded around by a Black woman. It's undignified."

"That so."

"You must understand, Marshal. How can she touch me like that? So roughly!" he grimaced as Mary pulled him along.

"Quit your whining, Al," she said. "You've been making such a fuss all morning." She glanced over at the marshal. "I can't stay long. Train leaves in a half hour, and I need to get my stagecoach rolling this evening. The mail never sleeps."

"Indeed it does not," Marshal Davenport muttered, wincing at the thought of all the correspondence he had yet to read.

Al squirmed. "As a white man, surely you understand the indignity of this all. Besides, this is the South! *She* should be the one in chains."

"Well, it's more West than South," Marshal Davenport replied, pausing to spit on the dirt road, then pointed over to the jail as they rounded the corner. "You see that, Al? The Stars and Stripes still fly above my jail. You can complain all you want in there. You won't be getting out any time soon, unless it's to

Belly Through the Brush

hang." He glanced over at Stagecoach Mary and took a firm grip of Al's other arm. "We've got it from here, Miss..."

"Fields," she replied. "I appreciate it. I'll need to be on the train soon."

"Right, wouldn't want the mail to be delayed on my account," Marshal Davenport muttered, and then a thought occurred to him. "That's dangerous work. Have you had any run-ins with the gangs out here?"

"A time or two, but I have sent them packing," she said, tapping her shotgun. "The worst I faced was a lone man. You've heard of Lester Reyes?"

The marshal nodded. "The Demon, they call him. I've heard plenty of rumors about him."

"Yeah, well this Demon tried to hold up my stagecoach not too long ago. The rumors are true, Marshal. That man has no soul. While passing through the New Mexico Territory one night, Lester rode up on my stagecoach by himself like a one-man army."

Deputy Milton grunted. "I heard about him. A Mexican, I believe."

"I never seen a man so determined to kill like him before. After shooting it out with a couple of my guys on horseback his revolver ran out of bullets. By the grace of God, I'm alive today, but I had the uncommon luxury of looking that fella in his eyes before injuring him."

"What did you see?" Marshal Davenport asked.

"They say the eyes are the windows to the soul, and he had none when I looked."

"I wish you had killed that man when you had the chance," Marshal Davenport replied. "He's wanted dead or alive, with an $800 bounty on his head. He poisoned a town's water supply, killing over fifty people. The ones who didn't die were left shitting themselves for months."

"That's not including the number of folk he killed with his pistol," Deputy Milton added.

"I tell you what," Marshal Davenport said, "I'm rounding up a posse to take down the gangs in the area. It's clear you can handle yourself. I'll offer much more than you'd make as a stagecoach courier."

"Oh? Whiskey in the deal too?" Mary grinned.

Marshal Davenport chuckled. "As much as you can handle."

"That would put quite a strain on your funds. But..." she hesitated. "No sir, I couldn't possibly accept. I took this work on after being freed from slavery, and I am not about to leave it now."

"I see. Well, I suppose you better get back on the train."

Mary nodded. "Until next time, boys. I gotta get going. Thanks for the offer though."

Marshal Davenport pulled the silent Al Crosby along, as Deputy Milton pushed open the creaking jail door. The Yuma jail was empty and neglected,

Belly Through the Brush

cobwebs in the corners and the smell of mold permeating throughout.

"Do you see how she treated me?" Al grumbled, then sniffed at the jail. "Disgusting."

"Well, get used to it. At least you have it to yourself for now," Marshal Davenport said as Deputy Milton shoved Al into an empty cell. "I mean to fill this up in the coming days." He spat on the floor. "Both the jail and the graveyard."

Chapter 9:

The New Recruits

Henry's low moan echoed through the shack as Jake set the wooden bucket in front of him. They'd caught some rats over the past few days, Jake practicing with his father's old rifle, and he'd collected enough that Henry could have a good meal.

Or would if he had the appetite for it, Jake thought, glancing over at Lucille beside him. It still seemed strange to him, that Lucille had returned the next day, smelling of soap and flowers. *Why'd she come back?*

"Oh, Henry," Lucille said in a sad voice.

Oh, that's right. My dragon.

It was a strange feeling, to be jealous for a depressed dragon shackled up in a wooden shed, but there it was. Jake cleared his throat. "Mighty fine of you to be coming by."

"It's nothing, Jake." Lucille turned and smiled at him, and he had never felt better in his life, a spark of joy swelling in his chest.

"I do enjoy your company," he added after a moment. "They say there's been some folks talking about a dance coming up in Rattlefort." He paused. "I was—"

"Oh, he's eating!" Lucille said, half-rising, staring at Henry as he sniffed at the bucket. After a moment Henry withdrew his head and let out a sad mewling sound. "Oh..." Lucille sat back down. "You know, I wonder if perhaps you should let him out late at night. I think he wants to do his own hunting. And no one would see, after all."

"Yeah..." Jake nodded slowly. "I think my parents would agree to that." He patted the dragon's large leathery wing. "Don't worry, buddy, we'll let you go outside tonight."

***

"I rode around town, like you said, hat all tilted down and my coat scrunched up like it wasn't hot as blazes," Doc Otis said. "Didn't get a second look from anyone."

"Huh," Rawhide chuckled. "You have a plain face, Doc. No one would look at you twice."

"Nor you once if they could avoid it," Doc replied, then glanced back at the stoic Jimmy. "Word is there's to be a double hanging."

Jimmy nodded slowly. "What do you think, Doc?"

"I did not catch the name of Billy Wolfe, but it would not surprise me if they mean to hang your brother."

Jimmy breathed out. Then he pointed at the main square, visible from their position in a nearby bluff. "The scaffold's there. That'll be where it happens. Sam, give me your rifle," Jimmy said, extending a hand.

"S-s-ure, b-boss," Sam replied, handing it over. He'd had his rifle fitted with the new Amidon telescopic rifle sight for distant targets, and Jimmy raised the scope to his eye. He adjusted his position, keeping the rifle steady, and scanned over the outskirts of Yuma, Arizona. Some folk were out in their Sunday best, others going about their errands, but it was clear most of them were starting to congregate in the town square. Jimmy nudged the scope up to take in the scaffold.

"There we are," Jimmy muttered as his rifle scope took in Marshal Davenport's blurred form, a faint gleam on his badge, looking sternly at the audience. It would be a tricky shot from this distance. Jimmy grinned at the thought, but he didn't really consider it.

Belly Through the Brush

It will be much more sporting to have Agatha and Delilah gun that bastard down.

He adjusted his aim, spotting the deputy marshal, a man Jimmy only half-remembered. Instead, Jimmy focused on the chunky man being hauled up to the scaffold. He stared at the man, trying to place him, and finally recognized him.

"Ira Dotson," Jimmy muttered to himself. He was a renowned cattle rustler, Jimmy occasionally hearing stories of the families he'd impoverished throughout the West, and a thought struck him.

"What's he sayin'?" Rawhide Cooper whispered, a good deal louder than he might have intended.

"Hey Doc," Jimmy said, still staring down the rifle scope. "Ride on back into town and see what you can do to distract the lawmen there."

"No distraction better than a bullet to the head, Jimmy," Doc Otis replied.

"If it comes to it. Just get them out of the way."

He resumed looking through his scope. The mayor of Yuma himself was up there, along with another two men, strapping Ira up to a noose. The deputy marshal returned a moment later,

"Billy ain't there," Jimmy announced a moment later, baffled. *Where the hell did my idiot brother go this time?*

"Well... what are we gonna do, boss?" Rawhide asked after a moment.

Jimmy let out a low sigh, taking in the two wanted men being sized up for the noose. "I didn't come all this way for nothing," he said after a moment. "Ira Dotson I've heard about, and this other fella seems to be reckoned as worth hanging. I figure we can use new recruits."

He lowered the borrowed rifle, turning and handing it back to Sam. "Stay here and cover us," he said, Sam nodding and moving behind a boulder. He rested the rifle on it, training it on the square below. Jimmy glanced up the bluff, where Preacher was hanging back with a couple spare mounts. After a raid gone wrong, with Billy getting his horse shot down after fleeing a bank with just pocket change, Jimmy had learned to bring a spare horse around.

It was looking to be an especially good idea now.

"New recruits, I don't know, Boss," Rawhide muttered. "I like the gang the way it is now with just us."

"I don't come to you for advice, Rawhide," Jimmy replied. "Get on your horse and follow me," he said, mounting his own horse and starting down the sandy bluff overlooking Yuma.

"Yes, Boss!"

The two riders didn't attract much attention as they made their way through town, most of the citizens of Yuma busy as they went about their errands or hurried to attend the public hanging. They fit in well enough as they pushed forward. On the scaffold, the mayor was giving a long, rambling speech about justice as the second criminal was being fitted for the noose. Marshal Davenport kept a steely gaze on the crowd, Jimmy ready in case the lawman looked in his direction.

"Oh, I recognize that one," Rawhide mumbled beside him, nodding at the second criminal. "That's Albert Crosby. He's a murderer and a rapist. I wouldn't mind working with him."

Jimmy nodded, remaining silent, as the chatter of the crowd began to fall away. The hangmen were ready now, nooses tied firmly around the two wanted men.

"Justice is integral to a Christian society, and I hope and pray that you remember that this coming November, when I am running for re-election as your mayor." The mayor paused, clearly expecting applause, but there were only a few scattered claps. He twisted his mouth and glanced at one of his men. "You may do the hon—"

A shout broke the silence, a drunkard stumbling out of a tavern, hooting and hollering as he raised his hands in the air, trails of smoke rising from both. Unnoticed to all but Jimmy, Doc Otis stepped out of the saloon and disappeared into the crowd.

"I got two sticks of dy-no-mite aburnin' in my hands!" the drunkard shouted, ending with a hiccup, and then turned and fled down the crowded street. "Where will I go? Catch me if you can, Marshal, a-hee-hee-hic!-hee-hee!"

"Lord have mercy!" the mayor called out, as Marshal Davenport leaped into the crowd.

"Stop right there!" he shouted, pushing through the crowd, followed a moment later by Deputy Milton. They made their way after the drunkard, leaving the other men alone to look after the criminals tied to their nooses. Jimmy looked away as they passed nearby, then stuck a foot out as Deputy Milton ran by, sending the Kansan stumbling and cursing to the ground. He got up a moment later and trailed Marshal Davenport as he shouted at the drunkard, who sprinted down an alley.

Jimmy felt someone brushing beside him in the crowd. "So how was that?" Doc Otis's stubbly gray face grinning up at him from under his broad-brimmed hat.

"A hell of a distraction, Doc. You see to Ira and Rawhide will grab Al. Agatha and Delilah will see to the rest," he added, whipping up both his pistols. He fired both, each shot cutting into the rope and sending the struggling criminals to the grounds. Jimmy sprinted up as Rawhide punched the Mayor of Yuma off the wooden stage to fall stumbling back into the crowd.

Jimmy pulled Agatha and Delilah on the two hangmen. "Get out of here now or I'll send you both to hell."

As one, the hangmen turned and ran, as Doc and Rawhide hauled the criminals to their feet. Jimmy

Belly Through the Brush

scanned the crowd for would-be heroes, glimpsing an older man pulling his pistol out. A sharp crack echoed through Yuma, the man slumping to the ground, Sam Reeves taking him out with his scoped rifle.

"None of you get any ideas!" Jimmy snapped. He turned around to face the two criminals, their faces both bewildered and exhilarated. "The name's Jimmy Wolfe, and I'm recruiting for the Wolfe Gang. You can accept now or meet your maker."

"I'm in," Ira Dotson said in a rush.

"Good choice," Jimmy said as Doc cut away his noose and led him toward the bluff where Preacher waited with the spare horses. He looked over to Al Crosby. "Well?"

"I prefer going it alone," he muttered.

"I ain't even going to waste a bullet on ya when Rawhide has a knife," Jimmy said, "Go and cut—"

"No, no, I'm with you," Al said in a rush, smiling slightly. "Wouldn't want to disappoint after you came all the way here."

Jimmy spat on the wooden scaffold. "Don't make a habit of trying my patience, new guy. And I didn't come for you, I came for my idiot brother. Billy Wolfe. You seen him?"

Al shook his head.

"Ira, you seen him?" Jimmy called out, and the man paused mid-run.

"Ah, no Boss!"

"Well ain't that just something," Jimmy muttered, grabbing Al's noose and tugging him along, the wanted man choking as he tried to keep his feet. "I reckon your noose can wait a while, new guy. You're going to be my special project."

***

"Put your damn dynamite down!" Marshal Davenport hollered, chest heaving as he vaulted a bench and ran after the drunkard, chortling away merrily. There weren't any pedestrians here, and Davenport lined up his pistol now that he had a clear line of sight.

Marshal Davenport fired twice. The drunkard came to a stumbling halt, the flames that had been burning away on the wicks now snuffed out.

"Well there was no cause to shoot, Marshal," the drunkard said, turning with his hands still in the air. "You scared the hiccups away," he muttered.

"Throw him in the cell, Deputy," Marshal Davenport said as Deputy Milton approached, grabbing the man's arms and forcing him down into the dusty road. A few coins fell out of the drunkard's pockets as the sticks of dynamite fell to the ground. Up close, Marshal Davenport saw they were made of wax.

"Candles!?" Marshal Davenport roared. "Why would you do such a stupid thing? You made me think you were some kind of newfangled suicidal bomber!"

"Ahah… sorry, Marshal," the drunkard replied as Deputy Milton hauled him to his feet. "See, this peculiar fellow paid me a hundred silver dollars to distract you. A hundred silver dollars! Can you imagine, me, with that much money?"

"You're dumber than you look if you expect to keep any..." Marshal Davenport blinked. "Distract? The hanging!"

He turned around. Come to think of it, he had heard a couple shots in the distance, though it was a fairly common sound in Yuma. "Take him to the jail," Marshal Davenport ordered, before sprinting through the streets. He rounded the corner, seeing the crowd already dispersing, the ropes severed midway through and no criminals to be seen. He sprinted up the scaffold, peering over toward the nearby bluff, catching a glimpse of horsemen riding off into the sunset.

"Damn you, Jimmy Wolfe!" Marshal Davenport yelled. "I'll see you swing if it's the last thing I do!"

Chapter 10:
Teaching Ira a Lesson

Paper crinkled beside Jimmy as Doc Otis turned the page of his newspaper. "Well, it looks like Atlanta's fallen," Doc said. "That General Sherman, he's no shrinking violet, I tell you what. Give him command and the war will be as good as won."

Jimmy grunted. "Who cares what happens out East? Union, Confederacy, they're all the same." The sound of furniture chipping away was grating at him, and he turned to see Rawhide Cooper jabbing away between his fingers as he played five finger fillet with himself. "Will you knock that off?"

Rawhide paused, holding his Bowie knife in the air, then set it aside. "Well, alright Boss."

"Can't get any peace and quiet around here," Jimmy muttered. "It's enough to make one…"

Belly Through the Brush

He paused as the saloon doors swung open, a middle-aged woman in neat, proper clothing approaching him.

"Ah, Mrs. Orren," Doc said, setting his newspaper down. "What brings you to the Silver Springs Saloon?"

"It's practically the Wolfe Saloon by now," she said, glancing over at the proprietor, mechanically drying a mug as he stared fixedly at the wooden table Rawhide Cooper had ruined. "As a married woman, I wouldn't ordinarily set foot in such an establishment, but I have to say my part, seeing as you're what passes for law around here."

Jimmy grinned. "That's funny. Me, the lawman. Well, sure, Mrs. Orren. Say what needs saying."

"One of your new 'recruits,' this Ira fellow, he's stolen money from my bakery. I asked around, and I wasn't the first he did this to."

Doc frowned. "I heard the same, Jimmy. Was meaning to bring it up with you."

"That so." Jimmy mulled this over. They were thieves and brigands, after all, but Rattlefort was essentially a home base by now. There was no point in taking from the citizens of this town. At least, not without Jimmy's express permission. "Any trouble with Al Crosby?"

"He complained that my scones were too dry," Mrs. Orren replied. "Seems a disagreeable sort. But… no. He pays for what he takes."

Jimmy twisted his mouth. "And here I thought it was Al that'd be the problem. I don't suppose you know where Ira is now, Mrs. Orren."

"As a matter of fact, I seen him walking into Greenwood's Hardware Store on my way here. Likely he's causing a fuss right now."

Jimmy nodded, turning and spitting on the floor. The saloon owner made no reaction.

"Doc, take a gander over at Greenwood's and haul Ira over. It seems I've got to explain a few things to him. Rawhide, since you ain't doing shit besides tearing up that table, why don't you bring the rest of the boys over. Al in particular. I want him to see this." Jimmy rose from the table and fixed Mrs. Orren with a cold stare. The corners of his mouth turned up, but it wasn't exactly a smile. "I'll get your money back, Mrs. Orren. Let me know if you have any trouble with him again."

"I'm obliged," she said softly, turning and exiting the saloon, Doc Otis and Rawhide following close behind. Jimmy walked over to the bar and tapped the counter, looking the proprietor of the Silver Springs Saloon in the eye.

"What's the strongest thing you got?"

"Uh... well, I got some moonshine," the man mumbled. "You want a glass of it? Uh, on the house, of course."

"No, I want the whole bottle. Just leave it here," Jimmy said, already heading off. He made his way to

Belly Through the Brush

the bathroom in the back. There was no one around to bother him, though there was no saying just how much business the saloon usually had around this time of day. A few old-timers were drinking, along with a couple gentlemen Jimmy took for businessmen of some sort, and a pianist was keeping up a brisk tune. Jimmy was just cleaning up in the washbasin when angry voices echoed over to him.

"I'll do as I please, old man!" Ira Dotson shouted. "Hauling me into the saloon like that! Get your damn paws off me and move out of my way. The next time you step to me I'll kill you!"

Doc's familiar chuckle was the only response. "Come on then, kill me right now! Do you think I fear death, boy?"

"Bartender, a round of whiskey," Ira belted out, their voices echoing to the back of the saloon.

"Jimmy won't be happy when he finds out what you're doing," Doc cautioned.

"It's your word against mine then, geezer!"

Jimmy whistled to himself, glancing up at his reflection in the mirror by the washbasin. His black beard had grown out a little longer, his hair a bit tousled under his hat. *I'll have to do something about that. Just after I teach a lesson to Ira here.* Jimmy cracked his knuckles, then stepped out of the washroom, whistling to himself.

He looked over as the saloon doors opened once again, the rest of his gang filing in again, Sam out front

103

with his telescopic rifle and bandolier slung around his chest, Preacher still wearing his black clothing and preacher's hat, crucifix and pistol glinting in the light of the saloon. Al Crosby joined them as well, a repeater slung around his back, stained white shirt under two brown suspenders. Then last was Rawhide Cooper, the big man still playing with his Bowie knife, spinning it in the air and catching it.

A tough bunch, as tough as any I've worked with. But Doc is right, as usual. The Union is looking to win this war, and then they'll set their sights to the West. We need numbers—and fast.

Jimmy nodded at them, then sidled over to Ira at the bar. "Ira, which hand is your shooting hand?"

"Huh? Oh, my right hand. Why, Boss?"

"Well…" Jimmy took a seat beside him. "I like to know about my men. Be able to tally up their strengths and weaknesses. Send them on tasks that I know they can handle. And beat them down like dogs when they get ahead of their spurs."

"Makes sense," Ira said, nodding. "Hey bartender, another—"

"No, I've got this," Jimmy said, grabbing the bottle of moonshine. He uncorked it and poured a full measure into Ira's cup. "This here moonshine is the strongest stuff in the bar."

"Ohoh!" Ira said, grasping it. "So this is going to be one of those kinds of nights, eh Boss?"

"It sure is."

Belly Through the Brush

"Well, join me then, won't you?"

"I wouldn't mind one bit, Ira," Jimmy said as he poured himself a shot. "You see, working together like we are means profiting together. Acting as one. No going against my words."

"Sure, sure," Ira said. "Lots of profit to be had here."

"Well. Profit and loss are linked," he said, raising his glass, and they clinked it together. "To working together."

"To working together!"

They both took a long swig, emptying their glasses, and Jimmy slammed it down on the counter.

"Ooo-eee!" Ira exclaimed. "Feeling nice and toasty now."

"That's good, Ira," Jimmy said as he rose from his seat, winking his right eye over at Sam and Preacher, already standing ready beside them. "You're going to need it."

Sam and Preacher grabbed Ira, hauling him to the ground and pinning him down. The piano abruptly fell silent, the conversations of the others falling to a hush, as everybody looked over. Jimmy drew Agatha from his holster, standing over Ira as Doc approached the bar, grabbing the bartender's dirty rag from the counter.

"What are you doing?" Ira sputtered, and Doc forced the dirty rag into Ira's mouth. The cattle rustler was panicking now, fear clear behind his eyes, breathing fast.

"I told you Jimmy wouldn't be happy with what you was doing!" Doc shouted down at him. "Now stop resisting and bite down on this rag, boy! If you don't, it's gonna hurt," Doc Otis added, with a smirk on his face. "Though it's all the same to me."

"I-I-I'm sorry, Jimmy," Ira stuttered, muffled with the rag in his mouth, "I-I swear it won't happen again!"

"I know it won't," Jimmy said. "Now stop squealing like a little pig, Ira. This is what happens when you don't listen. I was clear about this, wasn't I? And didn't I say Doc spoke for me?" He glanced over at Al, gauging the man's reactions. *But he's just watching, cold as ever.*

Al met Jimmy's gaze. "You were crystal clear, Boss."

Jimmy nodded, satisfied, then looked back down at the struggling Ira. He shot him in the center of his left palm, Ira yelling in agony, and then Jimmy pointed at the bottle of moonshine.

"Soak that rag in the 'shine and wrap it around his wound," Jimmy ordered. "Doc, you cauterize…" he trailed off, noticing that Doc Otis was already heating a knife up by the fireplace.

"Already on it, Boss!"

Jimmy snorted over Ira's muffled screams. "You see, that's why I trust Doc. He knows what needs doing."

Belly Through the Brush

Doc approached with a glowing red-hot knife, kneeling down beside Ira as Sam grabbed the man's left hand, keeping it steady. Doc pressed it down, cauterizing the wound as Ira screeched yet again.

Jimmy looked over at Al, trying to see his reaction, but the man was as cold as ever. Then Al tapped his stomach. "It's making me hungry," he said. "Smells like roast pig."

Jimmy grunted, then looked back at Ira as Doc stepped away. "Well, come on up, Ira," Jimmy said, grabbing the man's uninjured right hand and hauling him to his feet. "Have another round with us," he added, guiding the sobbing man to a stool. Ira glanced over at Jimmy, then down at the counter.

"Hey Ira," Preacher snorted, taking a seat beside him with a grin on his face, the rest of the Wolfe Gang joining them at the bar, "if you let Jimmy shoot ya in your other hand then you'll be just like Christ when he was crucified."

A few of the others chuckled, but Ira remained silent, as the bartender passed out cups of whiskey. He and Ira shared the same pale, terrified expressions.

"No hard feelings Ira," Doc cut in after a moment. "We know you're a no-good thief. That's why we recruited ya! But you got to listen to the boss. Don't mess with the people of Rattlefort."

"But there was..." Ira mumbled, coming to a halt, then continued. "But I heard... Rawhide..."

Jimmy grimaced. "What did you hear about Rawhide?"

"I heard… he… killed a prostitute?"

Rawhide spread his arms wide. "I never killed no prostitute."

"What you heard was a rumor," Jimmy said. "People say crazy things sometimes."

"Oh." Ira nodded, taking another glass. "Alright, Boss."

"Now then. Speaking of recruiting, I've been doing some thinking lately. With things the way they are, and this Civil War looking like it's coming to an end, we should make the most of the time we have. What do you think about trying to unify all the outlaws in the West?"

The others looked over from their drinks, most looking vaguely skeptical.

"Unify?" Preacher asked after a moment. "Most of these gangs have some squabble or another with each other."

"We're all after the same thing, though," Jimmy pointed out.

Doc nodded slowly. "That could work. The easiest thing to do would be to gather up all the wanted posters we come across and send everyone worth a damn a letter of their own."

Jimmy raised his eyebrows, taking a swig of his whiskey and set it down. "Good thinking, Doc. Letter

Belly Through the Brush

writing, though? That could take ages, and I never had the knack for it myself."

"Leave it to me, Boss, if you don't mind me taking a small portion of our winnings for the costs. I did some snooping around the abandoned sheriff's office here, and there are all the bounties listed up until the war began. There are some newer ones posted around the Post Office too, and I can spread the word around to anyone who wants to earn a few coins writing letters and delivering them to towns throughout the West."

Jimmy nodded. "Take everything you need, Doc. More than that, promise some gold to those that show." He slammed a round of whiskey, feeling the warmth spreading through his body. "Well that settles it, then! A gathering of bandits; the most renowned and dangerous gunslingers in all the West coming to the first ever Outlaw Summit."

"Here?" the saloon owner sputtered, and the gang looked over as if forgetting he existed.

"Right in your saloon," Jimmy confirmed. "Well, you'll do a brisk bit of business, that's for sure."

The man nodded slowly, brightening up a bit. "Yes, sir. Good of you to draw some business to Rattlefort, and the Silver Springs Saloon in particular." He turned around. "Get on with it, man, strike up a jaunty tune!"

The piano began playing once again, Rawhide laughing at Al's joke, and the Wolfe Gang fell into excited conversation about the upcoming Outlaw Summit.

***

"Help me with the blanket," Jake said, grinning as Lucille and he unfurled it out. She'd been spending time with him all day, even helping out with their chores, and his parents had gone to bed earlier after they'd had supper together. Lucille and Jake approached on both sides of Henry, unshackled and awake now that night had fallen. They flapped the blanket once, then laid it gently on the dragon's back.

"What do you think?" Lucille said, stepping back. She smiled, the fading rays of the evening sky catching her pretty blonde curls. Jake felt a thrill rush through him. It almost didn't seem real; Lucille spending so much time with him.

"Let me just get Ulysses's saddle," he said, turning back into the shed and rummaging around. He hauled it out, smelling the familiar scent of aged leather and dust, returning to the open. He placed it on Henry's back, eyeing it skeptically. "Well, it's not ideal, and you'll have to squeeze in close…"

"I don't mind," Lucille said softly.

Hiding his smile, Jake worked eagerly to strap the saddle on, buckling it tight below Henry's back. The dragon rumbled, not irritated, but curious. "Let's try it out then," Jake said, cautiously putting one leg over and sliding on. He turned and extended her hand. Lucille approached, and he hauled her on behind him.

Belly Through the Brush

She kept her hands on his shoulders. "Alright, now... Henry, go ahead and fly!"

As if understanding him, the dragon leaped up, flapping its wings again and again, ascending into the air around the Mullens farm. The saddle lurched, Jake straining to keep in place, Lucille shrieking giddily behind him. They turned in the air as Henry banked to the side, providing a majestic view of the fields around them. Henry kept it steady as they sailed through the air, the breeze rippling through the air.

"It's so wonderful," Lucille said in his ear. "Look!" She pointed outward, and Jake glanced over, to see the distant lights of Rattlefort. Henry began to descend slowly, flapping less and less, before landing just outside the stable and rocking them both back and forth.

"What a ride, huh?" Jake said, as they clambered out.

"Yes... I should be going though. Ma will start to worry."

Jake's heart was still hammering in his chest, and he stepped close to Lucille, smiling shyly over at him. "Before you, leave, though..." he leaned in, kissing her, Lucille's arms embracing him as Henry rumbled contentedly.

Chapter 11:
Posse Comitatus

"Dear... Mister... President..." Marshal Davenport said out loud, slowly scrawling the words. "Salutations. I urgently implore you..." he set the quill pen to the side, squinting to the far end of the dusty police station in Yuma, Arizona. His desk was littered with a few yellowed newspapers and bounties. The distant echoes of the drunkard's shouting could be heard over the hustle and bustle of traffic outside the door and the lawman turned to scowl at the prison cell.

I'll give him one more day and send him out with a kick on the ass and a stern warning. He's just an idiot who got paid off to create a distraction. Not like these outlaws we need to take down.

Marshal Davenport dabbed his quill pen in the ink well once more and resumed scrawling away, the letters looking barbaric given the recipient and the gravity of the situation. "More... weapons... to be sent..." he muttered to himself, talking off and on as he wrote. He leaned back in thought. "My regards, now let's see. That's R-E-G... A..."

His thoughts were interrupted by the door opening, Deputy Milton stepping in, his spurs jangling. Beams of light shot past him as he squinted into the dim interior of the police station. "You sure like it dark in here, don't you, Marshal?"

"Didn't realize the time."

"Yeah, well the four o'clock train just came into the station, and you'll never believe who showed up. You ever heard of the Swann Brothers?"

"Oh, they're..." Marshal Davenport tapped his fingers against his desk in thought. "They're bounty hunters, aren't they? Not sure that I've ever met them myself."

"Yes, and what a funny bunch they are! Anyway, they're hauling in Dale Chase, wanted for theft and murder. Twelve hundred dollars, the bounty says. I thought I'd run along and give you a heads-up."

Marshal Davenport grunted and waved Deputy Milton over. "Good of you to let me do that. Here, take a look. Is this too formal? Informal?"

Deputy Milton chuckled. "Jesus, sending a letter to the Rail Splitter himself! What exalted circles you run in."

"Well, it ain't like I met the man. Maybe I'll get a chance after this infernal war comes to an end."

"More than likely," the deputy replied, scanning the letter. "A request for excess weapons, either from seized Confederate stores or Army surplus, sufficient to field a thirty-strong posse. Marshal, I hope you don't mind my saying, but your writing runs mighty close to illegible."

"Don't I know it," the marshal rumbled. "The teachers always said it was chicken scratch. I guess if I realized I'd write to the President one day, maybe I'd have tried a bit harder."

Deputy Milton shrugged. "Well, otherwise it's fine. Think we'll get those weapons?"

"Sure hope so, if we have any chance of wrangling up a posse worth a damn. Bring the letter over to the post office then, will you?" Marshal Davenport said, sliding it into an envelope. "I'll greet the Swann Brothers." He rose out of his seat as Deputy Milton hurried away with the letter. Marshal Davenport strolled along the stained and creaking wooden floor, pausing to spit, then grabbed the prison key and approached the drunkard.

He seemed sober now, having ended his hollering to instead stare plaintively at the lawman. "Heh... Marshal... you know it was all just a little misunderstanding," he rasped in a hoarse voice.

"No it wasn't. We've been over this, Horace," Marshal Davenport replied, weary of the conversation.

"One of the Wolfe Gang paid you to get my attention. And quite the distraction it was! Truth be told, you're lucky to be drawing breath, but I know you're just a dumb feller down on his luck. I can't say I've made the best decisions all my life," he said, unlocking the prison cell. "And this might be another bad one," he muttered, then rummaged in his pocket for a few silver dollars. "Here, take these," he added, pressing the coins into the smiling man's hand. "Sort yourself out. I don't want you to just go and drink these away."

"Of course not, Marshal! I wouldn't dream of it!" Horace said, almost hopping in his eagerness to get away as they approached the door. "You take care of yourself, Marshal. Yippee!" he said, jogging off into the distance. Marshal Davenport sighed and squinted at an approaching band of people.

One of them he took for a little boy, but most little boys didn't have a cigar clamped in their mouth and stubble on their cheeks. Beside him towered an extremely tall man, skin showing around his ankles where his pants fell short and his head somewhere up near the bright sun above, hauling the grimacing Dale Chase behind him. And last was a man of average height, one eye appearing to drift away. As he approached, Marshal Davenport realized he had a false left eye, along with some pockmarked scarring on his left cheek. This one approached, extending a hand outward.

"You must be Marshal Davenport! Gerald Swann."

"Pleased to meet you," Marshal Davenport replied, shaking the man's hand firmly. "I see you're here to turn in a bounty."

"We are indeed, sir," Gerald replied. "This scumbag ain't worth much in God's eyes, but I understand the government feels he's worth $1200 dollars," he added, yanking on the rope tied to Dale Chase's wrists.

"Dead or alive," Marshal Davenport confirmed with a nod. "You're a lucky man, Samuel, though I suspect a hanging in your future."

"The bitch had it coming," Dale said.

Davenport's whiskers twitched. "You can take that argument to the judge, son. Though I suspect you'd benefit from legal counsel." He glanced down at the extremely short man and back up at the extremely tall man. "Y'all are brothers?"

"Isaac Swann, the baby of the family," Gerald said, leaning over to slap the lanky youth on the arm. "And Calvin Swann, the eldest."

The short brother nodded, then spoke in a surprisingly deep and silky-smooth voice. "Pleasure to meet you, Marshal."

"Likewise," Marshal Davenport said slowly. "I have a proposition to put to you men. But first... well, why don't you lock him up, young man?" Marshal

Davenport said, handing the key over to Isaac. "Watch your head."

"Yeth thir," Isaac Swann replied, taking the key and hauling Dale Chase in. "Come on, Tham."

Davenport raised an eyebrow. "He bite his tongue or something?"

"Isaac? No, he's always talked like that, ever since he was just a little tyke."

Davenport's eyes drifted down to the diminutive Calvin, then jerked back over to Gerald. The middle Swann was rummaging for something and handed it over. Davenport blinked, unfolding the rumpled-up letter.

"What's this?"

"Only an invitation from Jimmy Wolfe himself to the first ever Outlaw Summit." Gerald paused. "We were thinking the government might benefit from this piece of information."

Davenport read it over once again. "The nerve," he muttered, then glanced at Gerald, trying to ignore the dizzying view of the false eye drifting to the side. "I'll throw in a hundred-dollar bonus for this, and I'll do you one better as well. How's about joining a posse with me and Deputy Milton?" he asked, spotting the deputy returning from the post office, kicking up dust in the warm Arizona afternoon. "There'll be enough bounties in one place to make you rich men three times over."

"I'm in," Calvin said abruptly. Gerald nodded slowly as Isaac returned, circling behind them. "How many men have you got?"

"You're the first ones," Marshal Davenport replied. "And I hope you take that for the compliment it is. I like a lean, mean band that can handle themselves. Well, are you in?"

"Leth do it, bwuthers," Isaac said enthusiastically.

Gerald grinned and nodded. "Of course, Marshal. The Swann Brothers are always ready for a fight!"

***

Sun Wong removed his bowler hat, wiping away beads of sweat that had accumulated even in the cold climate of the Tibetan mountains, and jerked it back down. He glanced over at his cousin Jun Zhao. It had been a long trip from San Francisco to his hometown of Guangzhou, and then to the mountains of Tibet with his steadfast cousin.

Jun Zhao led the way inside, already growing warm as if there was a natural heat inside. In a way, there was, although it was not from some geothermal process. "How has Xingteng been doing in your care, Jun Zhao?" Sun Wong asked his cousin in Cantonese. "I need her to get back my Feilong from Jimmy Wolfe. There's no telling what evil atrocities they've had him doing."

"Jimmy Wolfe," Jun Zhao repeated the unfamiliar name. "What a peculiar name, Sun Wong. How do you get used to them? I understand your English is fluent.

Your mother often speaks of nothing else but your circus in San Francisco."

"Well, I spend my time in the West of the United States, and they do as much grunting and growling as they do speaking," Sun Wong said with a chuckle.

"I see."

Sun Wong examined the dragon's den around them as they proceeded farther into the chamber. There was a pleasant, ambient heat now, and the stalactites dropped the occasional drop of water on them as they walked along. Jun Zhao brandished a glowing lantern to illuminate their path.

"It has been some time since I've been here last," Sun Wong mused. "Has Xingteng gotten over the disappearance of her child?"

"Unfortunately, she has not. We've lost a lot of men while trying to keep her restrained these last couple of months," replied Jun Zhao. "We've had to feed her a little less than we normally do to reduce her strength."

"That is to be expected, I suppose," Sun Wong said with a sigh. "She is probably still angry with us for taking away her egg."

Jun Zhao slowed, raising his lantern high in the air. A group of workers rose to their feet. A lantern flickered on a table where they had been eating their lunch, and Sun Wong saw forms moving in the darkness beyond, knowing that a significant number of workmen were constantly keeping an eye on Xingteng.

The light from Jun Zhao's lantern fell on a huge pair of closed eyes, reflecting off the green scales of a full-grown dragon. As Sun Wong approached, her eyes shot open.

With a rumble, Xingteng whipped her head around in irritation, heavy iron chains rattling as she struggled to move. Several groups of laborers struggled to hold the multiple chains that kept her bound in place. In irritation, Xingteng lurched to the side, sending a few workers sprawling as she yanked one chain close. She twisted her massive mouth back, biting on the chains and crunching down, until the chains snapped. Startled cries echoed out in the cave.

"Magnificent," Sun Wong said to himself, using English by force of habit.

Xingteng began building up fire in her belly, rearing back, panicked workers scurrying aside. It was then that a square-shaped ruby attached to Sun Wong's golden necklace began to glow brightly, illuminating the cave in a red hue. As it glowed, Xinteng's eyes turned bright red as well, and the dragon paused.

Sun Wong resumed talking in Cantonese, his tone confident and reassured. "Now I command you to obey me, Sun Wong; the living descendant of the Dragon Emperor, Jian Wong!"

Xingteng rumbled, this time gently, lowering her head and sniffing the air. She opened her mouth a fraction, a huge red tongue flicking out, as if taking in scents.

"Release the chains now."

Jun Zhao took a step forward, hesitation mixing with loyalty, and finally he nodded. "Workers, release the chains!" Despite his prodding, it took some time for the laborers to unhook the chains that kept her bound. Yet they noted her glowing red eyes and the way she no longer rumbled angrily from side to side. Whispers echoed throughout the cave as the last chains were released, the workers dragging them to the sides.

"Do you have a plan for Xingteng?" Jun Zhao asked in a low voice.

Sun Wong nodded. "We will use her to attract the brown-scaled male that has been flying over the Yarlong Valley." He adjusted his bowler hat, taking a long breath, smelling the acrid stench of the dragon's smoky aroma. She would benefit from spreading her wings in the fresh mountain air. "I believe that dragon is Feilong's father."

Chapter 12:
Outlaw Summit

"Fold," Jimmy grunted, staring over his cards at the punchably smug face of Ned Briggs. He smirked even wider, his young wife Shirley squeezing tight on his arm and letting out an ear-piercing banshee shriek as Jimmy tossed his cards aside.

"Ah, you did it, Neddy!" She grinned and kissed her clean-cut husband on the cheek. "Who's my Neddy Bear? Who's my Neddy Bear?"

"I'm your Neddy Bear, Shirley," he replied as he scooped up his winnings, flashing Jimmy a dazzlingly white smile. They were an attractive couple, it had to be said, and were renowned bank robbers. The air of honesty about them helped a great deal with their scams. "Another hand?"

"Ugh, I need a drink," Jimmy muttered, looking away as Shirley hugged Ned close. He walked up to the bar, where Al and Doc Otis were sharing a pitcher of beer, a stack of newspapers and wanted posters piled up on the counter in front of Doc.

"Whiskey, neat," Jimmy said to the proprietor of the Silver Springs Saloon as he sidled up beside Otis. He jerked his thumb back in irritation at Ned and Shirley. "Come on, Doc, these weren't the types I had in mind when I had you send off the invitations. A couple of bank robbers on the run? I'm looking for killers, Doc."

"Well, you'd be surprised," Doc Otis replied. "There are at least a dozen dead at their hands. Security guards, bank clerks, innocent bystanders, sheriff's. And it's not just Ned, either, that Shirley has quite the record. But... I get your point, Jimmy, I really do. They aren't exactly my type either, but I figured I'd throw a wide net and pull in whatever it caught. A husband and wife team of burglars don't exactly make for a renowned pair, do they?"

"They're card sharks too, I suspect, though I don't see how he's doing it," Jimmy muttered, more annoyed at the fact they couldn't tell how he was losing at poker than the fact that he'd been slowly draining money since the pair's arrival. He could be patient when it mattered, at least for a while, and gunning down his first guests would make this endeavor all a waste of time. "Anybody else in town? I'm sick of playing host to these two."

"You mean aside from the Deadly Six?" Doc Otis asked, with a faint chuckle. They had been the first to ride in, storming through town with the dust of Texas still on their ponchos and chaps. Their self-appointed leader Vincent had muttered something about "needing to lay low up North when we got your letter," but they'd holed themselves up in Madam Josephine's cathouse ever since arriving in Rattlefort.

"Yeah… they don't seem the chattiest bunch I've ever met," Jimmy muttered.

"Maybe we shoulda kept those Riley boys alive, eh Boss?" Doc Otis said with a grin. Jimmy simply shrugged.

"Don't think they would have responded to an invitation. Anyway, I prefer them six feet und—"

"B-Boss!"

They turned to see Sam Reeves storming into the saloon, rifle strapped to his back, face all twisted in excitement. "S-so I was lookin' in my s-s-scope, and I s-saw a man. I re-re-recognized him, Boss!"

"Who?"

"H-His n-n-name is L-L-L…" Sam licked his lips as the silence lingered. "The D-D-D…" then he shook his head. "I n-need a d-d-drink," he muttered, pushing past and to the bar, but Jimmy grabbed him firmly by the arm.

"Just spit it out!"

"I believe he means me." Everyone turned to look at a figure in the doorway. A broad-brimmed hat filled the entrance, a flowing poncho on the man's chest, two revolvers strapped to either belt. He was a sturdily built man, his clothes dark leather under his poncho, and his thin smile seemed utterly lacking in warmth. "Lester Reyes," he announced in a Spanish accent.

Sam Reeves nodded. "The D-Demon."

"Tequila, if you've got it," Lester said, approaching the bar, his spurs ringing with each step.

"Right away sir," the saloon owner said, breaking out of his catatonic shock. Jimmy had been leaning against the bar, and now he took a seat on a stool alongside Lester.

"Glad you could make it," Jimmy said. "I've heard a lot about you."

Lester turned and fixed Jimmy with a cold stare. "Most of it's true. Can the same be said of you, Jimmy Wolfe?"

"Ah, I don't read the newspapers much. But I've seen my wanted poster. Murder, theft, so on and so forth. That's all true enough."

"You know, I seen your wanted poster as well, along with those of your lackeys. Such a small sum! Is that from a lack of enthusiasm or ability?"

Jimmy frowned. "Maybe your bounty is higher. I seem to recall that it is. And so… what of it?"

Lester grabbed his glass of tequila and took a long sniff. "Seems to me that if anyone should be calling an

Outlaw Summit... it should be me." He slammed the glass down and belched.

"You ride alone, don't you?" Jimmy asked. "And it's not like you have a home base. Rattlefort is our own little—"

"Boss!"

Jimmy looked over to see Rawhide Cooper entering the Silver Springs Saloon, Preacher right behind him.

"We have a mighty strange group approaching," Preacher said. "I never did see a more peculiar bunch on God's green Earth."

"Earth here is red," Lester said, half-turning in his seat and fixing Preacher with a long look, as they filed away from the entrance. "The blood red of Arizona... or of Hell."

Preacher grimaced, but before he could reply, the first of the new arrivals entered the saloon. An armed Black man, not too common a sight in the West, with a shotgun slung on his back. He took a few steps in, ignoring the mutterings of the clientele.

"Eugene Cook," Doc Otis announced, a stack of yellowed wanted posters in his hands. "Escaped slave and notorious killer," he said, then looked over as another man emerged, an unstrung bow strapped to his back with a revolver and tomahawk on his belt. "And Powaw Tom, a half-breed veteran scout and cattle rustler. Welcome to the Outlaw Summit." Doc's eyebrows rose as a third figure approached. "Vincent, of the Deadly Six. Good of you to join us."

A plain-faced man nodded. He seemed to be freshly shaved, though he sported a long, brown, waxed mustache. "Wanted to see what the commotion was."

"Will the others be joining us?"

"No. I speak for the Six."

Doc shrugged and glanced over to Jimmy, who clapped his hands and rose to his feet. "Welcome to the Outlaw Summit. Drinks are on me. First things fi—"

"Oh, fuck you and your Outlaw Summit," Lester broke in with a scoff. "I just wanted to see who would actually show up to this. You think you're tougher than me?"

Jimmy looked over. "There was a time when I would gut you six ways to Sunday for the stupid shit you've been saying just in the minute that I've known you," he said in an ice-cold voice. "And perhaps that time may come again. But right now we have more important matters to discuss."

"What, under 'flag of truce?'" Lester sneered.

"If you want to call it that." Jimmy spread his arms wide, taking in all of them assembled in the saloon, knowing he had to win over the new arrivals and his new recruits as well. Ira had a sour expression, still massaging his left hand, as the others took their seats in the saloon. "This Civil War is coming to an end, and we need to unify before Lincoln unites the country and begins to look West."

"Fuck Lincoln," Vincent swore.

Eugene glared at him. "Fuck you."

Vincent's face flushed red. "I will not be talked to like that by—"

"Shut your damn traps!" Jimmy yelled over them. "We need to stick together on this one. Any of you with opinions that strong had years to pick a side. You picked profit instead, and so much the better."

"This ain't your gang, Jimmy," Lester cut in. "You want to unite? Fine then. Let's do it American style and have a vote."

Jimmy paused. The saloon began to rumble, as the bandits warmed to the idea, and soon a chant broke out.

"Vote! Vote! Vote! Vote!"

***

"I'm glad you came to see me again," Jake said, still grinning like a fool. Lucille touched him gently on the arm as he urged Henry back inside the barn. "I was starting to wonder!"

Lucille smiled, listening to the familiar rumblings of Henry as he folded in his wings, clambering inside. She could tell the dragon's moods by now, and knew Henry was a mixture of emotions; energized by their third night flight, satisfied with the pronghorn he'd managed to snatch up, and grumpy about being shackled up once again.

"Ah, you know I only stopped coming by because Ma made me," Lucille said, patting Henry's wing.

"Oh... does she not like me?" Jake asked, confused.

Lucille chuckled. "No, silly. She's never said a bad word about you, and you know she can swear something fierce. Actually... she's seemed a lot quieter around me lately... like she's planning on something." Lucille shrugged. "Anyway, no, there's a group of Texan bandits who showed up yesterday and I've been busy just keeping the place clean. I could barely even get away tonight."

"Well..." Jake's heart thumped in his chest, chains rattling as he tried to shackle the dragon up. It fell loose from the spike they'd hammered into the ground, though Jake didn't notice, distracted with Lucille standing just a few feet away. "Mighty glad you came to see me again..."

"You already said that," Lucille said with a smile.

"Can I accompany you back into town?" Jake asked. "My chores are done, and Ulysses could use the exercise."

"Well... certainly!" Lucille replied. They made their way to the stables, where her borrowed horse and Ulysses were both sniffing at hay.

Inside the barn, time passed slowly, as Henry stretched himself out. He shifted, feeling the chains rattle, and noticed that it wasn't as taut as before.

Turning his head, he dragged the chains along the barn floor.

They weren't attached!

Henry dragged the chains to the barn door, pushing it open with his scaly head, gazing out into the night. The urge to fly through the night rushed through him. He could return before dawn, and then the humans could go about their routines once again. Rushing out, Henry flapped his wings, soaring into the air. The chains whipped through the wind behind him, slowing him down slightly, but doing nothing to stop him.

The Arizona desert loomed below him, open in all directions as by instinct he veered away from the glowing lights of Rattlefort. Dark shapes moved down below, gray-brown against the dull yellow of the plains, Henry watching in fascination as the creatures lumbered along in a herd. Ahead of them, the gleam of water reflected the moonlight. Curious, Henry took several passes around.

Aside from the buffalo, he saw several humans and horses tracking them from the side, but they were no longer strange to him and he paid them no particular attention. Instead he swooped low, sniffing as he dove near the buffalo herd, intensely curious about the big animals. They seemed too big to easily pluck up and feast on, and while he was able to produce a growing flame, Henry knew it wouldn't be enough to down any prey. The herd began moving, confused by the strange

Belly Through the Brush

presence that swooped out of the night, and Henry continued diving down to play with them.

The stampede of buffalo continued for another few miles, until they slowed around a watering hole. The first of the bison began to drink, the rest crowding around, until the whole herd was gathered there. Henry looped around, beginning to lose interest, and finally landed in a heap across from the bison. He stared at them with reptilian eyes from across the pond, his tongue flicking in the air to sense their presence. They just stared back, bovine and docile.

Henry huffed, scooting toward the pond, then extending his head down. He thought he heard some strange noises, but over the snuffling of the bison it was heard to be sure. Henry gulped down great quantities of water, quenching his thirst, leaning over along the edge of the pond.

A shout broke the silence, and Henry tried to look over, feeling something falling on top of him. He growled, lashing around, firing a quick blast of flame that illuminated a band of men wearing leather and beads. Several were tossing ropes and netting above him, and Henry tried to scramble away, his wings all caught up.

Panicked now, Henry whipped his head, catching one man and knocking him into the pond. But the others were all over him, talking to each other, pinning him down, and the only thing Henry could do was let out a screech of fright.

Chapter 13:

The Election

The peal of the church bell rang out across Rattlefort. By the time the six o'clock bell had sounded, Jimmy's gang and the others had settled themselves into the Silver Springs Saloon. Jimmy himself sat at the bar, nursing a whiskey, wondering why Lester hadn't yet showed up. In the distance, he heard Doc trying to win Ned and Shirley over.

"What can I do to persuade you?"

"Well, the thing is, Doc," Ned replied. "Everyone knows the Demon. With someone like that—"

Footsteps sounded as the Deadly Six stepped into the saloon, Vincent at the head of their number, reeking of tobacco smoke. As they took their seats at the only remaining empty table, Lester Reyes entered, a cold smile on his face.

"Gentlemen, let's make this quick. So far as I can tell, it's only Jimmy who thinks he's fit to challenge me for leadership of the Outlaw Union. Is that right?"

There were a few nods and mutters of agreement around the saloon as Jimmy rose from the bar stool. "I've led the Wolfe Gang for many years. You haven't led anyone."

It was a simple argument, but Doc had suggested he hammer home that point. Still, the room simply remained silent.

"Wolfe Gang," Lester repeated with a chuckle. "I heard you lost your little brother. Can't take care of your own too well, can you? Ira here tells me you're not even taking from the locals. I've known mayors who are more like bandits than you."

Jimmy scowled as a few others chuckled. "You ever heard of laying low? There will be no interfering with the people here."

"Laying low he says!" Lester jeered. "Shooting down the Rileys, raiding Yuma, and mailing letters all across the West doesn't strike me as laying low in the slightest bit. I think you need a change of leadership for the sake of your own people. It's too late for Billy, and you don't want ole Doc or Rawhide here getting gunned down. For all we know, there could be lawmen casing the place as we speak."

Jimmy scowled. "Don't talk to me of my own brother. That idiot just ran off. And the law is after each and every one of you, which is why I called this meeting in the first place."

"Runs in the family, I guess," Lester said, clapping his hands. "Let's end this farce with a vote."

"By all means," Jimmy grated out. He stepped up to the bar, then whirled around to face the assembled outlaws. His gang was crowded together, even his sentries pulled in, and he took in their grizzled faces. Ira and Al weren't among them, which didn't strike Jimmy as a huge surprise, but he began to wonder as he took in the others. Powaw Tom, Eugene Cook, Ira, and Al Crosby were all seated at one table in the back. Their expressions were hard to discern.

Ned and Shirley were also in the back, kissing each other and not being too discreet about it, one of the Deadly Six watching with a lecherous grin. The Deadly Six themselves were still strangers to Jimmy; a ragged and sweat-soaked bunch with stained clothes and what seemed to be perpetual scowls. Jimmy didn't care much for the way Lester and Vincent had been chatting it up earlier. Vincent himself lounged at the head of the table, idly fiddling with a rip on his shirt, the stain of dried blood around it.

"Raise your hand if you want me as the leader of the Outlaw Union!" Jimmy called out, hands resting on his twin holsters.

Arms shot up in the air—from his gang's table. Jimmy's mouth twitched in disdain as he saw the others remain motionless. Then he saw a hand lift up from another table. It was Al Crosby, though he didn't exactly radiate enthusiasm.

Still now, that was something.

Jimmy scanned the crowd, starting to feel some concern, as Lester walked up beside him, his spurs rattling.

"Not a bad showing, Jimmy, getting most of your gang to go along with you," Lester said, his voice heavy with sarcasm. "Though, like your brother, it seems you lost one," he added, nodding over to Ira Dotson. He was frowning over in stony silence.

"Well..." Jimmy muttered, stepping aside a few paces. "Let's see now..."

"What's to see?" Lester asked with a chuckle. "Not the fastest counter in the West, are you?" He cleared his throat. "All those in favor of me leading the Outlaw Union, I want you to raise your hands, and go ahead and hoot and holler while you're at it!"

Arms shot up, the saloon rocking as the Deadly Six stomped their boots in unison. "De-mon! De-mon! De-mon!" they chanted, hands raised in the air. Others joined them; Powaw Tom, Eugene Clark, and Ira in particular. The cattle rustler had his left hand in the air, still bandaged, the same one Jimmy had shot through. He waved and shouted with all the rest.

Seemed Ira was still a bit upset about the whole thing.

Shirley looked over in the back as if just noticing what was going on and tapped on her husband's shoulder.

"We'd best raise our hands, darling, I believe there's an election coming on."

"You felt that?" Ned blinked. "Oh, right!"

They raised their hands up, and just like that it was done.

Jimmy scowled over at Lester, who smiled back, his eyes still blank as ever. "You're outmatched, Jimmy. Everyone knows the Demon."

Jimmy grunted. "How much did you pay the Deadly Six?" he asked in a low voice, as the commotion continued, more than a few bandits already ordering celebratory drinks. If anything, Lester's cold smile only widened.

"Like I would waste my own money on the opinions of fools. I've left a trail of corpses all through Texas; they know all about what I'm capable of, but they don't know shit about you. Maybe if you weren't 'laying low' after every little train robbery you'd have more of a reputation, Jimmy."

Jimmy nodded, feeling his anger subside into simmering annoyance. Much as he hated to admit it, Lester Reyes had a point. Everyone knew about the Demon. Not only that, but Jimmy wanted Lester working with him; wanted him more than any other criminal this side of the Mississippi and outside of office.

"One thing won't change; don't mess with the people of Rattlefort. It's *my* town and I lay down the rules in here. Aside from that..." he stuck out his hand and gritted his teeth. "Congratulations."

Lester snorted, even as he shook Jimmy's hand, the two squeezing tightly. "What are you, their mayor?"

"It's a good base," Jimmy replied, the two finally releasing their grips.

"You have other schemes in mind, then?"

"I do." Jimmy hesitated. He had assumed that he'd be the one calling the shots, but there was no reason not to share his plans. "We need resources if the Outlaw Union is going to last, and if we coordinate our goals the Union Army will be too overstrained to do a thing to stop us. Say we split up in three separate groups and pull off three different heists all on the same day. We steal gold, ammunition, and horses—and then we bring it all back here."

Lester nodded slowly, chewing it over, as two rounds of whiskey slid over the counter to both of them. Doc appeared from behind the counter, as the proprietor hurriedly filled another half dozen glasses. "To working together," Doc Otis said, raising a glass of his own. Lester nodded, and the three raised their glasses, clinking them together and drinking them down.

"It's a sound idea," Lester announced, taking a seat at a stool beside Jimmy. "Did you have locations in mind?"

Jimmy nodded. "A particular bank in Colorado. There's plenty of gold and silver coins stored there. Then a train heist in Nevada. I've heard they're shipping in plenty of imported ammunition from the San Francisco docks and sending it east to the Union Army. And finally, the Carmichael Ranch in Northern Texas. Biggest horse ranch there is. And we do it all in, say… four days."

Lester nodded slowly. "I like it," he muttered, then turned around with a grin. "I like it a lot. Tom, get over here!"

Lester took a sip of whiskey, then glanced back at Jimmy. "Do you know Powaw Tom?"

Jimmy shook his head.

"Best damn tracker there ever was. Years ago… ah, it must have been a decade or more, he tracked *me* down."

"It was easy," a voice in Jimmy's ear announced, and Jimmy barely resisted spinning around in surprise. Powaw Tom stood there, still and silent. "I just followed the smell of blood."

Lester snorted. "The hell it was. Anyway, after I killed the old fool of a bounty hunter with him, Tom here showed a great deal of sense in negotiating an end to the standoff."

"No reason to kill you," he replied emotionlessly. "Only the bounty hunter could turn your corpse in for a reward. They'd laugh me out of town if I tried."

"You were never going to kill me," Lester replied, showing just a hint of annoyance. "Anyway, we've ran into each other plenty of times over the years." He paused. "Who was that old bounty hunter, again?"

"Jeremiah Swann," Powaw Tom replied. "His sons are in the business now."

Lester grunted. "Alright, I want you to hit the Carmichael Ranch and take a dozen or so horses. You know it?"

"I know it. That's a five-day ride."

"Four if you leave now, and that's when I want you to hit the place. You're taking the Deadly Six along with you, and I'm putting you in charge."

Powaw Tom thought on this for a long moment. "Vincent won't like that."

"I didn't pick you because I thought they'd like it. I picked you because you're the best."

Powaw Tom nodded. "True. I might need to make an example of one or two. Might be the Deadly Four by the time we get back."

Lester shrugged. "As long as they're deadly. Jimmy, I know you're no slouch when it comes to train robberies, so I'll want you handling that job. The bank heist will be mine," he added, as Powaw Tom and the Deadly Six began making their way out of the saloon. "We'll give them the extra time to work their way into

Texas, then split up tomorrow and hit the other targets four days from now. Now then. Tell me the details about this bank you had in mind."

***

"I would like to thee through the thcope," Isaac Swann insisted once again, trying to take it from Calvin, who jerked it away.

"Leave me alone, baby brother!" Calvin shot back at Isaac, his deep voice incongruous, as the short bounty hunter attempted to look through the telescopic rifle sight at the exterior of the Silver Springs Saloon.

Marshal Davenport bit back an oath. They had made their way to a gentle rise along the outskirts of town without being detected, the sentries nowhere to be seen. Now they were snooping in on the Wolfe Gang as best they could. Not for the last time, Davenport wished the government would send them new equipment like that.

I suppose they have bigger problems right now.

"Leave him alone, Isaac," Gerald—the middle brother—said. A long moment passed. "Can I see through the scope, Calvin?"

"Just a minute," he grunted. "It's opening up and... yes, oh yes. Oh yes..."

"You're not looking at the cathouse again, are you?" Gerald asked.

"That was one time!" he snapped. "No, there's a group leaving the saloon, and they look like they mean business."

"Let me see!" Marshal Davenport insisted, and Calvin grudgingly handed it over, the lawman resting the butt against his armpit and closing his left eye as he peered through it.

"Why doeth he get to thee?" Isaac muttered.

"'Cause he's a marshal, you big oaf!" Calvin shot back.

Through the scope, a party of riders materialized, a native scout at their head. Davenport gently aimed further behind, taking in the grim expressions of the riders. From his time memorizing bounty posters, a suspicion bubbled up in him, and he gazed at them intently even as he counted their number.

The Deadly Six. But what the hell are they doing here?

"That's not the Wolfe Gang," Marshal Davenport announced in a low voice. "But perhaps—"

He tensed as he heard a sudden sound, turning back along with the other bounty hunters, the loud pump action of Gerald's shotgun echoing out into the night.

"Whoa there, fellas," came Deputy Milton's voice from the darkness, as he pulled the reins of his horse. "It's just me!"

"Christ sakes, we almost killed you," Gerald said, lowering his shotgun. "We're all on edge with this many eggs in one basket."

"What are you thinking, Deputy?" Marshal Davenport added, scowling as he handed the rifle back to Calvin. "You have to announce yourself. We're scoping out Jimmy's little gathering in the Silver Springs Saloon."

"Er, sorry fellas," Deputy Milton replied, smiling back bashfully from atop his horse. "I ain't mean to startle y'all, but I just received a telegram from President Lincoln back in Yuma. Thought it'd be worth the ride to let you know."

"Well... we're kinda busy working out here, Deputy," Marshal Davenport replied. "I left you in charge for a reason." He paused. "But what's Uncle Abe have to say?"

"He said the war has stretched the Union's resources thin, but Colonel Thomas Abbott and a small platoon of soldiers are chasing Confederates looking to occupy the New Mexico Territory. We'll have to meet him at his outpost in order to get spare guns and ammunition."

"Confederates? So far west?" Marshal Davenport sighed. "As if this wasn't bad enough. Seems like the war is right at our doorstep, Deputy."

"They just left town," Calvin Swann announced, still staring intently down his rifle scope. He lowered it and glanced back. "What's the plan, Marshal?"

"The plan?" Marshal Davenport sighed. "Seems we have to leave these crooks alone for now. Lead the way, Deputy. I'm not about to second-guess President Lincoln."

Chapter 14:

The Bank Robbery

The day's warmth was still settling in when Jake finished looking after the chickens and made his rounds to Henry's barn, a pitcher of fresh well water in one hand. Whistling to himself and thinking about Lucille, he turned the corner to the barn—and saw the barn door swinging back and forth with the wind. The pitcher of water fell, spilling heedlessly into the parched dirt, as Jake wrenched the door further open. He stared at the empty space for a long moment, transfixed, until his father's voice broke him out of his stupor.

"Jake, once you're done feeding Henry, I'll want you to check on—"

"He's not here, Pa!"

Jake looked over to his father, pitchfork in hand, blinking over in surprise at him. "Did Billy somehow…"

They looked over to the adjoining shed, where Dorothy Mullens was emerging, brushing her hands. She had just made a hot breakfast of oatmeal and left a bowl for their prisoner Billy Wolfe, a common routine by now. By the way she frowned, it was clear she had heard, and Jake's eyes fell to the ground. He knew this was his fault.

I must not have locked him up tight after Lucille and I flew him around.

"Billy can barely work a spoon, so it wasn't him that took Henry. I figure Henry must have worked himself free." She sighed. "I thought he liked it here…"

"Over here, boy," Lawrence said, treading carefully as he approached the barn, kneeling and taking in the dirt imprints of Henry's clawed feet. Jake joined him, taking in the footprints as they led away from the barn. Together, the two paced out farther into the warm sand, the footprints clearer to see.

Up ahead, the ground was firmer, a semi-arid patch of earth that with constant coaxing could produce a meager crop. The crops themselves were partly grown, and Jake knew Henry wouldn't smash through them. Just shy of the crop field they spotted a large indentation in the ground—and then there was nothing. Jake winced as he looked into the distance,

Belly Through the Brush

the rising sun coming up above the nearby hills. He'd been hoping to picnic with Lucille in a meadow there, once his morning chores were completed, but it seemed that Henry had ruined those plans.

"Great," Jake muttered.

He turned and joined his father as they trudged back toward the farm, Jake already thinking ahead to how he would chase after Henry. *How hard can it be to find a dragon?* Jake gulped, thinking about the attention this might bring. He would have to hurry.

"What do you think?" his mother asked his father in a low voice as Jake hurried into the kitchen, grabbing a few things he would need.

"Henry's footprints stop at the end of the crop field, so he must've started flying east toward the desert," Lawrence said as Jake approached, his knapsack already rattling.

"I'm fixing to get him, Pa! Please don't try and convince me otherwise."

"I know," Lawrence said, sliding open a drawer in a dented wooden desk. He scooped up a few stray bullets, along with one of Billy's revolvers, and handed it over to Jake.

"Be careful, son."

"That won't do," Dorothy said, the loud sound of shotgun cartridges being loaded echoing inside the small kitchen. Keeping the barrel pointing at the wooden floor, she passed it over to Jake. "Henry is family. I just don't want you to go out there alone and unarmed."

"He ain't going alone, Mrs. Mullens," a voice interrupted them, and Jake turned to see Lucille standing outside, the early morning sunlight falling on her and lighting up her blonde curls with an angelic hue. "I'm fixing to go with him."

Jake smiled despite himself.

"Are you sure Madam Jo… I mean, your mother would be okay with this?" Dorothy asked.

"I'm a big girl, and I don't care what she says. Henry could be in danger!" Lucille replied. "Plus, she gave me a derringer to protect myself after Pearl died."

"Better hurry then," Lawrence said gruffly. "I want all of you back by nightfall, you hear?"

"Yes, Pa," Jake replied, and he walked along with Lucille back to the barn. "I thought you wouldn't be coming over until later."

"And I thought Henry would be in the barn," she replied as Jake began saddling up Ulysses, Lucille's borrowed horse already saddled beside him. "Life is full of mysteries, Jake Mullens."

He smiled as he attached his knapsack to the saddle along with two canteens filled with well water. "Mighty glad you're coming with me."

"Let's make it quick, though," Lucille said as she rose to her saddle. Unlike some of the more prude women of Rattlefort, she didn't ride sidesaddle. Being the daughter of an unwed brothel owner brought with it at least a few advantages. "You promised me a surprise, and I am very much hoping this is not what you had in mind."

"Yes, Lucille," Jake replied, humoring her, as he mounted up and spurred Ulysses forward. They cantered toward the crop field, following the faint footprints, and Jake squinted into the distance. Past the nearby hills, there was nothing but desert around. "How hard can it be to find a dragon?"

***

"No masks?" Al Crosby asked in a low voice as the band of outlaws sauntered down the main street of the Colorado mining town.

Lester snorted. "Wear what you want; it makes no difference to me."

Ned chuckled beside them, arm circled around Shirley, already drawing attention from passersby. "This face is made for the newspapers," he said, tapping his freshly shaved jaw with his free hand.

"You're so right, Ned!" Shirley giggled. "We're going to be stars!"

"Huh," Eugene Cook said beside them, not even cracking a smile, his shotgun slung on his back. "A mask wouldn't do nothin' for me. There ain't too many Black outlaws in the West. Besides, the rest of you kinda… stand out."

"Guess that's how it's going to be then," Al muttered.

"Ned, Shirley, you two have such a... *presence* about you," Lester said in his Spanish accent. "I'll want you keeping the customers in line. No one in or out."

Ned and Shirley both chirped approval as they strode down the main street of the mining town toward the bank, clearly doing a brisk business in precious metals. The town was partly in the shadow of the mountains and snow still covered the rooftops, dripping down in the noon sun, turning the streets into a dirty morass. Rather than riding out directly, they had quartered their horses two blocks away in a stable on the edge of town. Once they made it there, it would be a straight shot back across the Rockies.

A man in a nice suit exited the bank's doors, a security guard casting him a wary look and a nod. Then the guard's expression tightened as the bandits approached, Lester at the head, flashing the cold smile that felt so jarring when combined with his dead eyes.

"We have business here."

"I'm going to need to ask you for your pistol, sir," the guard said warily, extending his open hand. "We've had trouble here before."

"This little thing?" Lester asked in feigned surprise, slowly pulling out his gun, hand around the barrel.

"Yes, and everyone else will need to hand over their weapons." The man paused. "What exactly is your business here?"

"Here you are," Lester said calmly, whipping up the pistol hilt and smashing it into the guard's nose, while he rammed the man forward through the door. The guard collapsed bleeding inside the bank, Lester stepping past, spinning his pistol around and aiming it at a frightened clerk. "I wish to make a withdrawal."

The others fanned out all around him, guns drawn, as the line of customers backed away in a rush.

"Oh my God!" someone cried out.

One woman shrieked as Lester paced forward to the counter, eyes fixed on the frightened face of the clerk, as one of the bandits silenced her. "Open up your safe."

The clerk licked his lips then nodded. Lester leaped up, sliding over the counter, and with one firm hand on the clerk's back they headed over to the vault. Eugene and Al joined him as Lester spared a glance back. Ned and Shirley had their guns trained on the cowering customers.

"Cooperate and no one has to die!" Lester shouted over the mumbles of the customers and clerks. Then he shoved his hostage forward. "Hurry up and open it."

"You keep screaming and I'll just keep kicking!" Shirley barked out from the lobby. Someone screamed, then it turned into a moan. "Don't test me!"

The clerk fumbled with his key, taking much longer than it needed to take, metal rattling against metal as it trembled. Finally he opened it up, stepping back, and the vault door slid open. It revealed a huge bounty; row upon row of boxes. Lester grabbed one at random, setting it down, the heavy load splitting open the wooden box to reveal gleaming gold coins.

Lester whistled, grinning as he brought out his potato sack, Eugene and Al already filling theirs. "I see the vault here truly is full! We might have to come back some other time."

Lester grabbed a heavy sack, slamming it on the counter and attracting the attention of the hostages along with Ned and Shirley. Ned whistled appreciatively.

"Now that's quite the haul!"

The others soon emerged with enough stuffed sacks for everyone, and Lester turned to the hostages, waving them to the back door. "Out thataway."

The guard was holding his bleeding nose, and muttered, "Juth leaf uth be. Go on…"

Lester reached down, hauling the guard by the scruff of the neck, half-dragging him to the back door until he stumbled to his feet. "All of you!" he bellowed. "Let's go! Vámonos!"

Prodded by the others, the hostages filed out meekly, Lester waving his pistol at the wall. "Against the wall. Move it, move it."

"You said no one has to die," the clerk sputtered, one step ahead of the rest of the stunned hostages. "You said—"

"Yeah, yeah, I say a lot of things," Lester said, stepping back as Eugene tossed two sacks of gold on the ground, turning to stare at a downcast young Black woman.

"Hey, boss," Eugene began, nodding over at the Black woman. "Let her go. She doesn't need to die. None of them need to die, but least of all her."

Lester snorted. "We all die. They can at least die knowing the Demon sent them."

"She's just a child," Eugene insisted in a low voice, as Al set the rest of the sacks of gold on the ground. "Let this one go here, Lester," Eugene said, his hand falling on his holstered pistol, ready to draw.

"My bullets don't discriminate against race, gender, or age. I'll shoot you right where you stand, Black man, so don't get any ideas."

Eugene gritted his teeth. "Just let her go," he repeated. "She doesn't know who we are, anyway."

"Oh, enough about that girl, Eugene!" Ned snapped. "What do you think, Shirley?"

"I don't think we should kill these folks, Ned."

"She's damn right, Lester, and you know it. There's no call for shooting them down. What do you think?"

"I think..." Lester paused. "That you talk way too much, cabrón."

"What do you mean by that?" Ned frowned. "Hey Al, what does he mean by that?"

"Enough," Lester said, stepping back from the hostages, hand on his revolver. "Dead men tell no tales. Six rounds and six hostages. This will be good practice."

Ned blinked. "Good practice for wh—"

Lester drew and fired in a mesmerizing blur, six rounds right between the eyes of each hostage from right to left, his left hand fanning the hammer as he shot. A silence fell, the air thick with gun smoke.

"Well this will be one for the papers," Ned said, grabbing a sack and hurrying away with Shirley, struggling gamely under the weight of a heavy sack.

"Enough with your talk of papers," Lester said, as Al joined the others, striding down the muddy street with sacks of gold on their shoulders. "We leave corpses, not witnesses."

"You didn't have to do that," Eugene grumbled.

"And you didn't have to join up with me," Lester said, already grabbing a heavy sack and slinging it on one shoulder. "And yet here you are, with a sack of gold for a few minutes' work. Beats slavery, doesn't it?"

Eugene stared for a long moment at the young Black woman, bleeding out along with the others, the side of the bank stained with spattered blood. Then he leaned down, hauled up the sack of gold, and joined the others.

Chapter 15:
Justice

The hot Arizona sun was blazing down something fierce as Jake and Lucille crested the hill. He paused a moment, sipping from his canteen, taking in the saguaros that dotted the landscape all around him. It was hilly and rugged terrain, though it sloped down to a flat desert up ahead.

"How are you holding up, Lucille?" Jake asked as he put the stopper back in his canteen, patting the solid Ulysses underneath him.

"I'm doing just fine, Jake," she replied, her brown hat giving her some protection from the sun. "Just a nice little ride in the countryside."

"I'll say. You're quite the rider, Lucille! Still, it's the heat of the day right now. What say we shelter for some protection from the heat?"

"Well..." Lucille looked over in the distance, then nodded toward a dry gulch. "That gulch right there would give us a bit of shade. Maybe we can let our horses rest for a spell too."

"I see it," Jake said, already urging Ulysses forward. "Let's go!"

His hooves clattered all around the silent land, the distant horizon a blur that seemed to hover and blur the more he looked at it. Jake was beginning to wonder if they'd ever find Henry.

No, I can't think that. We'll just keep pressing forward and find him, one way or another.

They gracefully descended from the rocky hill, delicately avoiding most of the scree, loose rocks tumbling down as they slowly made their way to the shade of the dry gulch. Jake leaned away from a saguaro as he passed by, the tall cactus bristling with needles. With careful movements, the two horses made their way down, and Jake hurried off. He tied their reins to a gnarled tree, careful to loop them nice and tight, enjoying the fresh breeze that blew through.

"Maybe we can take a break for an hour or so?" Jake suggested, taking his jacket off and placing it on a pile of rocks, the only shade from the harsh sun.

"Mind if I join you?" Lucille asked, taking something out from her horse's saddlebag.

"I was hoping you would," Jake admitted as Lucille approached with a blanket.

Belly Through the Brush

"Good! I thought I'd bring this along to make our rest stops comfortable," she said, settling herself on Jake's outstretched jacket. She spread the blanket out on both of them and rested her head on his shoulder. Despite the heat, she snuggled in close. "Where do you think Henry got off to?"

Jake had been thinking on this all through the ride, but now he was finding that he couldn't think about much else besides the fact that Lucille was right there beside him. "Well, you know how he loves to fly, and he's a hot-blooded creature after all. There are plenty of lizards and rattlesnakes out here in the desert. More than likely he's just enjoying himself on a really long joy ride. And with the heat we get here, no doubt it's letting him coast in the air," Jake added, watching a falcon circle lazily up high.

"Henry can't fly for hour after hour, though," Lucille said. "Or at least, I don't think so. He's got to rest some time."

"And so do we," Jake replied.

Lucille smiled, and they relaxed together, the time passing by lazily. After a while, dulled by the heat, the two fell into a contented slumber as the long day wore on.

***

"Excuse me, sir."

Jake blinked, waking up, trying to understand what he was seeing. There was a shaggy man looking down with a sunburned face and missing teeth. He looked desperate and pathetic as he held out his empty canteen, moving it back and forth.

"Could I trouble you for a sip of your water?" he asked.

"Uh... sure," Jake said by instinct, rising to his feet.

Lucille moaned, partially covered by her blanket, and the man's eyebrows raised high as he caught sight of her. Jake bent down to reach for the canteen. "I still have quite a—"

He felt a sudden pain on the back of his head, sprawling in the dusty rocks, and distantly heard a burst of noises. He wasn't sure just how much time passed as his head thundered away in pain. Then he felt strong arms hauling him up, as he blinked rapidly, still trying to get his bearings. "What..."

The bandit spun him around, and to Jake's surprise his shotgun was on the man's back, Lucille sprawled on the ground and pressing a hand to her reddened cheek where the man must have hit her. Before Jake knew it, he felt cords against his hands, which the bandit pressed against the gnarled tree.

"Don't you go anywhere, sweetheart!" the bandit called out, tying Jake's hands to the tree, so tight and quick it seemed second nature to him. "Got plans for you," he muttered.

"Shit," Jake said, only now jerking his hands away, the branch just moving slightly as he looked at Lucille rising to her feet. "Hey... hey!" Jake shouted at the man as he approached Lucille, cackling to himself. Lucille fumbled with the stocking on her left leg as the man approached.

"You don't want to do that," Jake said, thinking desperately, his hands twisting on the cordage behind him as his hands scraped against the desiccated tree. "Hey! You don't want to do that!"

"Oh, and why not?" the bandit jeered, looking back at him. "No, I think that I do. Watch and learn, you'll see how a real man—"

An explosion sounded, the bandit slumping forward, a surprised look fixed forever on his face. Lucille screamed at the same moment as blood droplets sprayed on her dress. She quivered, the dead bandit falling on her legs, the derringer she'd drawn and fired still smoking. Lucille set it aside, scrambling away from the man, hurrying over to Jake in a rush.

"Oh Jake," she muttered, squeezing him tight. "Oh Jake, oh Jake…" she shuddered and pulled back. "Let's get you cut free."

***

Marshal Davenport stood in the main street of Yuma, Arizona, staring in disbelief as a half-naked man capered across the way. He hiccupped from time to time as he sang to himself.

"Horace, you drunk idiot, I regret letting you out of my cell. It's clear you're not fit for civilized society. Still, I'm glad you're not getting in the way of this hanging."

Davenport turned, strolling back through the street. A few people were walking through town, a mule hauling a load of goods, but the traffic was pretty light around this time of day. That suited Davenport just fine. There was justice to be done, and this time he intended to take security quite seriously. Deputy Milton had the convicted murderer Samuel Chase with him, a bag planted firmly over the man's head, as the judge read the sentence aloud. The mayor had opted not to show up to this one.

So much the better, Davenport thought, scanning the crowd, noting the Swann brothers intermixed among them. He wasn't taking any chances this time. They had their eyes peeled for any potential raid; hands ready on the holsters of their pistols.

"… and, therefore, sentenced to be hanged until death," the judge concluded, nodding at Deputy Milton, who pulled the lever. Without any further ceremony, the latch gave way, dropping Samuel down. He struggled a moment, legs twitching jerkily and eventually falling still.

There was a scattered, almost respectful applause from the audience, much smaller a showing than the previous crowd had been. At once they began to disperse, chatting amongst themselves, Marshal Davenport nodding to a few of the locals who expressed their gratitude for bringing the man to justice.

"Well, I suppose the praise goes to you three," he said later, once the square was all but deserted.

"The government's ransom is all the thanks we need, Marshal," Gerald replied, falling in with Davenport as he strolled back to his office. "We're just eager for the next one."

"I understand that," Davenport said, raising a hand to hail Deputy Milton. "Deputy, help them with the burial," he ordered, continuing to walk down the main street. "The problem," he said to the three brothers, "is that we still need to build up our posse. But I want fighters I can trust by my side."

"We know," Calvin grunted in his deep voice. "We can be patient. But have you heard the rumors going around town."

"There's always rumors," Davenport muttered.

"Sightings of horse thieves in Texas. Another train held up along the railroad. There's something going on; more than usual."

"In my line of work you hear rumors all the time," Davenport said, entering the little sheriff's office. "I wouldn't put too much faith in it. Not till it's in the newspapers, that is." He paused, settling himself in his chair, while the others arranged themselves around the office. "Calvin, have you inventoried the weapons like I asked?"

"Of course, sir," the short Swann brother said, crossing his arms. "It's enough for a small army. Now all we need to do is…" he trailed off, turning to the door as a huge figure emerged.

"Well now, ain't that a sight!" Davenport announced as Stagecoach Mary stepped in, gripping a newspaper tightly. "How have you been doing Mary?"

"Not well, Marshal, not well," she said, slamming the newspaper on the desk. An even larger Black man entered after Mary, standing silent beside her, as Davenport glanced at the front-page article. "We want in," she said, as he scanned the report about a bank heist in a Colorado mining town. "Is your offer still available?"

"Certainly," Davenport replied. "To you, anyway," he added, glancing at the huge man standing silently beside Mary. He had a pained expression in his eyes, one that Davenport had recognized in others, and combined with his silence it gave him a very imposing air. "What's this news of a bank robbery in Colorado got to do with this?"

"This is my cousin Herbert. His daughter was killed in the bank heist… little Tammy. And if I had agreed to join you earlier…" she shook her head violently. "Jimmy Wolfe must be taken down!"

Davenport read it again, focusing on the details about the clerks and innocent customers murdered in cold blood, his temper rising. He noted the execution-style killings outside the back of the bank, the whitewashed wall splattered with their blood, the whole scene on the front of the cover. He couldn't even imagine how that must feel; to see your family dead on the cover of a newspaper, and he burned with righteous indignation. "That damned Jimmy Wolfe! How could he do this?"

"No, Marshal, you're wrong," Calvin said, chewing on a piece of straw. He leaned over. "Jimmy might be a murderer and a thief, but he kills only out of necessity. I suspect this 'Outlaw Union' split into different groups, as we saw during our stakeout. This must have been the work of a different bunch. No doubt Jimmy's so-called Outlaw Union was behind the bank robbery, but the executions were carried out by someone else."

"Lester Reyes," Stagecoach Mary grumbled. "That soulless bastard would be behind this. I wish I had killed that son of a bitch when I had the chance."

Davenport grunted. "Perhaps you are right. Either way, I will see justice done." He looked up at the man standing beside Stagecoach Mary. "I'm being very selective about my posse members, Herbert. These bank robbers… you're seeking revenge on them?"

"Justice," he replied.

"Hmm. Well said. And you'll stick with us till the end, even if it should mean your death, if it brings these outlaws to justice?"

"Yes."

Davenport tapped his desk a moment, then leaned back, resting his feet on the corner of his desk as he studied Herbert's expression. "Say no more. You're hired. Calvin, let them get their pick of anything we have in the armory. That's what it's for, after all."

"Certainly," Calvin replied, moving over to the back. "Welcome to the posse!"

Chapter 16:
Down Goes Ulysses

"Thanks Lucille," Jake mumbled, face crammed into her golden curls, as she sobbed in her arms. "You did the right thing. I... I just wasn't expecting..."

She squeezed him tight before pulling away, her eyes reddened. "I just can't believe it," she said. "I shot him... I killed him..."

"You saved our lives," Jake said, wincing as he rubbed at his palms, still marked where the coarse rope had been tied around them. The back of his head still throbbed in pain, but it was his pride that was wounded the most.

I should be the one to protect her.

"Thank you, Lucille," Jake replied. "You saved us."

Lucille nodded silently, wiping away at her tears and sniffing. "Ma always said a time like this could come, growing up as I am and working as a maid in a cathouse. Always expected it to be in Rattlefort on some night," she said with a final sniff, before staring down at the body of the dead bandit, the stench of blood and sweat thick in the air. "Not in the desert in the middle of the day."

"I guess it's always when you least expect it," Jake said, his voice dry and raspy. He patted Ulysses, the horse's flank hot even in the little bit of shade they had found. "Come on boy," he said, untying Ulysses' reins and leading him out of the dry gulch. Lucille had bent down by the dead bandit, wrinkling her nose at the stench, and worked the revolver free.

"It's hot," she muttered, wincing at the heat the steel pistol had generated as he stuffed it into Ulysses' saddlebag. "Better to have too many guns then not enough," she said as Jake raised his eyebrows.

"Well, you earned it," he said. Together he and Ulysses struggled out of the dry gulch, the horse moving slowly as they made their way out. To Jake's surprise, another horse was tied to the arm of a massive saguaro cactus. "That must have been the bandit's horse," he said out loud, looking around. There wasn't anything to be seen in the vast desert beside hills and saguaros.

Belly Through the Brush

The bandit must have spotted us ages ago. A rider sticks out like a sore thumb out here, and we're the only ones stupid enough to be riding around like this.

"I'll string this one along with us," Lucille added, untying the reins and clicking encouragingly as she pulled the other horse behind. "This heat can't be easy on you."

"Nor on Ulysses," Jake added, hauling himself up. He patted the side of his trusty old horse and stuck his hand out to Lucille. She grabbed it as Jake pulled, settling herself into the saddle right behind him. She held the reins of the other horse as they began moving slowly ahead.

"Henry, where are you!?" Jake called out into the distance all of a sudden, his patience running out. "Where could he be..."

"I haven't seen any trace of him out here," Lucille added. "But I'm looking, Jake. I'm looking."

Jake squinted ahead. In the distance the horizon appeared to blur, making a reflection, and the more he stared at it the more he was sure it was the reflected view of a lake. "Just keep on going, Ulysses," he said, staring intently into the distance. "There's an oasis up ahead. Once we drink our fill we'll be fine. Chances are Henry is just taking a long nap right beside it..."

***

"Golly, Marshal," Deputy Milton said, his eyes raised as he held his broad-brimmed hat in one hand, scratching at his tousled hair with the other. "Are you two pen pals?"

Marshal Davenport snorted and set the telegram down, but it did seem a bit unbelievable. President Abraham Lincoln himself had sent a message.

"I read something in the newspaper the other day about some kerfuffle with Attorney General Gates getting replaced, once he raised a fuss about being passed over for the Supreme Court. That's probably the only reason why the Commander in Chief would be bothering with a sorry ole lawman like myself."

"Huh. Didn't figure you for keeping up with politics."

Marshal Davenport sighed. "I guess I just keep hoping this war will be over soon. But the story is always the same. If it ain't blood and carnage in Virginia, it's bandits in Colorado. Anyway…" he studied the telegram for a long moment. "I'm to meet up with Commander Lester Abbot. He has a military post in the New Mexico territory."

"That so? I thought you'd be hankering to storm into Rattlefort."

"Rattlefort," Davenport muttered, half to himself, as he rose to his feet. "Now that's a problem with no easy solution." He opened the drawer, scooping the stray revolver rounds up into his hands, figuring it was better to be safe than sorry.

"We heading out now, Marshal? I can get our horses if you need to—"

Belly Through the Brush

"No, not *we*. I'll be making this trip alone, and I expect you to hold down the fort in my absence. Make sure there's no trouble in town and continue to hold weapons practice with the rest of the posse. I want them sharp and ready when it comes time to take on the Outlaw Union. Keep your eyes peeled for any potential members to add to our posse as well, Deputy, though I'll want the final say. Is that all understood?"

"It is, sir..." Deputy Milton said slowly. "Though I must say, I do protest your decision to leave us all high and dry. Besides, the posse can do their training plenty well without me, and I'm hardly a local in these lands. Looking after Yuma? I suppose that by itself is fine, but I know the others would be hankering to go with you. These are dark times, Marshal, and there are bad men afoot. Could you perhaps at least take some of the posse with you?"

"Somebody talking about us?" Gerald Swann said, his spurs jangling as he entered the Marshal's office, casually removing his hat and brushing the sweat off his brow and pockmarked cheek. "That Herbert's a better rider than you might expect, once we found a plow horse big enough to carry him. Lassoed a steed easy as you please, and even wrassled it to the ground."

"Good, I'm glad to hear it," Davenport grunted as he paused at the entrance, seeing the street beginning to fill with the other posse members, chatting away with each other. It warmed his heart to see them getting on so well, not to mention that their training was already yielding dividends. He didn't plan on going into a fight with a band of strangers with their own agendas... he had seen too often how that had ended. "I've just got an errand to take care of. Won't take me more than a few days, maybe a week at most. I'm leaving Deputy Milton in charge. I know that if he needs any help y'all will..."

Davenport trailed off as the others erupted with a series of grunts and sputters. It had been years since he'd had to deal with other people's opinions, aside from the civilians he dealt with on a daily basis or the wanted men he could safely ignore as he hauled them in, so he wasn't too sure what to do about this response. A posse was in a somewhat uncomfortable position of being not quite civilian and not quite a fellow law enforcement officer, and he didn't exactly know what to say. He glanced over at Deputy Milton, who was no great comfort.

Milton shrugged. "Told you they weren't gonna be too happy about you leaving, Marshal."

"Where are you going, anyway?" Stagecoach Mary asked. "We should at least know."

"*Weeeelllll...*" Davenport began, dragging out the word. "If you must know... I've been ordered by President Lincoln to report to an outpost in the New Mexico territory. Reckon you can handle yourselves without me for a while."

"President Lincoln?" Calvin Swann butted in with his deep voice. "Ain't he got enough problems of his own?"

"One would think," Davenport muttered, setting his hat on his head. The noon sun shone down its intense rays, and he was already starting to heat up. He didn't much care for the ride that was about to come, but part of him liked the idea of entering the wilderness once again and leaving the problems of Yuma behind. It was peaceful in its own way.

"I can ride with you," Stagecoach Mary said immediately. "It ain't safe out there. Herbert can come too; he's got himself a horse and everything."

Herbert grunted as he nodded.

"No, no, I don't want to hear it," Davenport began with raised hands as the Swann brothers echoed Mary's concerns. "Just help out Deputy Milton," he added, already striding to the stables and going through a mental checklist of what he needed. "I'll be quite alright on my own; I've ridden through this country hundreds of times on my own and done just fine."

***

Powaw Tom wiped his brow, squinting into the distance. This was hard riding by any measure, and not one that most could manage. The Deadly Six had been up to it, to his surprise, keeping an intense pace as they had ridden out of Rattlefort to raid the Carmichael Ranch. Sure, some of the horses had been played out over the long trek, but they had plenty to spare. Besides, they had gotten away cleanly, Powaw Tom scouting out the periphery before the Deadly Six had rushed in and quietly and efficiently led their captured horses out.

It was a success by any measure—but they were not yet back to Rattlefort.

Powaw Tom stared at the form materializing in the distance. He had seen more than his fair share of mirages and knew from hard won experience just how to tell the difference. This rider up ahead was real, however, and Powaw Tom raised his hand for the Deadly Six to slow. The Texans did so with barely muffled oaths.

"We've been riding all day and now you want to stop?" Vincent began, face flushed red from the heat. "Ain't even like there's a stream around—"

"Hush," Powaw Tom said, pointing into the distance and ignoring Vincent's sputtered protest. "See that? The rider over there."

"I don't see no…" Vincent trailed off as he squinted into the distance for several long moments. "*Could* be a rider," he admitted.

"It is," Powaw Tom replied, looking back at the other members of the Deadly Six. He knew they were saddle-sore and tired, but they carried themselves high in their saddles, several of the bandits peering over into the distance to look for the indicated rider. Trailing along behind them on rope were over twenty or so horses of good stock.

"We're crossing into Arizona now," Powaw Tom announced. "So we'll play it safe. Skirt along the gulch here," he said, pointing at a dry gulch that cut through the dry landscape, "and then turn north as it curves away. I'll make sure whoever this is hasn't seen anything and catch up with you."

"Catch up? Hah!" Vincent said. "There's no catching up to the Deadly Six."

"Is that so?" Powaw Tom asked, and despite himself he thrilled to the idea. "A hundred silver dollars if I catch up with you before you make your way back to Rattlefort."

"Done," Vincent said, "but I want to make sure we take care of whoever this is. I'll have two of mine stick with you."

"They'll just slow—"

"It ain't just a rider," one of the Texans said, a lean man with a patchy blond beard. He had been staring into the distance for some time.

"Two riders?" Vincent asked, as the blurry shape began to grow. "Who'd be fool enough to sit two riders on one horse out here?"

"No, it's a wagon," Powaw Tom said. "Best steer clear before it comes closer."

"We're going," Vincent announced. "Leroy, Fritz, stick with the Indian. We'll meet you back at

Rattlefort," he said, spurring his horse forward, a clatter of hooves following along with him.

"The name's Tom," he muttered. His father was a member of the Powaw tribe, though his mother was a white woman, and both groups had shown a mutual degree of disinterest in welcoming him as one of their own. He glanced over to the lean man with the blond beard; Leroy, according to what the others had said. Fritz, a man with a pince-nez and a long black hat, sidled alongside him.

"I'll trust you boys on this one," Fritz said in a German accent. "My eyesight isn't what it once was."

Leroy had unstrapped his rifle, a telescopic sight attached to it, and kept steady as he looked through it. Finally, he let out a low whistle. "Well, ain't that something! I knew there was quite the gleam coming from the wagoneer. That there is a lawman, and no mistake."

Powaw Tom kept his opinion to himself, trusting his own senses over what the Texan might think he was seeing. "Looks like whoever it is could be coming from Yuma," he said slowly. "That might be Marshal Davenport. Let's follow him... but keep your distance. Chances are he's up to something."

***

Mile after mile they went, the sun beating down mercilessly. Jake felt he had lost track of time. He had certainly lost track of Henry, if he had ever had it to begin with.

Still... just a bit farther...

He squinted into the distance, seeing another lake, and hating himself for falling for the illusion half a dozen times before. The first one had been a mirage, along with all the others, and still they continued on their trek. The further they got, the—

Jake felt a wobble, glancing down at Ulysses, then felt it again.

"You alright, b—"

Just like that, down went Ulysses, Jake and Lucille toppling to the ground along with him. Somehow he staggered out in time, Lucille falling to the side, as Ulysses spasmed on the ground.

"Oh no," Jake muttered. "Oh no..."

He winced as he took in Ulysses' shattered front legs, the poor animal panting heavily on the dusty ground.

"He's all played out," Lucille concluded sadly, and they watched Ulysses for a long moment, Jake knowing what he needed to do but not wanting to do it. The bandit's horse stood still as if in shock, Lucille finally reaching for its reins, and making calming sounds as he took it a few paces away. Jake reached for his revolver, taking in the panicked eyes of Ulysses as he kicked and bucked on the ground.

"I'm sorry," he muttered, placing his revolver above his horse's head. "So sorry."

A single shot rang out and the wounded horse's thrashing stopped. Jake looked away, then approached

Lucille, who was staring at the ground. She crouched down and raised something in her palm. Jake worked his dry throat, not knowing what to say, as Lucille turned around. A single scale gleamed in the middle of the dirt in her hand.

"Henry was here," she said.

Jake blinked. He had scarcely even hoped to find any sign of his dragon after all they had been through. Yet it was definitely one of Henry's scales. He coughed.

"I'll get Ulysses's saddlebags," he said in a ragged voice. "We still have the bandit's horse."

"We'll find Henry," Lucille said in a firm voice, grabbing his arm and staring intently into his eyes. "We'll find him, no matter what!"

Chapter 17:
Outpost Ambush

Marshal Davenport pulled off his broad-brimmed hat, letting the cool evening breeze ruffle his hair. The intense heat of the desert had died down, and with night approaching the Marshal wanted to finish his business. Fortunately, the military outpost up ahead was clear to see.

A bit too clear. I guess they're none too worried, with the Confederates on the run.

The wagon rattled as his sturdy horse continued to pull it forward. Marshal Davenport twisted in his seat, taking another glance back. There wasn't anything out of the ordinary, as far as he could tell. Still, a feeling that he was being watched continued to pester him.

Must be nothing.

Marshal Davenport spurred his horse forward, placing his hat back on, and cantered down the sandy hill toward the stockade. It was a rough encampment of timbers, with a large wagon inside along with several tents. A man stepped out in a faded blue coat, a musket slung along his shoulder, looking a bit out of place in New Mexico. He turned, surprised to see Marshal Davenport's approach, but he showed no great alarm. If he'd been posted as a sentry, it didn't appear as though he was a particularly diligent one. Still, Marshal Davenport gave no particular reaction as he slowed his wagon and inclined his hat.

"Is Colonel Abbott here?"

"He sure is," the soldier said slowly. "Are you the lawman that was coming by?"

"I am indeed."

"Take your wagon 'round the other end of camp," the soldier said, pulling out a wad of chewing tobacco and nodding over in the indicated direction with his blue kepi hat. "Thought there'd be more of ya. The Colonel has a few boxes of powder and shot for you," he added, popping the tobacco in his mouth and entering the encampment. Marshal Davenport jerked his reins to the side, and his worse began taking it around the small military post. By the time he pulled up near a boulder, dusk had well and truly settled. He hopped down from his wagon to see a tall, dignified man approaching.

"You must be Colonel Thomas Abbott," Marshal Davenport said, approaching with his hand extended. He was no military man, and held no particular rank, so a handshake seemed fitting enough. The officer's eyes crinkled as he shook Davenport's hand, his gray mustache twitching under shining blue eyes.

"None other! We have quite the shipment for you, courtesy of the President himself. Come with me, Marshal."

Together they strode through the camp, Colonel Abbott limping slightly, a few other soldiers looking over in curiosity beside a campfire. Their stew boiled over the smoking fire. A large tent lay just behind it, the sides flapping gently in the cool breeze.

"Yes, he said you could supply my posse with a few cases of ammunition. I reckon you have some to spare?"

"Indeed we do. You two," Colonel Abbott said, pointing out two men beside a large tent, who rose from their place by the fire. "Start loading up the boxes of ammunition."

"Yes, sir," they replied, quickly hurrying over to a few crates stacked nearby.

"Do you have pickets out?" Marshal Davenport asked, scanning the soldiers around him. They seemed more like boys out on a camping trip.

"Hmm? Oh, I have cavalry sweeping the area. Some of the Chowilawu Indian's have been spotted nearby, but we drove back the Confederates for good.

Hah! Ended their war, I should say," he added with a beaming smile. "You should have seen how I led from the front. Routed old Johnnie Reb along the Rio Grande, eh boys?"

A few of those around gave out ragged cheers, one or two raising their bowls as a mess cook ladled out their stew. Marshal Davenport got the sense that they had heard the Colonel's stories more than a few times already. Today alone.

"Fix bayonets, I said, and then we—"

"I'm in a bit of a rush, Colonel," Marshal Davenport broke in. "I hate to be rude, but it's quite a ways back, and it's tricky enough riding at night without a loaded wagon."

"You won't be staying? You're welcome to, you know."

"I mean to see this job through soon as I can."

"Very well then. Would you like any provisions for the road? Sergeant, get the man some dinner."

"Well, much obliged," Marshal Davenport said as the cook approached with a bowl in his hands.

"It's nice and wa—"

The cook's words were silenced abruptly as he jerked back, a bullet smashing through his neck and spraying blood on the wall behind him. The crack of a rifle shot sounded at the same instant, and Marshal Davenport scrambled to the side, a bullet whizzing by just overhead. Without pausing to think, he sprinted

past the startled soldiers, diving into the tent as another bullet thwacked into the ground just beside him.
What the hell? I've got to get out of here!

***

Leroy pulled the lever of his telescopic rifle back, a cartridge casing pinging on the boulder he was using for cover. "Not sure if I got him," he muttered even as he loaded another bullet. Powaw Tom pulled his bow to full strength and loosed, the arrow arcing up before slamming into a soldier's chest. The man lurched onto the campfire, shrieking as he ran into the hot stove pot. Then he slung his bow on his shoulder, stalking forward at a rush, tomahawk in his right hand and a revolver in his left.

Another bang sounded from Leroy's position.

Then Powaw Tom reached the stockade; a low point that he'd scouted out before, and easily pulled himself up. He caught a glimpse of Fritz storming into camp from the side, mounted on his horse and firing away, squinting down his pince-nez as he aimed. He was yelling as loud as twenty men, just like he'd said he'd do once they had decided on the attack.

Could be twenty bluecoats in here, but we have the element of surprise.

Powaw Tom hopped inside, rushing forward. A cut suddenly formed in the side of the large tent, and Marshal Davenport came barreling out, knife in hand but headed away. Powaw Tom shifted and threw his tomahawk. It spun end over end, just barely missing

Marshal Davenport and slamming into the wooden stockade, sending splinters flying. He cursed, shifting his revolver to his right hand, but by the time he raised it Marshal Davenport had disappeared.

Powaw Tom hurried toward the gap in the stockade. The two soldiers loading the wagon hurried inside, glancing around in surprise at the sudden attack. Powaw Tom whipped his revolver up and fired, fanning it back with his left hand as he pulled with his right, downing the soldiers in a spray of gunfire. As they collapsed to the ground, he caught a glimpse of Marshal Davenport cutting away the horse from the wagon. He pulled himself up, riding bareback into the distance. Powaw Tom snapped his revolver up and fired. Or tried to.

It clicked—and clicked again.

Empty.

A tall, distinguished looking man burst out a tent, a rifle in his arms. He glanced over at Powaw Tom in rage.

"I'll kill you, you Indian son of a b—"

Powaw Tom flung out his second tomahawk underhand, the sharpened point spinning and cutting into the man's gut. He collapsed in a heap as Powaw Tom began hurriedly reloading his revolver. In the fading light, he saw forms rushing past, the rest of the soldiers opting to flee from the sudden attack. Then Fritz trotted into the center of the encampment, firing a final shot at one retreating bluecoat, before peering over at Powaw Tom.

"That you, Tom?"

"It is."

He approached the horseman as they stood before the largest tent in the very center. Powaw Tom bent down toward the dying officer, retrieving his tomahawk and wiping the blood off on the man's uniform.

"Lordie, how they run," Leroy announced as he strolled into the camp, telescopic rifle slung on his back.

"Let's burn it down for good measure," Powaw Tom said, striding over to the campfire. He grabbed a thick log, tossing it against one of the tents. It began to smolder and burn as the flames licked the side.

"Well now, what do we have here!" Fritz called out, his German accent thick even in his excitement. "Come on over, take a look!"

Powaw Tom approached as Fritz tore off a canvas cover, revealing a large swiveling artillery piece with what looked to be a half dozen thin barrels. A hand crank sat beside it, and boxes of ammunition were stacked right next to the artillery piece.

"A Gatling gun!" Leroy cried out. "Oh, I heard tell of those! They spit out bullets like nothing else."

"Really," Powaw Tom mused, glancing back outside the camp at the wagon. His decision was made in an instant. "Alright, we'll load this up in the wagon with some ammo. Better hurry before the fire spreads and they start popping off." He grinned. It might be that he wouldn't beat Vincent back to Rattlefort, lugging that thing with him, but it seemed more than worth it.

"Let's go!"

***

"I sure hope they found Henry," Dorothy said, pausing from reorganizing the Mullens family pantry as their freshly baked cornbread rested on the table. "He hasn't been with us for very long, but it's hard to imagine going without that little critter."

"He's a big fella now," Lawrence pointed out. "I'm sure they're fine. More than likely our Jake and Lucille are out joy riding with Henry and Ulysses. You know how a young couple can be," he added, patting his wife on the back. She just shot him a sad smile and said nothing further.

"I'll check on our other guest," Lawrence said, grabbing a plate of cornbread and exiting out the farm. He whistled to himself as he walked. Keeping the plate steady, he opened the door to greet Billy Ward. Their prisoner moaned softly. The chains rattled as he blinked over. His skin was paler than usual and sweat beaded his brow. "You don't look too good, Billy," Lawrence said with a frown, kneeling and setting the cornbread beside the man.

He barely stirred.

One eye slowly opened. "You gotta help me," Billy croaked out. He rustled now, clambering to his feet and wearily sinking into the old wooden chair beside the straw mat he'd been sleeping on. "I just don't understand it," Billy muttered, shaking his head. "I felt fit as a fiddle yesterday. But my fever's gone on all day, and it hasn't broken yet. Think you can get something to numb the pain? Whiskey maybe? Opium?"

Lawrence sighed. Dorothy had her suspicions after hearing about Billy's problems in the morning. Lawrence had to admit he'd been skeptical as well, but he'd felt Billy's burning forehead. There was no faking that. Even with a full workday at the farm, Lawrence had checked on the man with increasing worry throughout the day.

As if I didn't have enough to worry about.

"I'll get you some medicine," Lawrence muttered, rising to his feet. "Reckon if I head out now I can make it to Rattlefort before the general goods store closes."

"Thank... you," Billy muttered, his chains rattling. "You're good people. I... I see that now."

Lawrence nodded, unconvinced. He left the outbuilding and looked up at the afternoon sky. Then he began trotting forward, the jog soon turning into a run. With Ulysses out faithfully helping Jake and Lucille, the only hope of getting medicine for Billy meant going on foot to Rattlefort. It wasn't a trip he'd made without a horse in ages, but the exertion helped wipe away the worries. Lawrence gritted his teeth, breathing in and out at a steady pace as he ran along the rutted path.

Where are you, my boy? Come back to me soon.

Chapter 18:
The Chowilawu Indians

Jake staggered forward through the fading light. He paused, wiping his brow of grit and sweat, holding the reins of the bandit's horse. Lucille, trailing right behind him, bumped into Jake's shoulder.

"Pardon me," she said in an exhausted voice, sounding as if they'd bumped into each other on the streets of Rattlefort.

Rattlefort. How I miss civilization... or what passed for it there.

"We can't go on anymore," Jake said. "Not tonight, at least. Let's make camp here."

Lucille blinked for a moment, suppressing a yawn. Her expression changed from weariness to one of grim determination. "I'll make a fire," Lucille said, reaching for Ulysses's saddlebags. Jake watched, the saddlebags seeming strange on another horse. He kicked himself for bringing Ulysses out into the wasteland here just to die.

Where are you, Henry? Where did you fly off to?

Jake worked his dry mouth. "I'll start gathering firewood."

In truth, there was little that was usable out in the desert, and the fading light didn't help matters much. He gathered a growing pile of dry, scraggly sticks, then left to break off a bundle of branches from a pinyon tree. By the time he returned, hands chafed and feeling like a dried-out husk of a person, a low fire was burning away.

They rested in silence.

As the hours went by, Jake and Lucille scooted close together, though he could scarcely tell who had initiated it. Night fell, and her warmth beside him was like a soothing balm after all they had been through. At some point Jake nodded off, his arm wrapped around Lucille.

When next he opened his eyes, Jake faced four spear points hovering in front of his head. He blinked, looking up to see four Indian men keeping watch of him. The neighing of the bandit's captured horse broke the silence as a fifth came near, holding onto the reins.

Lucille came to with a start, gasping with surprise and tightening her grip around Jake. The Indian holding the reins had a bow strapped on his back and fixed them with a searching gaze. Then he said something to the others in a language Jake couldn't understand. The Indians didn't seem particularly impressed by either of them, based on how they sounded.

Jake and Lucille were soon twisted around, their hands bound with twine, and urged upward with impatient shouts.

"What's going on?" Lucille asked.

"I don't know," Jake admitted.

The Indian who seemed to be in charge pointed forward and then tugged at the captured horse's reins. Jake twisted around, glancing back to see another man putting out the fire. Then he was pushed forward. He half stumbled before recovering, keeping pace with the party as they marched through the desert. Night had fallen completely, but with the bright moon overhead reflecting off the sand, it was surprisingly easy for them to march.

Easier than during the day, at least. I wonder if we're in their territory.

Jake's head throbbed as they continued onward, the desert giving way to scrub brush as they headed to higher ground. The yellowed land turned green in parts, and the sounds of a creek served to waken him up. The Indian in the lead said a few words now, one of the others grabbing the reins of the bandit's horse and pulling it away.

"What tribe do you think they are?" Lucille whispered.

"I don't know."

They made their way up a mesa, where a profusion of juniper trees blossomed, and the air felt a good deal cooler in the higher elevation. Finally the game trail they'd been following opened up to a camp. Indians going about camp life looked over in surprise as Jake and Lucille were dragged over to a large tent. He almost bit his teeth as they were flung in past the threshold. He rose to his knees, blinking and adjusting to the gloomy interior.

He heard a few sharp words from the leader who'd brought them in. Around them were the others, spears readied, though they remained silent. And then Jake noticed an older man bending down to examine them both. Jake felt a sharp pain at his wrists as his bonds were cut free. He licked his lips. It was now or never.

"I... I come in peace," he said simply, moving his chafed arms forward and rubbing at his left wrist. "I'm just a farmer. My name is Jake Mullens. And this is my wife," he added, gesturing at Lucille as her own bonds were cut. A flash of surprise showed in her eyes, and then she nodded.

If there's anything I can do to protect her...

"I'm looking for my dragon that wandered off," Jake admitted, feeling silly to even say that. The chief was looking at him impassively. He raised his hands to form a big, flapping bird, then lowered it slowly as she caught Lucille's raised eyebrow. "Uh, could I... get some water?"

"I am Chief Sipatu of the Chowilawu," the old man said abruptly. "What is this 'dragon' you speak of? I have never heard of such a creature before," he said, a dumbfounded look on his face. Jake mirrored the look.

He speaks English quite well.

"Oh… it's very good to meet you, Chief, sir," Jake said in a polite tone. "You speak the language of our country quite well."

Chief Sipatu snorted. "*Our* country?"

"A dragon is like a big, scaly creature with wings," Jake said quickly, looking to brush past the faux pas. "I found him as a baby, and well, we really bonded. But he ran away… or, um, flew away," Jake rambled on. "I don't suppose…"

"You mean the sky lizard?" the leader of the band who captured him asked. Jake was surprised once again, and he wondered if he'd said anything that the man might have overheard earlier.

"That sounds like Henry," Jake agreed. "You saw him?"

"Ah, so that was it, Atohi," Chief Sipatu commented, casually filling his pipe with tobacco and lighting it with the embers of a fire smoldering at his feet. "Yes, of course. That strange story you told to impress the village."

"It was true," the other man replied in annoyance.

"Though many of us doubted it." Chief Sipatu paused. "But I can doubt it no longer. It seems you are telling the truth, Jake. Where did you see this sky lizard, Atohi? This so-called 'dragon,'" asked Chief Sipatu, puffing tobacco smoke from his clay pipe.

"At the camp of our enemies, the Kestejoo tribe," he replied. "Beyond the watering hole where the buffalo go to drink, I saw them capture the dragon."

"Mmm... that's troublesome," the chief said, pausing a moment as the smoke drifted away. He fixed his stern gaze on Jake. "You see, the Kestejoo are a violent tribe that refuses to deal peacefully with outsiders. They are even known to eat human flesh. I don't know if we can help you save your sky lizard without taking casualties," said Chief Sipatu, passing his clay tobacco pipe over to the man next to him. "We've been at war with them over territory for many years, and I'm not willing to sacrifice the lives of my kinfolk."

Facing Chief Sipatu, Jake sat quietly for a long moment.

Henry must have been caught by surprise, or otherwise he'd fight them off. I'm surprised he hasn't started a wildfire of his own. He must be tied up... but if we could get to him without the others noticing... he grinned, looking over at Atohi and the men who'd snuck up on him in the night. Atohi tilted his head, surprised at Jake's smile.

"I understand your concern, Chief, but my dragon can breathe fire. My grandfather always told me that within chaos there is opportunity. And there's nothing more chaotic than Henry."

Both of them, if Mother's stories are to be believed.

"What are you suggesting, Jake?" Atohi asked, accepting the clay pipe from the man next to him. "An ambush?" He put the pipe to his lips and inhaled deeply.

"We'll do this just the way you crept up on us. If I can get close enough to free Henry's bindings, I'm sure we can burn down the camp of the Kestejoo tribe from within and cause chaos. You wouldn't mind that, would you?" Jake asked, with a smirk on his face. Chief Sipatu smiled genially in response. "At that time all you have to do is attack with a small group of men and pick them off one by one."

Lucille crossed her legs, grabbing Jake's hand and squeezing tightly. "It's a small risk with a great reward," she added.

"Hmm…" Chief Sipatu glanced at Atohi, who nodded almost imperceptibly. He turned and spoke with the others, gesturing to demonstrate as he went on. Finally he fell silent. It took a few moments, but the others went along with him, silently signaling their agreement. Only when it was clear and all in agreement did Chief Sipatu nod at Jake.

"We will do this. Now, drink water, have a meal with us, and rest through the heat of the day. Tonight we strike; to free your dragon and rid ourselves of the Kestejoo threat once and for all."

***

"Why do I even assign you to sentry duty," Jimmy said, his tone light and conversational as he emptied a revolver on the table, "if you're just going to get drunk and fall asleep?"

He paused, waiting as Sam Reeves sat slumped on a dining chair against the rickety old table of their desert outpost just outside Rattlefort. A snore was his only response. Jimmy sighed, carefully plucking one bullet from the pile and giving it a kiss. He stuck it in one of the revolver's chambers and gave it a spin.

"Tell me, Agatha," Jimmy continued in the same coldly pleasant tone, "if Sam lives out the day," he said, spinning the chambers once again. Then he whipped it forward, pointing it at Sam's snoring face, and pulled the trigger.

A single click sounded.

Sam snorted, raising his head up, blinking blearily into the distance and swiveling his gaze to take in Jimmy and the pistol in his face. "Wha… what?"

"You awake yet?" Jimmy asked, pointing the revolver up in the air and pulling the trigger a second time. A gunshot broke the relative silence of the desert outpost and Sam jerked to his feet.

"Uh, uh, y-yes Boss!"

"Good," Jimmy muttered, holstering his pistol. "Don't. Fall. Asleep."

"Jesus, what was that?" Doc Otis called out.

"Making sure no one's sneaking in," Jimmy said.

"Who'd be stupid enough to try?" Doc Otis said, rubbing the bridge of his eyes, bundles of bills, coins, and gold bullion bars stacked in front of him. "Dammit, Boss, you made me lose my count."

"Show them how it's done, Shirley," Ned said, taking a seat at the table. Shirley beamed wide beside him but made no move for the table as Doc Otis continued shaking his head in annoyance.

"Come on, Ned, don't be silly. I can't count that high, I only got the ten fingers."

"And the toes, darling, don't forget the toes. Such sweet toes you have."

Shirley chuckled, pulling in close.

"B-B-B-Boss!" Sam called out. Jimmy Wolfe turned back in a flash, to see Sam pointing out in the distance. "R-R-Riders."

Powaw Tom rode ahead, two other members of the Deadly Six spurring their horses on as it pulled a wagon behind them.

"No Vincent yet?" Powaw Tom asked, pulling up at the desert hideout. A smile spread across his broad features. "I knew I'd outride him, even with the weight I was carrying."

"Oh?" Jimmy asked, peering over at the wagon as it rumbled closer. "What did you get me?"

Fritz and Leroy grinned from their place at the wagon. Fritz hopped down in a hurry, barely keeping his black hat on, and hurried over the back.

"Take a look, Boss," Powaw Tom said as he inched his horse over. "Courtesy of our good friend Marshal Davenport, last seen riding hell for leather and leaving this for us."

Jimmy approached, curious, and watched as Fritz whipped the coverings off. He grinned back at Jimmy, the afternoon light reflecting on the glass and wire of his pince-nez. But his eyes were fixed on the shining steel barrels of the Gatling gun.

Jimmy let out a long whistle, unable to say anything further. He shook his head in disbelief. "Good job," he said finally. "That's just what we need to make the Outlaw Union a reality."

"B-B-Boss!" Sam called out. "M-More!"

Jimmy glanced over to see the outlines of a couple dozen horses illuminated on the nearby bluffs. Even at this distance it was clear to make out Vincent and the other members of the Deadly Six with him.

"We brought back more than twenty horses from the Carmichael ranch," Powaw Tom continued. "These fellas didn't even slow me down too much," he added, with a hint of grudging approval.

"Wonderful," Jimmy said, grinning at the arriving horses. "I think it's time for Phase Two of my plan…"

Chapter 19:
Rescue Mission

Jake shivered in the desert night, though it wasn't due to the cold. Somehow the idea of rescuing Henry at night and fighting off the Kestejoo warriors had seemed all well and good in the light of day.

But now?

He tried to keep his mind focused on the present. Atohi stalked past a large saguaro, the massive cactus limbs just about the only thing he could see in the darkness. Jake scooted forward—and then barely bit back a yelp. Slowly, painfully, he reached down to where a small cactus had embedded its spines into his left shin. Without the benefit of light, it took him a minute, but he had soon removed the spines and continued padding forward behind Atohi.

The pain remained, but it at least helped crowd out his doubts.

Jake bit his lip, reaching Atohi as the scout peered over at the encampment. The barest light now reflected back at then, but Jake tried not to look at it, as staring at the smoldering campfire would ruin his night vision. Instead he stared fixedly forward into the empty desert, slowly breathing in and out.

Jake had first found Henry in a situation like this after all, sneaking into the outlaw camp in the desert outside Rattlefort. He wondered now if the Wolfe Gang still used the old outpost, with its old and half-rotted timbers bleached by the sun. More than likely they did. Jimmy Wolfe wasn't known for his fanciful airs.

Staring into the distance, Jimmy blinked as he saw the barest hint of motion. For a moment he thought it was a coyote, but when it was followed by another Jake realized they were Indians from Atohi's tribe. The scout crouched down low behind the boulder and spoke now in a soft whisper.

"The Chowilawu warriors I brought with me have surrounded the camp. We are not strong in number, but we are brave. I do not want to lose my men, Jake. You understand?"

Jake nodded.

"This will require all of your focus." Atohi sighed. "And even then... well." He paused, and Jake realized that the light from the campfire was swelling. He risked a glance up, wincing at the brightness as he saw some of the Kestejoo tribesmen tossing fresh logs on the fire. The flames, which had previously been close to unnoticeable, now reached new heights as two men dragged a solid log into the campfire. It was beginning to resemble a bonfire now.

"What are they doing?" Jake asked.

Atohi chuckled to himself as they watched over two dozen of the Kestejoo tribesmen surrounding the fire, chatting away without a care in the world. One man approached, with a metal chalice in one hand. Jake blinked.

Is there... blood on his chin?

His guts twisted as his thoughts were confirmed by Atohi.

"Ah, I see. The chief is trying to make the other Kestejoo believe that dragon blood will make them immune to fire. You see the black-looking dirt around the campfire? It's actually soot."

"I get it," Jake muttered, his eyebrows arched downward in growing anger. He clenched and unclenched his fists, seething within. "They'll drink Henry's blood first and step in the soot before walking through the fire. That way their feet won't get burned."

Atohi grunted. "Yes, it's an old trick. It's a tactic used to boost a tribe's morale. But... if they keep draining the dragon's blood..." he glanced over at Jake's scowl. "I mean, Henry's blood... then he will eventually die."

I'm not going to let that happen, Jake thought, shifting his gaze to where the first man had come from. Unbidden, a smile spread across his face and he jerked his right hand forward, pointing into the darkness.

"Look, Henry's over there," Jake replied, with his left arm over Atohi's right shoulder, guiding his eyes through the darkness with a finger. To the left of where the Kestejoo were gathered around the campfire was Henry's large and distinctive form, lying hopeless alongside a huge boulder. A net covered every inch of his scaly body and his mouth was bound with rope. The nose of a dragon was far superior to that of humans and he quickly picked up Jake's familiar scent. His long neck arched upward as he lifted his head to glance in their direction, sniffing away. His thin red tongue stuck out, helping him smell the air.

"Let's get closer," Atohi whispered as the Kestejoo Indians danced around the enormous campfire. "Quietly now."

Atohi weaved his way forward. Jake crept close to where Henry was tied up, quietly making his way nearer, bellying through the brush. As Jake drew closer, he couldn't hide his emotions, tears trickling down his face, hidden by the night. Henry's face turned to look at him as Jake approached, tongue flicking out from time to time, but making no other particular reaction.

"Found you, bud," Jake whispered, with a finger over his mouth, signaling for Henry to keep quiet. "We're gonna get you out of here."

Henry's scaly head nodded as if he understood Jake's words. After being captured and bound for so long he understood the situation and kept quiet. Atohi handed Jake a hatchet and they both cut the net and bindings covering Henry's mouth. The dragon jerked his head around, pausing only to nuzzle Jake's shoulder.

"I missed you, bud," Jake said softly, his dirty face still marred by tear streaks. Atohi slashed down, cutting the rest of the rope and tossing the material aside.

Then, in a fit of rage Henry quickly rose up and roared loudly, flapping both of his enormous wings. The chanting died away at once as the Kestejoo Indians looked back in surprise at the freed dragon. With a power flap of his wings, Henry kicked up a gust of wind and sand which whipped outward at the Kestejoo who were still dancing. The gust was powerful enough to put out the massive campfire and the area was left in darkness.

Jake clambered on Henry's back, returning to his familiar position. In a brief moment of silence all the Kestejoo could hear the command Jake uttered to his pet dragon.

"Henry, burn them all!"

In the darkness of the night the Kestejoo Indians could see the red and orange embers of fire building up from Henry's belly as he opened his mouth. Sweeping from right to left, Henry breathed out a stream of fire that roasted everyone in its path.

Atohi scrambled to the side, looking frightened to his core as he watched members of the Kestejoo turn into ash piles before his very eyes. Then Atohi blew his bull horn and gave the signal for his fellow Chowilawu to attack. Arrows streamed out of the night in ones and twos, hitting the panicked Kestejoo even as the tribesmen rushed for the weapons.

"Up we go!"

Henry flapped upward, gaining altitude as he spun in a leisurely circle. Jake clung to his dragon's neck. The camp was easy to see now, lit by the spreading fire that illuminated the figures rushing away. Henry swooped down again, and his rampage of fire continued as he sent a stream of fire pouring downward, then rose and took to the night sky once again.

Jake twisted over, trying to get a sense of the chaos below. He heard as much and saw the Chowilawu Indians rushing in on horseback, picking off the scrambling members of the Kestejoo tribe with bows and arrows. Henry dove down and killed most of them, making it easy for the Chowilawu, but every time his fire drew close to the women and children on the other hand of the sprawling camp, Jake tugged him away.

"No boy, not them!" he shouted, and the dragon ceased his fire abruptly. Henry rumbled as a part of howling Chowilawu rushed by, but the dragon could tell that they were a different group and held back his flames. Jake braced himself as Henry swooped over noncombatants fleeing for safety, but he didn't need to worry.

Henry understood intuitively as his eyes scanned the scattering Indians below him. He made a grunting sound after a moment that Jake took to mean all those still fighting had perished or been routed.

"Good boy," Jake said, slapping his dragon's long neck. "I'm sorry I couldn't come to you sooner," he whispered. Then he urged Henry forward, spotting the Chowilawu encampment by the several glowing campfires that lit up the darkness. The lengthy journey was significantly shortened by riding on Henry, and he soon slowed and reared up, his claws digging into the open ground in the center of camp as the dragon landed gracefully.

"Henry!" Lucille called out, running over to join them. Jake slid out along Henry's scaly hide, stumbling into Lucille's arms. They blinked, both startled by the sudden embrace, and then Henry's tongue lapped across both their faces. Jake and Lucille giggled as they separated.

"It's good to see you, big guy," Lucille said, and Jake noticed now that she had a pot in her hands. "Cactus slime and ground herbs," she said, grabbing a chunk and slapping it on a red cut on Henry's wing. He let out a low moan but stayed still as Lucille carefully applied the remedy to the dragon's wounded wing.

Chief Sipatu approached as more of the Chowilawu gathered, looking at Henry in utter astonishment. He smiled, watching as Jake and Lucille reassured Henry, tending to the dragon and chatting with him as they worked.

"It's truly amazing to see the bond you have with that sky lizard," he said. "Jake, I am glad we could work together in this. If ever you're in trouble, we are ready to come to your aid."

"Thank you, Chief," Jake replied, carefully dabbing at a scratch on Henry's snout. "We'll let Henry rest up, and when he's ready we'll head back." He sighed. "I think my parents must be worried by now..."

***

"Well... he seems to be in stable condition," Doctor Rawlins announced, leaning back on the wooden stool.

"Glad to hear it," Lawrence murmured. It was odd, but he really meant it. Even after all the Wolfe Gang had put them through, not to mention Rattlefort itself, he saw more than a little good in Billy Wolfe. It seemed time away from the gang was helping Billy grow in this way... even as he suffered from this malady. "For your discretion," he added, adding a couple extra silver dollars to Doctor Rawlins' extended hand.

The man nodded, glancing briefly at Billy, who was speaking to Dorothy about something. "You know," Doctor Rawlins said to Lawrence in a low voice, "it seems like Jimmy Wolfe has given up looking for his brother. It seems they have bigger plans afoot."

Lawrence nodded. "Plans that don't involve us, I hope."

Doctor Rawlins sighed. "So far the people of Rattlefort are doing well enough," he said, rising to his feet. "I'll keep your secret safe, and he's in the clear. But... well, you can't keep him here forever."

"I know," Lawrence muttered as the doctor left. He approached Billy, who was feebly sipping at a bowl of soup. The one-time bandit lowered it apologetically.

"You know, I was thinking," Billy mumbled. "I'm sorry my gang and I burned half your crops down. I know that was a rotten thing to do... I realize now that y'all are some good folks. You could have left me to die from that illness but y'all didn't. It means a lot to me."

"Glad to hear it," Lawrence replied, waiting for the expected request. It wasn't long in coming.

"Now, if you could just find it in your hearts to let me go, I'd be mighty grateful," Billy said. "I won't tell Jimmy I was here if you let me go. I promise."

"It's not that simple," Dorothy said, glancing at Lawrence. "You've seen Henry, who is family to us," she continued. "We can't afford to let you tell the world that a dragon is on our farm."

"God knows what Jimmy or anyone else would do to Henry," Lawrence chimed in. "Much less the government if they find out. Hell, they'd probably have him burning down Richmond. No, if it was just a matter of trust, I'd let you go." He paused. "When Henry is big enough to fend for himself... we will let you go, Billy," Lawrence said. "That's a promise."

Chapter 20:
Battle in the Sky

    Mr. Sun Wong soared through the clouds, his silk shirt rippling in the winds. He felt Xinteng's grumbling as he steered her through the Yarlun Valley, but it meant nothing to him. He'd beaten her spirits down, after all, and took her child away to the American West.
    Before those damned bandits managed to seize it.
    Sun Wong didn't know quite what had happened after that. News was hard to get out here. All he did know was that Bailong, Xingteng's former mate, nested in these regions.
    So where are you hiding?
    He pulled on his attached reins, Xinteng rumbling in annoyance even as she followed along. She jerked

her head to the side, as if glancing around. Her rumble fell away at once.

That's peculiar...

Sun Wong's eyes widened, a mixture of adrenaline and paranoia surging through him as he suddenly jerked the reins to the side. Xingteng protested even as she followed, and then a brownish blur soared past right above where she'd been a moment before. Huge talons flew by, but they pulled up just in time to avoid raking Xinteng's back.

Sun Wong stared over in shock even as Xingteng banked away, and then he fought for control as he saw the smaller, brown dragon circling back up in the distance.

Why did Bailong try to attack Xinteng like that? They've mated before. Unless...

Realization followed, along with anger. Xinteng wasn't Bailong's target. It was the rider.

The nerve!

Bailong was approaching now, heading directly for Xingteng. Sun Wong glared in annoyance. If that was how the beast wanted to play it, then it would be a battle in the sky.

"Fire!" Sun Wong called out. Xingteng rumbled in protest, jerking her head from side to side. Angry now, he gripped the red, glowing dragon amulet that hung around his neck. "You *will* obey me," he hissed. "Fire!"

Xingteng fired at once, a long-range effort that Bailong could have avoided. Instead he flew straight through it, taking the flames along its scaled body even as he opened his mouth wide. The glow of embers could just be seen. Sun Wong ducked low and jerked the reins to the side as a blast of fire surged overhead, turning the chilly air into an oven. His left shoulder smoldered where it had caught fire, though it was soon put out as Xingteng banked to the side, the high winds whipping past.

Unbelievable, Sun Wong thought in outrage. It was clear that Bailong had avoided hurting Xingteng but was instead aiming directly at him. *He doesn't want to risk injuring the only female dragon left,* Sun Wong thought to himself. *And they can blast fire at each other plenty of times before seriously wounding each other. Therefore...*

Sun Wong gritted his teeth, now pulling the reins up completely. Xingteng rose, higher and higher, heading directly for the sky. She couldn't resist Sun Wong's orders now. Bailong streamed past, moving too quickly to fire, and twisted in the air as he tried to follow.

Just like I want you to do.

Sun Wong jerked the reins down, and Xingteng abruptly dove down. The wind streamed past as they hurtled toward the ground in a high-speed nosedive.

This succeeds or I die.

Sun Wong tore his gaze away, looking upward to see Bailong in hot pursuit. Then he twisted his reins to the side, directly at a mountain peak. Xingteng twisted in the air, and Sun Wong could detect her panic as she soared toward the mountain. Sturdy as dragons were, the impact itself would not kill her... probably.

Bailong clearly wasn't taking that risk.

He soared down at high speed, swooping around just as Xinteng approached the jagged, sharp rocks of the mountain slope. The male dragon rammed into Xingteng, breaking her fall and reducing the impact. Sun Wong held on hard as he rocked in place, almost knocked off Xingteng as the two dragons tumbled toward the ground, falling into a meadow of melting snow and dirt. Xinteng rammed the ground, and Sun Wong finally spilled loose, plopping into the mud.

He breathed out from the impact, hearing both dragons groaning from the crash. Putting the pain aside, Sun Wong staggered to his feet, wiping a bit of mud from his silk jacket. He approached Bailong, laid out on his back, looking a bit stunned but otherwise unhurt.

They are remarkably tough creatures, these dragons.

Sun Wong stepped forward, gripping his amulet and raising it high as he fearlessly approached Bailong. The dragon was smaller than Xingteng, his scales differing shades of brown, and his yellow eyes swiveled over to stare down Sun Wong.

Belly Through the Brush

"Rise and obey me," Sun Wong called out with his glowing red amulet raised, his voice echoing out through the mountain valley. "The last living descendent of the Dragon Emperor, Jian Wong!"

***

The dancing had begun hours ago, with the arrival of the successful Chowilawu raiders, and as dawn approached it grew louder and louder. Jake patted Henry's scaly neck. He fought back a yawn as Lucille clambered on behind him, and Jake smiled as he felt her hands on his back. The first rays of dawn were shining now, illuminating the celebration.

"It's time to go, Henry," Jake said. At once the dragon sprung up, and the dancers called out in one final goodbye. Jake caught Atohi's normally stern face beaming up at them, Chief Sipatu waving along with some of the others—and then Henry soared away.

The first few miles passed in silence as they enjoyed the wind fluttering their clothing, savoring the cool sensation. They knew from experience that the Arizona desert would soon become a furnace. Jake's steady gaze swiveled from side to side and soon he spotted a faint trail of smoke in the distance. It seemed like a single campfire, though what it was doing out in this wilderness was beyond him. He stared at it, wondering if someone was out there in the wastes.

No doubt whoever it was wouldn't last long.

Sighing, Jake urged Henry to bank to the side. The young dragon was more than willing to check out whatever it was.

We'll just look down from above, Jake thought to himself. *No one can know about Henry. Not after all we've been through in trying to get him back.*

They saw the outline of what looked to be a dead man, slumped down on the Arizona sand, which was already growing hot. Henry circled over the man like an enormous vulture as Jake and Lucille stared down in curiosity.

The dead man stirred. He turned, raising one hand up to shield against the sun. A beam of light reflected off the star on his hat and Jake felt a sinking feeling as he recognized the man.

"Marshal Davenport!" Lucille confirmed, yelling it in Jake's ear and causing him to wince. He turned back at her.

"Yeah, but…"

He stared into her eyes for a long moment. In them he read her trust; her sense that Jake was a good man. He swallowed.

"If we… help him out… then he'll know about… Henry…" Jake trailed off as the dragon continued circling in the air.

Lucille just stared back. Jake sighed. In the back of his mind, he knew that it was only a matter of time before someone saw Henry. He was only getting bigger and bigger. At this point… there wasn't much more that Jake could do to protect Henry.

"You're right," Jake croaked.

"I didn't say anything."

"I know," Jake replied with a sigh, pulling down on Henry's reins. "But you're still right."

***

Marshal Davenport had led a decent life, by most measures. Even a long one, as far as these things went. Dying out in the Arizona desert was a fate he couldn't truly claim to be surprised by.

He was a careful man in most ways, and that had taken him pretty far in life. It had taken him out of the military outpost when the poor militiamen there were getting butchered. It had even been enough to ride hell for leather on a stolen horse out into the night.

But if he'd been a truly careful man, he might have paused to examine just why his horse had limped so much. He'd been plenty careful of the stunningly accurate fire that had hounded him out of town and had opted not to stop for a damn thing. But if he had, he might have noticed the bullet lodged in the horse's flank, noticed the loss of blood and the way it wobbled…

The sad fact of it was that he hadn't been as careful as he should have been.

Instead he'd been spilled from the saddle all at once as his borrowed horse had collapsed in the night. Marshal Davenport had almost broken a leg of his own from the sudden fall. He hadn't had much choice after that either. He'd had to shoot the poor animal dead and put it out of his misery. If it meant his pursuers got him, then so be it.

Yet as the days had dragged on, walking through the Arizona desert in night and day, he was beginning to realize he wasn't being pursued at all. In fact, he had the opposite problem. Alone in the desert, with not a drop to drink, he'd barely managed to scrape up a small campfire before collapsing.

With the sun's approach he wasn't too surprised that the vultures were circling. He squinted. One of them, anyway, and a big bastard at that. He felt for his revolver as it came nearer.

Now that there was a mighty *big bastard of a vulture...*

The creature landed in the sand beside him, spraying him with rocks and gravel. Squinting, he looked over to see a massive, scaled head looking straight at him.

If Marshal Davenport had anything left in him, he reckoned he would have pissed himself just then. As it was he just opened his dry mouth again and again.

This thing taking me down to Hell?

A young woman hopped down, followed by a man, and Marshal Davenport stared in surprise as she opened her canteen. "Drink this, Marshal!"

He closed his eyes, drinking thirstily, coughing after a half dozen quick swallows.

He opened them again as if to confirm.

Yep, that hell beast is still there.

Marshal Davenport felt something at his boots, jerking them away as the hell beast sniffed at it. "What the hell is that thing?" he hollered, reaching for the hilt of his pistol. The creature's eyes followed his movements, its mouth half opening and beginning to swell and rumble, a fire brewing inside it.

"No, Henry! He's a friend!" the young man shouted, stepping in between the two of them. Davenport was relieved to see a familiar face appear from behind the fire-breathing dragon that was staring him in his eyes.

"Hey you're the Mullens' kid, right?"

"Yes sir. Jake Mullens."

"And I know this young lady is Madam Josephine's daughter," said Davenport. "But what on Earth is this creature? It keeps watching me like a goddamn hawk."

"He's my dragon Henry, and he don't fancy people reaching for guns too much, Marshal. Just don't make any sudden moves, and we'll patch you up and give you a lift back to Yuma."

Davenport sat quietly as he pondered to himself. *So it's taking me to Yuma instead of Hell. I reckon that's an improvement.* Jake patted the dragon on the head, and it seemed to be calming down. *With this fire-breathing critter helping us we might be able to stop them.*

"Hey kid," Marshal Davenport said, warily rising to his feet and keeping his hand well away from his revolver. "I'm starting a posse to take down Jimmy Wolfe's outlaw union. He's in cahoots with some very dangerous fellows including the likes of Lester Reyes, 'The Demon.'"

"The one they call El Diablo?" Lucille muttered.

"That's right. The devil himself. He just murdered a group of innocent people during a bank heist recently and God knows what else they got planned. I could sure use your help, Jake." He nodded over at Henry. "Well, you and your friend here."

"I don't know, Marshal. Last time I checked, dragons aren't immune to gunshots."

Marshal Davenport snorted, trying not to wobble too much. "Last time I checked, you owed me a favor. Remember that sum of coins I gave you for the Riley Gang bounty?"

"I hear ya, Marshal, but if I get involved in your fight word about Henry is going to spread like wildfire," said Jake. "How am I going to protect him th—"

To Marshal Davenport's surprise, Lucille stepped forward, grabbing Jake by the arm. She whispered, but the Marshal could just about make it out.

"If you're fixing to marry me and start a family one day it better be in a world where people like Jimmy Wolfe and Lester Reyes don't exist. This is not just the Marshal's fight either. It's Rattlefort's."

Jake sighed at the bittersweet words of Lucille. "You're right," he said heavily. "Again." He fixed the Marshal with a firm stare. "Alright, sir. Henry and I will join your posse."

Chapter 21:
Back Home

The wind whipped away at Marshal Davenport's increasingly thinning hair as Henry soared over the desert. "We better land out here!" Marshal Davenport called out, pointing to the bluffs just outside Yuma. "We don't want to rile up the townsfolk!"

Jake nodded, and Henry began a low, swooping dive to descend. The late afternoon was turning to evening, and already the town was beginning to light up, tiny pinpricks of lantern light visible along with the adobe and wood buildings. Henry beat his wings a final time, scattering dirt and rocks down the slope of the bluff, and his clawed feet scraped the ground as they came to a final stop.

Taking a deep breath, his heart still hammering away from the intense experience of dragon flight,

Marshal Davenport carefully slid down. His right hand rested a moment on Henry's scaly body, and he tapped the dragon twice, shooting Henry a tentative smile. The dragon just tilted his head, flicking his tongue in and out as he scented the air.

"Well, I've gone bull riding before, and I've certainly ridden my share of horses. But," he coughed, "there ain't been nothing half as exciting as a ride on a dragon, and that's a fact."

Henry made a rumbling sound that Marshal Davenport took for approval. Jake and Lucille both slid down on either side. The young man looked over at Marshal Davenport. Jake's eyes were shining, and the enthusiasm he had felt infectious. The dragon's low rumble continued as his head shifted forward, resting on Jake's left shoulder.

"Y'all wait right here while I fetch the posse. We don't want Henry to put the town in a frenzy," said Marshal Davenport, wiping sweat as he tried to avoid Henry's gaze. "Won't be but a minute."

Jake nodded, even as his dragon nuzzled him, and Marshal Davenport turned to the steep slope of the bluffs. He carefully clambered down, then picked up speed, scree and dirt clattering down to the ground along with him. Reaching the bottom, he staggered forward, feeling a pebble lodged in his left boot. He ignored it, already shifting into a steady jog as he entered the familiar town of Yuma.

A few of the citizens looked over at Marshal Davenport, one or two calling out to him, but he didn't have time to reply. Instead he made a beeline straight for the old jail which he'd turned into an office of sorts. To his surprise, Isaac Swann was standing outside the door, a cigar glowing in his hands. The tall bounty hunter looked over, straightening as he approached.

"Marthal."

"Good to see you, Isaac. Is everyone here?"

"Jutht about."

Marshal Davenport made his way inside, eyeing Deputy Marshal Milton, who was leaning back in his desk. The Kansan took his boots off the desk, straightening up and shooting his boss a wan smile.

"Marshal! How did the transfer go? You need any help unloading? Calvin and Gerald are out—"

"No, I won't be needing any unloading done," Marshal Davenport grunted, taking in the silent Herbert along with Stagecoach Mary, who were looking up from their card game. "That damned Jimmy Wolfe got the jump on me and sent a few of our boys to early graves. But never mind that. There's something I need you all to see. Come along now," he said, waving them outward.

A deep voice sounded from outside.

"I got the provisions you asked…"

Calvin trailed off, looking up at Marshal Davenport. The short man was loaded down with a rattling pack. Beside him the one-eyed Gerald stared over expressionlessly, his hands full of canned goods.

"Set them in here," Marshal Davenport said, moving past Deputy Milton and to the desk the man had just vacated. Marshal Davenport scowled at the fresh dust on his oak desk and brushed it away. It was mercifully empty, at least, as apparently no telegram had come in since he'd been gone. The Marshal opened a shelf, pulling something out and putting it in the pocket of his jacket. The cans rattled as they were all stacked together beside Calvin's pack.

"What's going on, Marshal?" Stagecoach Mary asked finally.

"Better if you see for yourself," he replied, leading them outside. The posse continued silently along the streets of Yuma, the baking streets below them slowly cooling down as evening settled in. When he reached the bluffs, he hurried up, grunting with exertion as bits of rock and dirt trailed down wherever he set his boots. "It's just us!" he called out.

With his focus on the ground ahead of him, Marshal Davenport found himself startled once again as he made his way to the top of the bluff. Henry looked over, slowly spreading his wings out wide even as Jake patted one leathery wing, shushing him like a nervous horse.

"Well, I never," Stagecoach Mary whispered, stepping forward slowly.

"It's alright," Jake said with a grin. "Just let him smell your hand. Once he knows your scent and that you're friendly, you'll all be fine. The name's Jake Mullens, by the way. Pleased to meet you all."

As Marshal Davenport made the introductions, Henry sniffed the extended hands of each posse member. Surprised though they might have been, Marshal Davenport knew that he'd picked right. They hadn't shirked or backed down at the thought of having an enormous lizard place his nose just above their hands, and there weren't too many people he could say that about. But Henry soon shifted back to Stagecoach Mary, who beamed widely as she stroked the dragon's muzzle. Soon enough she was giggling, the big, stern-faced woman quickly giving in to playing with Henry.

"You might be a big and scary looking dragon, but I know you wouldn't harm ole Mary, would you?" she asked, smiling as Henry behaved like a playful puppy in the hot sand.

"Seems like Henry really likes you, Ma'am," Jake muttered softly. He smirked as if at a joke, but Marshal Davenport got a sense that the boy was a bit jealous.

"He sure does," Lucille chuckled.

"Oh, just call me Mary," Stagecoach Mary replied, grinning as she ushered Herbert forward. "Come on now, Herbert, give him a pet!"

The huge man merely stood there immobile as Henry sniffed him once again.

"I reckon I won't," he intoned after a moment.

"Well, I'll give the little feller a pat on—"

At Deputy Milton's approach, his spurs jangling with each step, Henry seemed to rear up. Stagecoach Mary looked over, rearranging her clothes. Henry rumbled as he stared down into Deputy Milton's eyes.

"Easy boy!" said Jake, rubbing Henry's wing in a comforting motion. "No need to be so defensive."

"Heh... sorry there, partner," Deputy Milton said, gazing up at Henry as the dragon slowly calmed down. "No need to get nervous. We're all on the same side."

The dragon's head nodded once.

Marshal Davenport patted his pockets, then reached inside his jacket. "Speaking of which..." he pulled out the small bible he'd taken from his desk. "It's time we do this formally. I'd been meaning to wait until a proper time, when I gathered a posse who can take down Jimmy Wolfe for good." He stared into the eyes of everyone around him, letting the moment linger. "And I know you're the ones who can do it. Mary, let's start with you. Step forward, please."

Going off half-remembered instructions from years back, along with a bit of improvisation, Marshal Davenport swore in Mary, Herbert, Calvin, Gerald, and Isaac as U.S. Deputy Marshals.

"Tho help me God," Isaac concluded, stepping back and smiling down at his brothers, all newly minted deputy marshals.

Marshal Davenport shut his bible. "Well, that settles it. Now you're all officially—"

A grunt sounded, followed by the briefest puff of fire, which illuminated the small gathering. Everyone looked over in surprise at Henry, as a bit of smoke wafted up.

Marshal Davenport blinked at the dragon. "Jake, what's wrong with him?"

"I don't know either, Marshal."

"Hmm, I think Henry wants you to swear him in like everyone else," said Lucille.

Henry nodded his head decisively.

"Well, I reckon there's no law that says a dragon can't be deputy marshal," Davenport replied, walking over nervously with the small bible still in his right hand. He extended it over.

Henry placed his huge claw on it, causing Davenport's knees to buckle from the sheer weight. Like he observed with everyone earlier, Henry stood still and upright on all fours proudly. All except Mary looked on in amazement at Henry, muttering that they couldn't believe how intelligent he was. Even Jake could only chuckle to himself.

"Do you solemnly swear to fulfill your duty according to the tenets of this oath?" asked Marshal Davenport, in an exasperated tone, feeling slightly ridiculous.

Henry nodded his head in response to Davenport's words before shifting his eyes over to Jake for approval. Jake grinned back.

"We've got to get going, Marshal. I'm sure our parents are pretty worried about us," said Jake. "We'll meet after I take care of some business."

***

Lawrence settled down in his chair, sighing to himself contentedly as he finally finished another day of backbreaking farm work. He'd thought it would have been easier, and if Jake had been back with them it really would have. But Lawrence Mullens was getting on in years, and Jake was growing into a fine young man. And the way he looked at Lucille... well, Lawrence might be an old codger now, but he remembered the feeling. He grinned over at his wife Dorothy, who was soaking a rag in a bucket of water.

"We've been together a while, ain't we?"

"Hmm? Yes," she replied distractedly, raising the rag above the bucket and squeezing some of the water up. "Billy Wolfe is still running a fever, but he does seem a bit better than before. I'll just check up on—"

The door rattled from a heavy impact, followed by another. Lawrence rose at once, cursing to himself. If the Wolfe Gang were here... he looked over to his wife, who was already scurrying away to the guest bedroom where they were now keeping the bedridden Billy.

"I'll keep him hidden!" she hissed.

Lawrence nodded, rushing over to grab his pistol. By the time he reached the door, his wife had joined him as well, a shotgun in her hands. He kicked the door open, surprised to see Olive, Goldie, and Madam Josephine. She looked none too pleased.

"Dorothy, where's my Lucille? She better not be here at this farm foolin—"

Click-Click.

The sound of Dorothy's loaded shotgun stopped Josephine from completing her sentence.

"Don't come to my farm and beat down my door. And don't even think about insulting my son."

After a brief moment of silence Madam Josephine grabbed the tip of Dorothy's shotgun and wrenched it down to point at the ground.

"I ain't seen Lucille in days and folks in town say she has been spending a lot of time with your son. My motherly intuition is telling me she is here!"

Madam Josephine, Olive, and Goldie push their way past Dorothy and Lawrence at the front door. They headed straight into the room of the recovering Billy Wolfe.

"Now hold on just a minute," Lawrence sputtered. "You can't just—"

"That you, baby girl?" Madam Josephine asked as she yanked back the covers. "Oh, my Lord…"

"Billy Wolfe!" Goldie hollered.

"Madam Josephine, get away from him. He looks sickly," Olive whispered in Josephine's ear. A familiar rumble sounded in the distance, and Lawrence paused, looking out the nearby window.

"What is the meaning of this, Dorothy?" Madam Josephine demanded as Billy Wolfe cringed back, crawling back on his sick bed. "Did this two-timing scumbag hurt my Lucille? I'll kill him!"

Her hands jerked forward, wrapping themselves around Billy Wolfe's neck. He sputtered as Dorothy moved to intervene. Lawrence moved over to the open door and smiled broadly.

"They're here!"

Henry had descended into the dirt near the house, and Lucille and Jake were both clambering down. They hurried over to join them just as Madam Josephine scurried back to the porch. She stumbled on the wooden front porch before lifting the front of her long dress up as she hurried down a small flight of stairs.

"Lucille Elizabeth McDermott! Where have you tw—" She paused, finally noticing Henry, and let out a shriek. "What the hell is that? Lucille, get away from it now!"

Olive screamed out behind Josephine.

"M-m-monster?" Goldie muttered, fainting immediately after exiting the door. Lawrence lunged forward and caught her just as she fell.

"Easy there," he muttered, setting Goldie down on the porch. Beside her Josephine had dropped to her knees in fear.

"Don't worry, Mama!" Lucille said as she hurried over. "I had to help Jake find his dragon after he'd gone loose."

"His… his dragon?"

Lucille nodded, then patiently explained as Madam Josephine stared in stunned silence at Henry, who still kept his distance. Lawrence rushed over to his son, wrapping him up in a hug.

"Are you alright, my boy?" Lawrence asked, disengaging after a moment. "Where's Ulysses?"

Jake sighed. "I've been better. And Ulysses… well…"

The two of them explained what had been going on while their parents listened, feeling a mixture of sadness, surprise, and pride.

"A deputy marshal," Dorothy murmured. "Well, I'll be. You're a lawman just like your grandfather. I never dreamed something like that would happen… pinch me, Lawrence." She squealed. "Not so hard," she muttered.

"Sorry," Lawrence replied. "Let's go check on Madam Josephine."

They gathered around the front porch, where Olive and Goldie were listening in silence as Lucille came to her conclusion.

"Sorry for not telling ya, Ma," said Lucille. "It was a spur-of-the-moment decision, and I had to help Jake find Henry."

Madam Josephine licked her lips, having finally found her voice. "I see," she said, sounding unconvinced, but she nodded at Dorothy and Lawrence. "I apologize for barging in like that. You know how it is when your child is in danger…"

"We do," Dorothy agreed. "Indeed, we do."

"Well, I'll stay quiet about this. About all of this; Billy and Henry and the whole lot. Come on now, Lucille, girls. It's back to the cathouse tonight. Oh, Jake, a word if I might."

Lucille nodded, and accompanied Goldie and Olive as they made their way over to the carriage they'd used. Madam Josephine guided Jake over to the barn as his parents returned to their house. She sighed.

"I want you to swear to me that you'll protect Lucille."

"I swear I'll protect her even if it costs me my life, Ma'am."

She nodded, trying to assess the young man. "Do you like my daughter, Jake Mullens?"

"No, I love her!" he replied. Madam Josephine caught a glimpse of her daughter peering over, her porcelain features breaking into a smile as she eavesdropped on their conversation. Madam Josephine couldn't help but smile. She sighed to herself, thinking that her daughter deserved a better life than she'd had.

"I'm glad to hear it, Jake Mullens. Very glad indeed."

Chapter 22:
This Means War

The wind whipped around Jake as he held himself close to Henry. The cowboy hat his grandfather had once worn in his days as a sheriff bucked on his head like a mustang. His new badge twisted against his shirt and Jake pressed a hand against it. The star of a deputy Marshal was cool to the touch. Below them stretched the Arizona countryside, with Rattlefort identifiable only by a few pinpricks of light that broke through the night. That was all Jake needed though, as he noted the familiar bell tower and the Silver Springs Saloon nearby, glowing yellow through its windows.

"Right behind that building, Henry!"

Moving more silently than one might imagine for a creature of his size, Henry sailed down, gliding gently in the air until he raised up his talons and came to a sudden stop in the alley behind it. His massive wings were left extended, just above a dry goods store and the Silver Springs Saloon, and he delicately brought his wings in close and ducked down as Jake hopped off.

"Just wait here, buddy," Jake said as he patted Henry's neck. Jake took a moment to fight down the fears that were threatening to overpower him. He thought of Lucille; of his family, of the good people of Rattlefort who needed the Wolfe Gang gone. "Let's see if we can't get rid of these pests."

Jake strolled down the alley just as the saloon door burst open, Rawhide Cooper striding outward with his spurs jangling, shooting a frustrated look back inside. Jake darted back into the shadows, but Rawhide clearly hadn't noticed.

"Rawhide, don't you go running away from this whipping!"

Jimmy's holler from inside the saloon chilled Jake's soul. He heard a burst of laughter from within as he crept to the door. "I had you beat on the flop! Don't stop giving away your money now!"

"I know y'all are cheating!" Rawhide called out at the entrance, jabbing a finger inside for emphasis. "I'm going back to the hideout. You bastards took me for everything."

"Don't let the door hit you on the way out," Doc Otis chuckled.

Jake watched the grumbling Rawhide storming out and gave him a few seconds. Then he strolled boldly forward, making his way into the Silver Springs Saloon. Preacher was still cackling away, holding his stomach, but the rest of the laughter had finally died down. Jake caught the barest glimpse of motion in the back as Henry tracked his movements through the cracks of the broken saloon windows. The proprietor of the bar paused from nervously cleaning a mug and held out his hand; a faded white rag dangling from it.

"Now, I don't want no trouble, young man…"

Jake ignored the barkeep and focused on the men scattered around the poker table. The Wolfe Gang was a mess. They'd already gone back to squabbling over their chips. A stout fellow sitting alone at the bar frowned over at Jake.

"Who the hell are you?" he slurred in a strangely baby-like tone.

"Easy, Ira," the barkeep cautioned.

"Shut up. Was talking to…"

Jake passed Ira by, heading toward the poker table. A blank-eyed Sam Reeves was staring aimlessly at one of the windows as he drifted into a drunken stupor. He snorted, looking over and blinking as he stared at Henry through the window for a brief second. He stumbled and fell from his leaning chair at once.

"Hahaha!" Preacher McGowan erupted in laughter.

"Is there ever a time you ain't drunk, Sam?" Doc Otis muttered. "Or sleeping?"

"I just saw a dr-dr-dragon!" Sam Reeves stuttered, his right finger pointing at the boarded window near him as he sat up on the wooden floor. "A r-r-real life dr—"

"I told you to stop drinking so much. It's messing up your head!" Jimmy shouted, while tossing his cards in frustration at Sam. "Help that fool up to his feet, Preacher." Jimmy squinted from the poker table as he noted Jake's approach.

Jake tilted his grandfather's cowboy hat lower. "Howdy boys."

Jimmy scoffed, looking a deal less intimidated than Jake might have hoped. "Is that you, Jake Mullens?"

"Sure is."

"You here to lose some money on this poker table?" asked Jimmy, his elbow jabbing Doc Otis in his right side as they both smirked. "Got a spot for you, kid."

"I'm here to deliver a message from Marshal Davenport."

"That's obvious," Doc pointed out, rubbing his gray beard. "I see that new shiny badge on your chest."

Jimmy glanced down at his cards and sighed in exasperation before looking up at Jake. "I told that old fart already. No offense, Doc," Jimmy added. "We ain't turning our guns in for no presidential pardon."

"Oh, the Marshal is well aware of that," Jake snorted. "We're past any chance at redemption." He spun a chair from an empty table nearby and took a seat. "This time he said to tell you that Rattlefort is not a home for the Outlaw Union anymore. Y'all need to leave or else you have to suffer the consequences."

"What consequences? Powaw Tom made a fool outta him and damn near killed him to boot, the way I hear it," Doc Otis chuckled, as he stood up from the poker table. Picking up his cup of moonshine Doc slowly made his way to Jake's table. Doc's right hand casually drifted down, gripping the handle of his pistol as he took a seat.

"I wouldn't do that if I was you Doc," muttered Jake. Doc just chuckled. Cupping his hand towards his mouth, Jake whistled loudly.

"And what's a dumb young whippersn—"

In the blink of an eye, Henry's large head smashed through the side wall of the Silver Springs Saloon, sending splinters flying in all directions. The dragon bit and grabbed Ira Dotson's upper torso before yanking him out of the establishment with blinding speed. The Wolfe Gang sobered up pretty quickly after that.

"What in God's name was that thing?" asked Preacher McGowan. He stared at the enormous hole in the wall near the bar as the saloon owner backed away, dropping his empty mug to shatter on the ground. He rushed away, running through the spreading pool of beer and back to safety.

"L-Like I told you it was a dr-dr-dragon!" Sam shouted.

"Whatever it is just snatched away Ira," said Doc Otis, slowly cocking back the hammer of his pistol.

"That's right, and it could happen to any one of you," Jake snorted as he looked Doc in the eyes. "If ya move an inch you're dead."

Doc leaned back, studying Jake for a moment. He seemed to consider something.

"Don't try—"

Doc quickly drew his pistol from his holster, faster than Jake had expected, but before he could point it at Jake, Henry's head broke through the opposite side of the saloon. Henry roared, a blast of flames soaring outward. In seconds Doc Otis was wrapped in flames, turning into a pile of ashes before everyone's shocked eyes, his moonshine feeding the growing fire.

"No, not Doc!" Jimmy cried out, rushing over to the steaming pile of ash where Doc Otis had once been. Tears fell, almost unnoticed, sizzling as they dropped onto the smoldering remnants of the man.

"Hellfire," Preacher murmured, glancing over at Jake. His hand hovered near his pistol and then jerked aside at once. An uncomfortable silence lingered.

"Alright," Jimmy said, his voice now as cold as ever, even as tears weaved their way down his face. He stood, unashamed, glaring at Jake. "We'll leave

Rattlefort. But just know that this means war, Jake Mullens."

***

Rattlefort, AZ
1845

The cough sounded ragged and wet. Jimmy hesitated outside the doorway.

"Is she gonna be okay?" Billy Wolfe asked quietly. He was just ten years old, and Jimmy didn't know what he'd do if they lost their mother. Their father, Frank Wolfe, had been killed before Billy was born and Jimmy could scarcely even recall the man. At fifteen, Jimmy reckoned he would do alright on his own if it came to it, but Billy…

"We need a doctor, Jimmy," Cooper said. "She sounds a lot like Ma and Pa did when they got black lung."

Billy's eyes widened, swelling up with emotion and barely suppressed tears. Jimmy glared at Cooper. He was thirteen, and he'd been taken in under their mother's care a few years back after Cooper's parents had died. Cooper was about the meanest, orneriest kid Jimmy had ever met. Sometimes he liked that about him.

This was not one of those times.

"Ain't like we got money," Billy managed.

"Wait here," Jimmy said, carefully entering the bedchamber. "Here I am, Ma. With a fresh cup of water like you asked for. Anything else you need?"

She coughed. "Just... take care of the boys. When I'm gone."

"When you're gone? Ma, don't worry," said Jimmy, as he held his mother's hand. "Cooper and Billy are going to help me get some money for a doctor."

"Ain't no doctor worth a damn in Rattlefort."

"I hear there's a doctor passing through. We'll get you sorted out, don't you worry."

She coughed as Jimmy turned away. He shut the room behind him and looked at the others.

"We gotta rob a store. It's the only way."

Billy squirmed, looking down at the ground.

"With what?" Cooper asked.

"This for starters," Jimmy said, lifting up his shirt to reveal his father's old pistol stuck in his trousers. "I found it this morning in my Pa's old things."

Cooper nodded thoughtfully. "I guess I got that hunting knife. Been wanting to use it somebody," he added with a savage grin. "Cut 'em up real good."

"I... I'll just stare at 'em real mean-like!" Billy suggested. "And... well, I could carry the money!"

"Fine," Jimmy stated. "But we don't have time to mess about. I don't know how long that doctor's going to be in town. So let's go!"

The three of them left their small shack along the edge of Rattlefort, striding through the small frontier town. Cooper whistled as they turned a corner, nodding over toward a tall, blonde woman walking past.

"That there is just the finest piece of flesh I ever did see," he murmured. "*Josephine.*" He whispered it like it was magic. "A woman like that sure gets me in the mood for fightin' and f—"

"Keep focused on the job," Jimmy grunted. "Christ, you're just a kid."

"Pff, you ain't much older than me. Besides, you're just saying that because Delilah has you whipped."

"Shut your damn trap!"

"There she is!" Billy squeaked.

From out of Mrs. Orren's bakery there emerged the young Delilah Evans, a couple fresh loaves of bread in her hands. She smiled, surprised to see Jimmy, and he melted as he took in her shimmering white teeth and red hair.

"Well now! Where are you all headed to in such a hurry?"

"We're fixing to rob the general goods store," said Jimmy, with Billy and Cooper following behind. He lifted his shirt to reveal his father's pistol tucked in his waist. He never had much of an art for deception.

Her eyebrows rose high. "Are you kidding me, Jimmy?"

"You're looking mighty fine today, Delilah," Cooper snorted, examining her figure. His eyes fixed themselves on her breasts and he grinned wide.

"Shut up, Cooper!" she replied, folding both her arms in anger. She looked over in dismay at Jimmy. "You could go to jail if you get caught by Sheriff Mullens."

"That old fool Halfwit Henry can't even shoot the tail off a donkey. And we have no other choice. Now move out the way, Delilah."

"No."

Delilah moved to block Jimmy's path every time he took a step.

"Okay, I ain't fixing to ask twice. Cooper, grab Delilah and kindly escort her back home."

Cooper eagerly wrapped his arms around Delilah from behind and hauled her away. She sputtered, her shoes kicking up dirt.

"Unhand me this instant. James McGregor Wolfe! If you go through with this I'll never speak to you again."

Jimmy worked his dry mouth, spitting on the dirt street. He ignored Delilah, instead studying the general goods store. "Billy, keep watch here. I'm going to circle around while we wait for Cooper to get back." He glanced back to see Cooper leading her away. "It's best if we just keep her safe," he murmured. "This is no kinda life for her."

"Are we... crooks now, Jimmy?" Billy asked, staring at his boots. He seemed so little next to Jimmy. After a moment, he patted his younger brother.

"Not just yet, Billy. But one day everyone will know about the Wolfe Gang. And we won't *ever* need to worry about money again."

Chapter 23:
Doc Otis

Rattlefort, AZ
1845

A knock sounded on the door of the Rattlefort sheriff's office. Henry blinked, raising his head blearily from his table. He sniffed and took in the stink of whiskey. As he slid his half-empty bottle aside, Shcriff Mullens heard a few shouts in the distance. The knocking persisted once again.

"Come in," he grunted, settling himself in his chair. "It's not locked. I think."

The door opened, and one of the carpenters in town stuck his head in. "Sheriff, there's quite the racket going on over at the dry good store."

"I hear it," Sheriff Mullens said, weaving his way to the entrance even as his head throbbed from last night's drinking binge. There was definitely shouting coming from within the store just across the street.

"And about that travelling Doctor," the man pressed. "I swear he's a fraud. Charges top dollar for potions and tinctures and what have you. A friend I know bought some snake oil for some warts on his... anyway, just said it stung like a son-of-a-bitch when he dropped the snake oil on and didn't do nothin'."

"Might take a few days," Sheriff Mullens said, glaring down the road at the wagon hitched up near a saloon. The words "Doc Otis' Miracle Elixirs and Other Various Tonics" were emblazoned on the side in a splash of gaudy yellow and bronze paint. "Looks like he's ready to leave at least. I'll give him another warning." Henry pulled at his gun belt, adjusting it beneath his pot belly, the suspenders keeping it in place over his plaid shirt. He might not be in the best of shape, but he had two revolvers with him, and the skill to use them both. "Now let's see what all the fuss is in here."

He paused at the door, listening for a moment.

"I know you got more in there!" a boyish voice demanded. "Every last silver dollar!"

"Now hold on—"

Henry didn't hesitate. Gun drawn, he pushed his way in, aiming down the sights of both revolvers at a teenager standing on the counter with a bandana across his face. Catching a flash of motion, his left arm swiveled to take in a boy of perhaps ten or eleven, standing open-mouthed with a bag full of money. He dropped the sack, coins spilling on the ground, and raised his mouth even as the teenager made no move.

Behind them, the proprietor of the store looked over in relief, brushing her chestnut brown hair out of her face.

"Hold your horses!" Sheriff Mullens called out. "If you two even flinch I'll shoot you down right where you st—"

The sound of a cocked hammer cut him off, and then Henry felt cold metal pressed against the back of his head.

A third bandit? But where did he come from?

The young man on the counter frowned, looking puzzled over his bandana.

"It seems like the tables have turned against you, Sheriff."

Delicately, Henry turned partway to see a middle-aged man standing behind him, his eyes barely visible between his hat and a wrapped handkerchief that concealed his features.

"Better lower your guns before I blow your brains all over this pretty wood floor."

"Alright now, take it easy. Nobody has to get hurt."

Sheriff Mullins slowly lowered his weapons to the ground.

"Now scoot 'em to the side with your feet," the man instructed, tilting his brown leather hat even lower to conceal his salt-and-pepper eyebrows. "Hey boys, hurry up and get me a bunch of that opium while you're at it."

"Sure thing, mister!" the boy on the counter hollered after a moment, though Sheriff Mullens reckoned he still looked more than a bit puzzled by this turn of events. The two boys glanced at each other before shrugging their shoulders at the same time.

"Boys, grab that lady behind the counter. We'll bring her along just in case the Sheriff tries anything funny."

"I got it," the older boy said, grabbing a few bottles behind the counter.

The younger boy grabbed a few small boxes, along with a few fancy-looking packages of goods almost at random, filling his sack until it strained fit to bursting. As they made their way to the exit, the older boy waved the proprietor of the general goods store away with his pistol. "You heard the man, lady. You're coming with us!"

"You won't get away with this," Sheriff Mullens vowed. "I'll be coming after you."

"Not any time soon," the middle-aged man growled. "Stay inside and count backwards from one hundred. When you reach zero, then you come out. But I'll be keeping time too. If you get too excited and come out too soon, the lady gets it in the back of her head."

"Oh my," the woman murmured as the boys bolted out of the store.

"Fine," Sheriff Mullens grunted. He felt the pressure of the barrel leave the back of his head and heard the door slam behind him. Yet he made no move, counting down from one hundred.

I will get you, you bastard.

***

"Let me go already, you big goon!"

"No, no, not just yet," Cooper said, scanning left and right. They were close to the outskirts of Rattlefort by now; behind an abandoned shack that Cooper had identified as a good spot for a hideout some time ago. He hauled Delilah behind the half-rotted and wind-scoured wood to keep her away from prying eyes.

"What do you think you're doing? Let me go right now, Cooper!"

"I know you're Jimmy's girl, but…" He rolled her over onto her back before using his weight to keep her pinned down to the hot sand. "We can still have some fun. Right?"

"I think not!" she said, spitting up at him. He grimaced, wiping it away, and then winced in agony as her fingernails tore against his face. Seeing red, he shoved her down as he grabbed his knife. "C'mon, don't be like that, Delilah!"

He gritted his teeth, trying to keep her down as she struggled to get him off of her.

"I just want a little sample, that's all!"

"Go to hell!"

He brought the knife up to her neck just as she jerked her head forward, the blade cutting into her throat.

"Shit," he muttered as she whipped her free hand up at him, clawing his face once again, sending a rush of pain and rage coursing through him.

Then everything went red.

***

"Get out of here," Jimmy rumbled in a voice deeper than his own, tapping his pistol against the woman's shoulder. The proprietor of the dry goods store took off running without another word. Jimmy glanced back at his brother and the older man, the two of them striding forward at a quick pace toward a wagon parked by a saloon. After a moment, Jimmy followed, jerking his bandana off and stuffing it into his pocket.

The older man had already unhitched his horse and clambered up, urging it on speedily toward the bluffs outside of town. Billy had joined beside him, his wide eyes staring at Jimmy over the bandana they'd made of their family tablecloth. Jimmy climbed onto the back, holding on to the bottles he'd taken as the wagon rocked back and forth, heading out of town quickly.

Jimmy peeked in the back, taking in the crates and the rattling of bottles with unfamiliar colors every shade of the rainbow.

Just who is this fella?

Before he expected it, the wagon slowed and came to a halt on the dirt and rocks outside Rattlefort. Jimmy hopped down, making his way toward the front.

"That's one hundred," the older man said, sliding out of his seat. He'd taken them a bit outside town to shield themselves behind a low hill; the dirt and saguaros blocking the view of town. "Now then," he said, pulling his own bandana off, "What the hell were you boys thinking? You always need to have a lookout when doing things like that."

"Thanks, Mister. We were gonna have one but got sick of waiting around for him to get back. If it wasn't for you we'd be on our way to jail right now," Jimmy admitted, handing him a few bottles of opium.

"Don't mention it. Why rob the general goods store anyway? You boys desperate for coin?" the older man muttered, while pulling out a medical bag from his wagon.

"Our mother isn't feeling too well and we need money to pay for a traveling doctor that's passing through," said Billy as he pulled off his bandana.

"Well, today's your lucky day. Doc Otis, wandering miracle worker, at your service."

Jimmy's eyes opened wide. "*You're* the traveling doctor?"

"Yep."

"Billy... give him the bag of money," Jimmy said. "All of it." He tried his best to hold back his tears as the doctor's eyes widened. "Here you go, Mister. You can have it all if you just take a look at her. I'm not expecting miracles, but I'm sure praying for one."

Doc Otis remained silent, looking at the sad expression on the boys' faces. For a second his stern expression softened into one of pity. "Keep it," he said as he climbed aboard the wagon. "I'll take a look at her. Just show me the way. Might need to beat a hasty retreat out of town if the lawman puts two and two together."

He extended a hand and helped them both up.

"We can circle around the outside over here," Jimmy pointed out. "There's an abandoned shack we like to play around, and it ain't too far from home."

Doc Otis nodded, spurring his horse onward and following their directions. They rumbled along until they approached their mother's house, Jimmy's heart in his throat.

"Jimmy!"

They saw Cooper approaching, his face ripped and bloodied. He had a deeply guilty expression, looking away as the wagon slowed.

"Uh, I, um… I…"

"Boy, you're looking like somebody tanned your raw hide," Doc Otis observed.

Billy burst out laughing. "Hahah, *Rawhide* Cooper!"

Cooper winced, attempting a smile. "Well… you see… the Hilton twins ganged up on me. And, uh…"

"We don't have time for this," Jimmy replied, hopping off the wagon. "Doc, come on!"

He hurried into the door, the others close behind, and then Jimmy rushed upstairs and opened the room. "Ma, we're back! Billy and I brought a doctor for you. Everything's going to be alright now."

There was no reply.

"Ma?"

Doc Otis quickly made his way past Jimmy, moving beside the silent woman and placing two index fingers on her neck. He checked her pulse. Jimmy stared down at his mother.

Was she always that pale? Why ain't she saying nothing?

Doc Otis sighed. He then proceeded to lift up her lifeless right arm before letting it go. "I don't rightly know what to tell you boys," said Doc Otis, shaking his head from side to side with a look of uncertainty. "It's too late."

"Nonsense, Doc. She's just sleeping," Jimmy replied in a whimpering tone.

"Ma's dead!" Billy cried, spinning around and bumping Cooper's shoulder as he stormed through the door. Jimmy just stared blankly, silent tears dropping down his face and chin. Doc Otis covered Agatha Wolfe's face with a blanket and left the room silently. Cooper shot Jimmy another guilty look, glancing away, and the two boys followed after the doctor. Billy was sobbing to himself out on the veranda.

"She's gone, but we still got each other. Right Billy?" Jimmy asked, wrapping his arm around Billy's shoulder, the younger boy's tears flowing like a river.

"What are we gonna do now?" Billy replied. "We're all alone!"

Doc Otis made his way out of the house, with Cooper following behind, staring down at the ground. "You boys can follow me if you want," the doctor said after a moment. "But we gotta leave now."

"Are you sure that's okay, Mister?" asked Cooper, perking up a bit. "We don't wanna be a burden, but… I reckon I need to get out of town."

"Call me Doc Otis," he replied, smirking at Cooper. "Think I'll call you Rawhide. And I wouldn't mind the extra company," he added, glancing at the others. "You boys got a lot of potential."

His comforting words weren't enough to stop the boys' flowing tears, but it struck a chord in the depths of their hearts.

"Before we go, we need to bury our mother," Jimmy announced, rising to his feet. "I think… by that shack on the edge of town."

"I don't think you should go there!" Cooper said in a hurry. "I mean. Cause. She deserves to be buried on her property," he added, pointing at the garden. "You know how she loved her flowers."

"Yeah," Billy muttered, sniffling and wiping his eyes. "I'll get the shovel."

"Maybe I could… say goodbye to Delilah," Jimmy mumbled, his eyes welling with tears again. "Apologize to her for being the way I am…"

"I wouldn't do that if I were you," Cooper replied. "She called us criminals and said she doesn't ever want to see you again."

Jimmy's heart hurt so much that this last injury didn't bring out anything more than a shrug. The next hour was spent in a blur and a flurry of dirt as the boys took turns digging a hole in the garden. All the while, Doc Otis prowled the perimeter and tended to his horse, until he seemed satisfied that there was no one in pursuit.

"May God welcome you, Ma," Jimmy said as Billy shoveled the last bit of dirt over her grave.

"Amen," Doc Otis added agreeably. "I'll do my part, Mrs. Agatha Wolfe, to see to the education of your waifs."

"You don't mean schoolin', do you?" Cooper asked warily.

Doc Otis snorted. "Oh, I ain't fixing to teach you school stuff, Rawhide. But you will learn quite a few tricks of the trade. Science, medicine, how to add and take away… mainly subtracting stuff from others and adding it to the wagon," he said, jerking a thumb back at his traveling wagon. "None of this robbery at gunpoint business, at least not for a while. You don't want to make too much of a fuss. Tinctures, laudanum, and snake oil. That's where the real profits are. Help me gather up a crowd in the next town so I can sell to morons all over these United States." He looked at Jimmy. "You got quick fingers, boy?"

"None faster!"

"Good, good, you can pick some pockets while they're not looking," Doc Otis mused, rubbing at his salt and pepper beard. "Yes, I think we could make a killing together…"

Chapter 24:
A Plan of Retaliation

Rattlefort, AZ
1865

Jimmy rode through the streets of Rattlefort, his eyes downcast as the flood of memories from twenty years ago rushed through him. He glanced over at Rawhide Cooper; the closest person to him now, with Doc Otis gone. Rawhide nodded back at him as they ambled along.

"Damn shame," he said, breaking the silence that had settled in around them ever since streaming out of the smoldering Silver Springs Saloon.

"And with Billy still gone too," Jimmy added, twisting irritably in his saddle. "And not knowing how or why…"

It put him in mind of his first love, strangely enough. Both gone; plucked away by the Grim Reaper without Jimmy even noticing. Ever since Doc Otis had been burned to smithereens, Jimmy had been in an unusually melancholic state, remembering how he'd first turned to crime and met his mentor.

"You said you escorted Delilah back home before being accosted by the Hilton twins?"

Rawhide blinked in surprise. "Well, what... what in the hell has brought this on? We've been over this a dozen times."

Jimmy scratched at the stubble on his chin. They'd eked out a living along with Doc Otis, growing up as pickpockets and burglars before graduating to stagecoach robbers and horse thieves. It had been three years before Jimmy had snuck back in, with the half-baked plan of surprising Delilah and trying to woo her away into joining their gang. In the end it had been him that'd been surprised; stunned by the story of her discovery in a shallow grave outside town. She'd been murdered; raped too, some said, though Jimmy could never be sure with gossip of that sort.

He let out a long sigh. "Just thinking of old times." He'd vowed to put down whoever had killed her, naming his two pistols after the most important women in his life in a fit of passion, but the years had brought nothing but dead ends. And, slowly but surely, he had given up all hope of revenge.

"We'll make better times; newer times," Rawhide insisted. "That's the way of things. You want something bad enough, you just gotta grab it and make it yours." He shot Jimmy a vicious grin.

"Reckon so," Jimmy muttered, still uncharacteristically downbeat.

"I don't see you moaning over Ira," Preacher McGowan pointed out, mounted on his gray sorrel as they rode through Rattlefort.

"No, you don't," Jimmy replied, spurring his horse. Together they stormed out of town, making their way to the hideout. A man Jimmy didn't quite recognize guarded the entrance, waving them in after a moment. He had a pince-nez, and Jimmy took him for one of the Deadly Six. "See to our horses," Jimmy snapped as he dismounted and handed the reins over. The man frowned but took the reins all the same. Jimmy pushed his way inside.

Ned and Shirley were in the corner, chuckling to themselves as they shared a joke. Jimmy felt a pang of envy and looked away, his expression hardening as he saw Lester Reyes puffing at a cigarette in the center of the hideout. The man patted at a sleek, black table in the middle of the hideout, where the others were gathered.

"Do you like the table?" Lester asked, pouring a glass full of tequila. "I decided to do a bit of… shopping," he said with a cold grin.

"While you were shopping, we received a message," Jimmy grated out as he approached the table, his gang trickling in one after the other. "From a farm boy turned deputy. Marshal Davenport wants us to clear out. More than that… he sent a dragon as a show of strength. Burned Doc to a crisp."

"And Ira," Preacher McGowan added helpfully.

Lester chuckled. "A dragon?" He tapped his glass. "You've been drinking too much, I think. There's only one demon in Rattlefort."

"They can vouch for me," Jimmy growled. His men gave the others serious nods, and the expressions of the other outlaws turned from jovial to confused. "I don't know about you, but I'm going to gut this Davenport for killing Doc Otis."

"Vengeance!" Lester puffed at his cigarette, then smeared the embers on his new table. "Can you believe this idiota?" He shook his head. "That's why you're not fit to be a leader, Jimmy."

"Oh yeah?" Jimmy glared at Lester. "And why's that?"

"You let emotional attachments cloud your judgment," said Lester. "Doc knew the risks of being an outlaw. And you should have killed that beast right then and there."

"Emotional attachments!?" Jimmy repeated, his sorrow turned into rage. "You know, I'm just about sick and tired of you. I ain't never taken insults from nobody, and I ain't about to start today!"

Jimmy drew Agatha and Delilah from his holster, Lester whipping up his own pistol, and the Wolfe Gang quickly following suit as they all aimed at Lester.

"Whoa, hey now!" Vince called out, the others looking uncertain.

Powaw Tom stepped in front of Jimmy, both of his hands slowly guiding Agatha and Delilah back to his holster. "Don't do it, Jimmy."

"Hahaha... look at you pendejos," said Lester, setting his revolver on the table and blowing smoke from his cigarette in Jimmy's direction. "You think I fear death?"

"Get out the way, Tom. This ain't got nothing to do with you," said Jimmy, gritting his teeth.

"I know," Powaw Tom replied calmly. "But Lester wasn't the one who killed Doc. Channel that anger toward the ones responsible."

"I agree!" hollered Ned, watching the argument unfold with Shirley sitting on his lap.

"Ooh, darlin', don't yell in my ear."

"Sorry, Shirley!"

"If you're gonna shoot, shoot the dragon," Eugene chimed in, sitting on a crate in the corner as he drank whiskey from a bottle. "Not each other."

The Deadly Six remained silent, unwilling to comment on the petty squabble. They took their cues from Vincent, who crossed his arms and looked disapprovingly at the standoff. After a moment, Jimmy holstered his guns, the mood in the hideout relaxing slightly. Preacher and Rawhide lowered their guns, following Jimmy's example, and Sam and Al Crosby also did the same before taking seats at the table.

"Cigarette?" Lester asked idly, handing one over when Al Crosby stuck his hand out. Lester settled back in his chair, the rest of the group hanging onto his words. "I'm still the leader, and I say we strike now," said Lester. "Since they drew first blood we'll hit 'em where it hurts the most."

"What's the plan?" asked Powaw Tom.

"First, I'll cause a diversion and get Davenport and his posse to come running back to Rattlefort," Lester replied. "Jimmy and his gang can stay here and guard the stolen loot. This is technically his hideout, after all, and we don't know if they'll strike here next."

"Damn right it's my hideout," Jimmy mumbled under his breath.

"Meanwhile, Powaw Tom and the Deadly Six will go and plant dynamite at the Marshal's office in Yuma. As soon as Davenport returns and trips the wire, kaboom!"

Vincent nodded. "Easy as that, Boss."

"And w-w-what will we do about the farm boy and his dragon?" Sam Reeves asked.

"Absolutely nothing, at first! Jake and his dragon might be the brawn but Davenport is the brain," said Lester with a grin as he glanced in Sam's direction.

"I like this plan," the usually silent Al Crosby cut in, blowing a cloud of smoke from his cigarette. "Even though I don't like you," he added to Lester, who shrugged.

"I don't care if you like me. You know not to mess with the Demon." Lester tapping his fingers on the table. "We will cut off the head and watch 'em fall apart."

"I'll d-d-d-drink to that," Sam said, reaching over for the bottle of tequila.

In a flash, Lester pulled a knife out and slammed it into the table, wood chips flying from the blade, which was just an inch away from Sam's hand.

"You have to ask first," Lester said calmly, glancing at Jimmy. "Is your whole gang so rude?"

Sam's eyes widened. "P-p-p-p…"

"Please?" Lester suggested, wrenching the knife out, whirling it around, and jabbing it back in its holster.

"N… never mind," Sam said, lurching abruptly from his seat. "I d-don't feel like d-d-drinking."

"Well now, praise the Lord," Preacher McGowan said in astonishment as Sam Reeves left the table. "I never did see that man refuse a drop of liquor."

"Don't praise the Lord, Preacher," Lester said in his Spanish-accented, coldly tranquil voice, "praise the Demon." He raised his glass up high, winked at Preacher McGowan, and threw it back.

***

Henry's claws slid on the dirt for a pace before he came to a stop. By the time Jake clambered down, his father was already peering out the door.

"Oh, Jake! Are you staying tonight?"

"Yes, Pa," Jake said, patting Henry. "I'll get you settled in for bed later on. You know not to stray away now, right?" he asked the dragon. "Upon your honor as a deputy, if nothing else." Henry licked Jake's face, and he chuckled as he stepped back. "Okay, you understand then."

Henry's head bobbed up and down.

Jake turned and walked toward the door.

"We were just eating," Lawrence said. "I think there's enough for us all."

Jake nodded, then froze in place as he saw Billy seated at the dinner table. The pale-faced bandit shot Jake a quick smile and waved a spoon in greetings. Dorothy looked over from her seat.

"Oh, Jake! Come and join us for dinner."

"Um, yes, Ma," Jake muttered, taking a seat and eyeing Billy Wolfe uncomfortably. "But what's he doing here?"

"He's been getting a lot better. Well enough to eat with us, anyway… and he's promised to change. Haven't you, Billy?"

"Yes, Ma'am," Billy replied in between bites of his dinner. "Good to see you, Jake. I know you agree with me that we need to let bygones be bygones."

Jake mumbled something as he took a seat. Under the hard stare of his mother, Jake nodded, then grabbed a dinner roll. By the time their meal had finished Jake had warmed up to Billy. A little bit, at least.

"Sorry to be such a burden," Billy said, patting his stomach. "But it's so hard to resist your cooking, Mrs. Mullens!"

"Oh, you're such a dear!" Dorothy replied with a smile. "Come back any time!"

"Just not to burn our crops again," Jake muttered, then noticed his mother's stare and almost choked on his food. "Um... I'm kidding."

"I wouldn't do that now," Billy said, carefully wiping at the corner of his mouth and folding up his napkin. "You're good people. But I think I'm ready to go, if you're fine with that."

Jake's parents exchanged glances and nodded together.

"Are you ready to walk, though?" Lawrence asked. "I know you were sick for a while. I don't want you to think you're unwelcome. Another week, even another day, could help you build up—"

"That's kind of you, Mr. Mullens, but I feel like I'm ready. I know where to go for some sleep and food to get me on my feet again."

Lawrence frowned. "Where's that?"

"You know I can't say exactly," Billy said, rising to his feet. "Thanks again."

Jake shifted in his seat, then he rose along with Billy.

"I'll show him out."

Jake led Billy outside. Henry, roaming around the farm and sniffing at the buildings, turned to look at Billy. Jake could tell he was skeptical.

"I know," Jake said to Henry, then he turned to Billy. "Before we let you go, Billy, remember that there's always a choice. You can choose not to be an outlaw, the same way my parents chose not to let you die."

"I appreciate that, but Jimmy is my brother, and I'm the only family he's got."

"You know I'm a deputy now, Billy," Jake added as he patted his gleaming start. "I'll look the other way this time," said Jake, patting Henry on top of the head outside. "But if you go back and join your brother I'll be forced to take you down with him."

"I understand," Billy replied, tilting his hat at Dorothy and Lawrence in gratitude as they looked on from the porch. "Do what you have to do," he said, turning and walking away from the farm before fading into the distance.

Chapter 25:
Casualties of War

"Ride like the wind!" Lester called out as the wagon rolled by, fully loaded with explosives. Vincent raised his hat up high and shot Lester an enthusiastic grin. "But don't hit any potholes or start any fires. That thing could go boom!"

Vincent nodded, then turned to face forward, whipping his horses forward. Flanking the wagon were the other members of the Deadly Six, along with Powaw Tom. He rode along silently, his face dour and expression unreadable. Lester watched the group heading toward Yuma, then turned back to face Jimmy and his gang. Jimmy still had that same annoyed look on his face. It privately amused Lester, to think that this upjumped bandit figured himself to be an equal to the Demon.

"Sure you can handle guarding the hideout?" Lester Reyes asked, unable to resist poking at Jimmy's ego.

"Of course," he muttered.

"We're all loaded up!" Ned called out from the driver's seat of the Outlaw Union's second wagon. Shirley sat snuggled up right beside him with a shotgun in her lap. "Want a ride?"

"I'll just walk alongside," Lester said, pointing forward. "Vámonos!"

He strode along the wagon as it rumbled along toward a hill overlooking Rattlefort. In the distance Lester could make out a few citizens of Rattlefort going about their daily business. One or two looked over, but without much curiosity. They considered themselves neutral; thinking that they could just outlive whatever government claimed hold here.

Idiots, all of them. They don't know the Demon.

The wagon lurched forward, slowing as it strained up the slope. Ned whipped the horses as they pulled against the sand and dirt. Eugene Cook emerged from the other side of the wagon just as Lester did, and together they both rammed their shoulders against the back of the wagon, pushing forward. Finally the wagon lurched forward, making it past the steepest segment of the hill and then rattling forward. The wagon moved forward for another minute or so, Lester carefully watching to make sure it wouldn't tilt over on the steep slope, before it finally lurched to a halt.

"That should do it," Ned called out. "A fine view of Rattlefort, just like you wanted. We're at the peak."

"Fine driving, Ned!" Shirley added.

"Thanks, doll!"

"Good, good, let's unload it," Lester said, waving them over. He trotted to the back where Eugene was already removing the canvas covering. Revealed within, gleaming in the Arizona sun, where the barrels of their captured Gatling gun. "A fine sight," Lester said, smiling as he took it in.

Once Ned and Shirley joined them, they began pulling away at it, dragging the Gatling gun into a commanding position on the heights outside Rattlefort. Ned paused, wiping his brow, as Lester swiveled the Gatling gun around to test its aim. Eugene approached with a box of ammunition, stacking it beside the growing pile. Rounds upon rounds were already linked up to the gun itself.

"I reckon you gonna shoot that dragon with this if it shows up," Eugene said, placing a hand above his eyes as he squinted into the Arizona desert around him. "Right?"

Lester chuckled, gripping the hand crank and drifting the gun barrels around, focusing on the main entrance of the town's dry goods store.

"Just watch, cabrón. There is only one way to strike fear in the hearts of men, and that's with terror." He let rip, cranking the Gatling gun as round after round sped into Rattlefort, shredding into the side of the church and ricocheting off the plaza. He turned the gun slowly, raking the town from one side to the other with hundreds of bullets as he shredded homes and businesses to pieces.

***

Billy staggered through the desert, sweat streaming his face. The journey from the Mullens farm had proven to be a good deal longer than he'd remembered, and his fever-wracked body hadn't been able to make it back overnight. So now he struggled in the hot Arizona sun, still wondering what he should do with himself. Motion caught his eye in the peripheral, and he turned to see a large patch of shadow moving quickly over the hills, a rippling wave that went over scrub brush and cacti. Glancing up, he saw a large bird in the distance.

No, it's Henry! That damn Jake Mullens is tracking me. Better not lead him directly to the hideout…

Summoning his reserves of energy, Billy turned to the side, striking off in what he knew was the wrong direction. But he was not about to betray his gang. After a moment, he squinted back up in the air, shielding the hot sun with his right hand. Billy's change in direction seemed to have attracted the dragon, which was now coming closer.

That dragon sure looks different from here, Billy Wolfe mused even as he kept walking through the desert. *It looks like a light green color. Maybe I'm just seeing things...*

His eyes widened as the dragon surged forward. "Oh hell," he muttered, feeling a surge of fear inside of him. He rushed forward, stumbling on a prickly pear cactus that sent needles into his right leg. "Dammit, dammit... stay away, you damn dragon, I'm feeling too hot out here already. Don't burn me up any more..." Billy stumbled over a dried-out log, falling into the hot sand. He raised his arms up to cover his head as he felt a sudden hot gust of air, then felt a growing sense of dread as he heard the dragon landing beside him.

Finally he rolled over, squinting over to take in Henry and Jake...

Billy blinked. "What the hell?"

That ain't Henry and Jake!

The dragon was a shimmering light green, with an ornate saddle atop it; dark leather but splashed with bright red and gold designs, along with strange markings of black atop white. It looked like some kind of unfamiliar language.

The rider slid off his mount, approaching Billy Wolfe with a contemptuous raise of the lip. He was a dignified-looking man of middle age with a tipped bowler hat, and Chinese too, Billy figured. They weren't too common out here aside from railroad crews, but this man had a distinctly Imperial look to him... definitely not some laborer.

"Do you know who I am?" the man asked as he approached, carefully removing slim leather riding gloves and stuffing them into a shirt pocket.

"Look, sir, please don't hurt me," Billy croaked, sluggishly rising to his feet. "I-I thought you were someone else at first."

"Someone else?" the man replied, peering over. A ruby amulet in the shape of a dragon glowed brightly at his chest as he spoke. "And who do you mean? Does he have a dragon?"

"Uh, yes. There's only one person with a dragon in these parts, and that's Jake Mullens."

"Jake Mullens," the man mused with a faint Chinese accent. "Tell me, boy, what is your name?"

Billy licked his chapped lips. He felt reluctant to answer and paused to brush off some sand. The dragon snorted, craning its long neck around to stare intently at Billy. It was definitely bigger than Henry. That ended his reluctance; Billy quickly deciding not to give the man any trouble, and he soon fell to stammering out an answer.

"B-B-Billy Wolfe."

"Wolfe?" the man blinked and snorted. "You're just the man I'm looking for," he replied sarcastically. "Wonderful. Your brother's gang of idiots robbed my train, killed my workers, and stole my baby dragon. Does the name Sun Wong ring a bell?"

Billy just stared and shook his head. "N-no, sir. We r-rob lots of trains."

Belly Through the Brush

"Hmm. Now then," Sun Wong said, coming in close. Despite his lack of apparent weapons, Billy cringed away. He waved the dragon over as he stepped near. "Do you think I should punish you and your brother Jimmy Wolfe? Xingfeng!" Sun Fang let loose a few unfamiliar words, and suddenly the dragon leaped forward, gathering up Billy in her huge, open jaw. Billy dangled from the dragon's mouth, shrieking in surprise and fear.

"Oh, Lord," he muttered, saying a few prayers as he dangled in the air. Sun Wong said something else in Cantonese, and Billy tumbled to the ground. He stayed there for a moment, then finally rose to his knees.

Sun Wong chuckled. "Don't worry, I won't kill you right now. It seems this Jake Mullens you spoke of stole my Feilong from under your noses. So here's what I want you to do. Tell Jimmy he has six days to return my Feilong or else. I'll be waiting for him in the Dragoon Mountains."

"Y-yes sir," Billy muttered as Sun Wong donned his riding gloves again. He approached Xingfeng, pulling himself back up onto the saddle. Then he clicked his tongue, shouting out something in Cantonese, and the huge dragon slammed her wings to the ground, knocking Billy back a few paces into a saguaro and scouring him with sand. By the time he blinked enough grit out of his eyes to see, the dragon was a small dot in the sky, whirling away from Rattlefort.

"There's… two dragons now?" Billy muttered, wincing as he reached back to pull out the cactus needles. "Well ain't that just…"

He trailed off, hearing the sounds of gunfire in the distance. To his surprise, it sounded more rapid than anything he'd ever heard before and just continued. He squinted at the faint outline of Rattlefort in the distance, where a plume of smoke was barely visible. Then he hurried forward, staggering through the desert.

What the hell is going on?

***

What the hell is going on?

Peggy Riley thought quickly as the bullets ricocheted through town. For an instant, the vision of her fallen gang flashed through her mind as she rushed for cover. The Riley Gang, cut down in a hail of gunfire by the Wolfe Gang in these very streets. Yet this time, as one of Madam Josephine's prostitutes, she had a different crew.

"Stay down!" she shouted, falling back into her old gunslinger ways as she rushed back into the general goods store she'd just left. Bullets slapped at the plaza all around her, a stray round going right through the neck of Mr. Orren as he peeked out of his bakery. Despite herself, Peggy spun around, debating whether to help. Then another hail of bullets carpeted the area, shooting right through Mrs. Orren's Bakery and cutting down a couple other citizens.

Then Peggy barreled forward.

"What's going on?" Olive asked, peeking out from the general goods store. "Peggy, what's—"

Peggy was a heavy gal, even after months of losing weight, and easily knocked Olive back into the general goods store just as the rain of bullets smashed into the shop. Rounds sliced all around them, cutting into the glass windows and wooden walls like a knife through hot butter. A spray of blood landed on Peggy as an older man reeled back, his chest riddled with a few rounds, and still that infernal chattering continued as bullet after bullet pelted the store.

Then, like a hurricane, it moved on to devastate some other part of Rattlefort.

"My... my arm," Olive gasped from under Peggy. She slowly raised herself up to see a grisly wound on Olive's left forearm. They both stared at it in shock as moans echoed inside the general goods store.

"Don't worry," Peggy snapped, quickly rising to her feet. She hurried over to where the store clerk kept their bandages. Peggy stepped over an unmoving corpse she suspected was the clerk, but she didn't glance down, instead focused on doing what she still could. She snatched up the bandages and a jug of moonshine for good measure, and then she rushed back to Olive, mechanically dousing the arm with a quick splash of the liquor.

"Drink this," she said, forcing another measure into Olive's mouth, as her eyes widened. "It'll dull the pain."

Peggy set the jug down, then quickly wrapped Olive's wound, thinking back to her years as an outlaw. There had been plenty of times when the Riley boys had been shot, bleeding like stuck pigs and howling at the moon, and Peggy had learned to keep her cool and just concentrate on what she could do.

"There," she said, cinching it up tight.

"Madam Josephine," Olive said with a gasp, pointing outward. "She was… in the open…"

Peggy winced at the thought. "I'll check on her," she said, already taking her moonshine and bandages. She rushed out, quickly spotting the elegant older woman with her long blonde curls, twitching on the plaza outside with a pool of dried blood below her. "Madam Josephine! I've got you!"

Peggy began a quick examination of the wounded woman, who moaned at the touch. "It's just your thigh," she concluded, already pulling up Madam Josephine's bloodied dress. "It's not as bad as it seems!"

"That damn Jimmy Wolfe," Madam Josephine muttered between gritted teeth as Peggy set to work. "I know it was him. We'll have our revenge. We'll… ugh… kill that bastard!"

Chapter 26:
Billy's Back

Marshal Davenport led his posse atop a government-issued horse, standing high in the reins as he glared forward into the Arizona sun. His face bore a permanent scowl ever since he'd heard the first reports of the massacre at Rattlefort, a few rumors brought by those fleeing the town. It had taken everything he had not to ride right into town, going hell for leather with a six shooter in each hand and righteous fury in his heart.

But patience will win the day...

"Just up here," he grunted, snapping a hand forward to indicate the dusty, windswept Mullens farmstead. He twisted back in his saddle to take in his posse. Stagecoach Mary rode her horse well enough, though her cousin was clearly not a natural in the saddle, even if they'd managed to wrangle a stout plow horse strong enough to carry him. The bounty hunters looked back at him stone-faced, alert and ready even after a hard day's riding. Deputy Milton brought up the rear, scanning the bluffs and ravines nearby with professional caution.

They're a good bunch, Davenport thought to himself. *Would hate to get them killed. I wouldn't bet against us, that's for sure... but it's the dragon who can really bring this Outlaw Union to an end.*

Davenport's sturdy horse galloped along, turning off the main road and approaching the farm buildings. It seemed strangely silent; with Lawrence and Dorothy clearly off on some errand or another. Davenport gritted his teeth, hoping they hadn't been in Rattlefort when the firing had begun.

A white horse was stabled outside, snorting and neighing as the riders approached. The dragon, Henry, lurched over from behind the cover of the barn and sniffed the air. Despite himself, Davenport felt a twinge of fear, but instead he merely inclined the brim of his hat as his horse slowed.

"Hello there, Deputy."

Henry nodded back. Despite the dragon's reptilian features, Davenport fancied that he detected a hint of approval and pride. A few bits of hay drifted down from Henry's head and the dragon sneezed, producing a faint plume of drifting smoke. Davenport slid out of his saddle and tied his horse's reins to a hitching post.

"Jake here?"

Henry nodded again, raising his right wing toward the open barn he'd emerged from. Davenport walked past at a steady trot, the spurs in his boots ringing with each step.

"Jake, you in there?"

"Huh?"

From within the dark interior, two forms raised their heads, blinking over blearily. Lucille was nestled against Jake's chest, and now she blushed prettily as she rose to her feet. Jake followed along, brushing some hay out of his head and shooting the Marshal a sheepish smile.

"Oh, sorry, Marshal. Guess we had a nice nap."

Davenport smiled, his stony exterior giving away to a moment of affection. They made quite the pair as they stood there, brushing hay off their clothes, but the moment couldn't last.

"Well, I'm sorry to bother you, Deputy…" Jake snapped to attention at the title, "but have you heard about the shootings over in Rattlefort?"

"I thought I heard some gunfire in the distance," Lucille said, her voice sleepy. "But the way it kept repeating, seemed like it was something different…"

Davenport sighed. "It was. A Gatling gun—and aimed at the people of Rattlefort."

"What?" Jake snapped, all sleepiness disappearing from his features.

"That's why I'm here," Marshal Davenport continued. "We need to put the Outlaw Union down once and for all. Are you with me?"

"Of course," Jake replied, already marching forward to Henry.

"Ma!" Lucille squeaked. "Tell me, Marshal, has anything happened to my mother?"

"I don't rightly know," Davenport answered. "We pulled up short... have to keep a low profile," he said, though it pained him not to check on the wounded.

Lucille bit her lip, placing a hand on Jake's arm. "I need to go see her," she said earnestly. Jake nodded, and Lucille rushed for her horse, passing through the assembled posse as several of the riders hopped off their mounts to stretch their legs and drink from their canteens.

"I'm ready to burn them all," Jake said between clenched teeth as Henry let out a smoldering burst of smoke in agreement.

"That's good, but not just yet," Davenport said, raising a hand to block Jake's approach. "Your folks around?"

"They went to a ranch looking for a plow horse they heard was for sale. Nowhere near Rattlefort, thank the Lord, but..." Jake fell silent, watching as Lucille rode off in a hurry.

"Perhaps that's for the best," Davenport muttered. "You mind inviting us in, son? We've got an ambush to plan."

"You're kidding me, Marshal!" Jake snapped as the rest of the posse tied up their horses. "We need to go get those bastards now, and make them pay!"

Davenport let out a low sigh as Deputy Milton approached with a sour expression.

"Ain't your place to talk to the Marshal like that," Milton said, jabbing a finger forward, but Davenport stepped smoothly in front of the man.

"Well, it ain't like I don't understand how you feel," Davenport said as he clapped Jake on the back. "But this time we're gonna pick the battleground. Now, you're a local boy... where do you reckon we can lay an ambush?"

***

"I told you not to mess with the people of Rattlefort," Jimmy Wolfe hissed as the Outlaw Union gathered in their hideout. This time their smiles had died away as the outlaws stood or sat uncomfortably in a loose circle around a battered wooden table. Lester Reyes sat in the middle of the group with that same damned smirk on his face. "What was the point of shooting them? You're crazy!"

"You're weak, cabrón," Lester replied. "You act like the people here elected you mayor. What happened to being a bandit?"

"You're one to talk of elections," Jimmy huffed, eyeing those around him. "Outlaw Union!" he bellowed, his voice echoing around the hideout. "Many of you were strangers to me once. But you've seen what the Demon's leadership gets you. I want to bring this to a vote once again. Me or Lester—who do you want running the Outlaw Union?"

Lester's smirk faded away into a scowl. "Now wait a minute. We already decided."

"I didn't know you earlier," Ned cut in. He shifted in his seat, looking nervous, Shirley biting her lip beside him. "Except by reputation, anyway. Jimmy, I know you're not afraid to kill, but you won't do it for no reason," Ned continued as Shirley nodded along with him. "I'm here to make a profit, not murder just for the fun of it. I vote for you, Jimmy."

"Me too!" Shirley echoed.

Lester snorted. "Women can't vote."

"Y-you know how w-w-w-e're voting," Sam Reeves declared as the Wolfe Gang thumped tables and chairs with the butts of their weapons. Preacher McGowan rose, a grin on his head as he held up a length of rope. The hideout echoed with shouts now.

"The Deadly Six aren't here," Lester spat out, glancing around the room. "And neither is Powaw Tom." His eyes landed on Eugene, who remained silent. Jimmy raised his eyebrows over at the man.

"I didn't join up for this," Eugene Cook finally said, shaking his head. "Can't say that I know you too well, but I'll vote for Jimmy."

"This is no longer amusing," Lester grated out.

Preacher McGowan cackled as he tossed his lasso around Lester's unresisting torso. Instead, the Demon merely stared at Jimmy Wolfe, not making a move to draw and fire.

"You do not want to make an enemy of the Demon," he said softly.

"Tie him up," Jimmy Wolfe said, rising to his feet. A thin smile spread across his weather-worn features. This felt right, finally—to be the leader of his own little Outlaw Union.

"You're a bunch of idiots!" Lester suddenly sputtered as Preacher and Sam tied him up securely. "We have the Marshals right where we want them and Powaw Tom is planting the explosives in Yuma as we speak."

"Since when do I give a damn about destroying towns?" Jimmy snapped back. "We started as railroad stickup men, and we'll continues as—"

"Jimmy!"

"Praise the Lord!" Preacher McGowan squawked, the Wolfe Gang turning to stare in fascination as a rumpled Billy Wolfe emerged. Rawhide Cooper, who'd been left to keep watch outside, stood right behind Jimmy's younger brother. Rawhide beamed like he was bringing in Christmas presents as Billy shot the others an awkward smile.

"Billy," Jimmy muttered, with a catch in his throat. He'd privately given up his younger brother as most likely being dead. "Where the hell have you been?" he asked, puzzled.

"It's a long story, but I'll explain later," Billy said, looking over at the unfamiliar faces gathered in their hideout. "What's this? What's going on?"

Jimmy spread his arms out wide. "I formed an Outlaw Union, Billy. Surely you've heard about it? Hell, all of the West knows about that."

Billy scratched at his stubble haltingly, attempted to say something, but just managed to end up squinting in astonishment at the now trussed-up Lester Reyes.

"Uh, so..." His eyes widened. "Is that the Demon?" he squeaked.

Lester smiled, seemingly unbothered despite being tied up.

"The former head of the Outlaw Union," Jimmy said with a sniff. "Could have used another vote, brother, back when we first chose a leader. But I reckon it all worked out in the end... though this damned Demon shot up half of Rattlefort."

Billy nodded slowly. "So that's what I heard..." He blinked furiously, shaking his head as if to clear his thoughts, and then fixed his brother with a sincere stare as the others watched in growing curiosity. "Listen to me, brother, although this might seem crazy. I... I was visited in the desert by a Chinaman on a dragon. Mr. Sun Wong, the very man whose goods we raided from the train robbery all that time ago. He says..." Billy licked his lips. "He says we stole a dragon from him. Now you might think I'm crazy, but—"

"Stole a dragon?" Jimmy cut in. "A few days ago I'd have called you crazy, and I'll still call you an idiot, but we've seen a dragon. Only that boy Jake Mullens has it."

Billy bit his lips, looking strangely guilty, and nodded. "I've... heard that as well. Seems the Mullens boy stole it from us after the robbery."

Jimmy sighed, swaggering over to take a seat at the long table beside the motionless Lester. Ignoring the former leader, Jimmy grabbed an open bottle of tequila and took a shot. Then he leaned back, frowning at his younger brother.

"So let me get this straight," Jimmy said after a long moment. "You mean to tell me this dragon we saw was on that train from San Francisco that we robbed?"

Billy nodded. "Must have been little at the time," he added. "In a crate, most likely."

"And the Mullens boy took it out from under us?" Jimmy asked, swelling with anger as he glanced at his gang members. "Which one of you was on guard duty back then?"

"Yes," Billy said, fidgeting in place. "This Chinese fella is pissed off, brother, and he has an even bigger dragon." He tilted his head as he studied the silent bandits around him. "Wait, where's Doc? Looking after the wounded in Rattlefort?"

Jimmy let out a long sigh. Preacher McGowan spoke up after a moment.

"Sorry to tell you this, Billy, but that Jake Mullens made his dragon turn Doc into a pile of ashes. He's with the good Lord now."

"What?"

Billy blinked, lurching heavily into a seat. Wordlessly, Jimmy slid the bottle of tequila over, and his younger brother poured himself a strong measure with a shaking hand. Jimmy had known his brother for so long it wasn't hard to guess at Billy's thoughts. Doc Otis had been like a father to them and had looked after them for most of their lives. Now his life had been snuffed out entirely.

Yet Billy was a coward at his core, and his thoughts quickly turned to his own survival. "Call me crazy, but I think we need Jake Mullens' help," Billy said, wiping his lips with his jacket as he set his empty glass down. "As much as I hate him right now, he's our best chance of not getting burnt to a crisp."

Jimmy snorted. His brother had been back just a few minutes and already he was talking nonsense.

"Think about it, little brother. That's absolutely ridiculous. Jake won't just hand over his dragon, so what do you suggest we do? Join the posse?"

Unprompted, a wave of guffaws and chuckles echoed throughout the hideout. It grew to a clamor, Preacher McGowan cackling wildly as the assembled bandits laughed. At least, everyone laughed besides Eugene Cook, who twisted his mouth like he was tasting something sour.

"That's exactly what we should do," Eugene cut in once the laughter had died down. "Billy is right, the enemy of our enemy is our friend."

The laughing came to a halt, and the atmosphere suddenly turned serious as the others turned puzzled expressions at Eugene. Jimmy opened his mouth... then closed it, entertaining the idea despite himself as the silence lengthened.

"After the Rattlefort shooting I don't think we'll be able to make amends unless we give them something," said Billy in an unusually serious tone.

"What do you have in mind?" asked Jimmy.

As if by common consensus, the eyes of everyone there drifted toward Lester Reyes, tied up but still looking as unperturbed as ever.

"I say we give the Demon as a peace offering," Billy said softly. "After all, he was the one responsible... was he not?"

Jimmy whistled, adjusting his seat. "I thought you were joking at first... but you do make a good point, and we need to get rid of him one way or another. Seems Jake knows just where our hideout is. So..." he tapped the table a few times, then nodded decisively. "We'll turn Lester over to the posse. Hopefully Marshal Davenport will be willing to put bygones aside for now and help us take care of this Chinese fella. As soon as Powaw Tom arrives back from Yuma with the Deadly Six, we'll bring Lester to the Mullens farm and tell them about Sun Wong."

The assembled bandits nodded agreeably, then a popping noise sounded. Preacher McGowan grinned widely, his teeth a mix of yellow, black, and empty gums. He brandished an open wine bottle, setting it down on the table with a solid thunk.

"So our plan's settled, and now we celebrate the good Lord's bounty. Praise be, Billy's back!"

Chapter 27:

Call For a Truce

Jimmy Wolfe grimaced as dust blew back from the lead horse. It had been quite some time since he wasn't the one riding at the head of his gang, but Billy had insisted that he knew the way and wouldn't startle the Mullens. All the while, Jimmy stewed on the circumstances that had led to him seeking out a meeting with Jake Mullens.

He don't seem like much by himself, Jimmy mused. *But his dragon and the posse? Can't say I'd be too keen on taking them all on. We'd come out the winner, no doubt, but lose a few in the process. Billy says he means to parley. What would Doc do, I wonder? He was always a canny bastard...*

"Just up ahead, isn't it?" Jimmy called out, pushing up on his stirrups to get a better look. The distant outline of the Mullens household was just ahead, and Billy was hooting and hollering, raising his hat back and forth. "Do you think they're—"

A shotgun blast broke the silence. Smoke trailed from a barrel sticking out the window. Dorothy Mullens peeked out from inside.

"What are you doing back here, Billy? Don't make me regret looking after you."

"Easy, easy!" Billy called out, spurring himself forward even as Jimmy slowed. The others followed his example and together they stared at the farmstead skeptically.

Awfully quiet for a working farm, Jimmy mused, opting to keep his distance. *Lot of outbuildings…*

"We came to make a truce!" Billy called out, approaching the house as if stopping by on a social visit. "Keep your weapons lowered. That means all of y'all."

"What do you mean?" Dorothy asked, her voice carrying in the silence. "It's just me here."

Jimmy snorted, thoroughly unconvinced. The reflection of metal from the side of the barn house served as confirmation. "Marshal Davenport, I know your posse's lurking around!" Jimmy called out. Billy spun around in surprise.

Dumb as he is, likely my brother didn't even pick up on that.

"We're not fixing to fight you, Marshal, we're fixing to work together." Jimmy worked his dry lips as the silence lingered. "You know I ain't afraid of a gunfight with you, Marshal. This ain't no trick. This is a call for a truce."

The cellar door by the house creaked open. Marshal Davenport poked his head out, then stepped into the open. A gentle breeze rustled his clothes and marshal's star. Framed in the afternoon light he was the perfect target—almost like he was giving Jimmy Wolfe the chance to draw and end their feud once and for all. But Jimmy merely cantered his horse closer.

"Never thought I'd see the day," Marshal Davenport grunted, spitting on the ground. "Come on out, then!"

Rising from behind a boulder beside the road was an extremely short man and a tall, muscular Black woman. Both bore shotguns and had the look of people who knew how to use them. Rising up from behind a cactus, wearing a khaki poncho over his clothing, was Deputy Milton with a lever action rifle.

They had us dead to rights and no mistake, Jimmy realized with a grimace. The short man casually rested his shotgun against the boulder and flicked a matchstick up, which took fire at once.

"We were going to smoke these once we'd smoked you," he said in a surprisingly deep voice as he lit two cigars. "Guess this'll have to do. Here you are, Mary."

"Thank you kindly," the woman replied, her eyes never leaving the remaining Outlaw Union as they rode on by. They were a sizable force, with Ned and Shirley driving a wagon flanked by the Wolfe Gang, not to mention Powaw Tom, Eugene Cook, Al Crosby, and the Deadly Six. Yet more and more of the posse emerged, dusting themselves off from concealed positions or appearing from the barn house and main building.

Lawrence Mullens joined his wife on the porch as Henry craned his long neck out from the barn and began waddling over to join them. Jake Mullens strode beside his dragon, looking cocky as ever with his new deputy's star.

"Got a present for you, Marshal," Jimmy announced as the wagon trundled forward, Ned bringing it to a stop beside the house. Marshal Davenport tilted his head.

"The wagon you stole? The Gatling gun inside is US Government property."

"That ain't the only thing we have," Jimmy replied as Rawhide Cooper emerged from inside the wagon. He grinned savagely, holding the trussed-up Lester Reyes, with a knife to the Demon's throat. Lester looked almost bored. "Consider him a peace offering."

"Dammit," a one-eyed man swore at once. Beside him, an incredibly tall youth frowned. "That was going to be our bounty!"

"Keep dreaming," Al Crosby snorted. "You morons spent years eating my dust."

All at once the uneasy truce seemed to fade away, guns drawn and an uncomfortable standoff forming as the Outlaw Union and the posse pointed their weapons every which way.

"Hey, easy now!" Billy Wolfe called out as Lawrence Mullens gingerly led his wife back inside. "We're friends, alright? Or at least we can work together." Weapons lowered a fraction as Billy glanced around to fix his eyes on Henry and Jake Mullens. "Jake, I learned recently that you stole Henry from our hideout after the train heist we pulled off in Utah a while back. You raised him, so I'm here to let you know that his owner, a Mister Sun Wong, is pissed off and is looking to take Henry back by force if we don't hand him over in a few days."

"What?" Jake blinked.

"It's true! This Chinaman threatens to burn down Rattlefort and us with it, but we ain't folding. Jimmy and I grew up in Rattlefort and we ain't letting that happen. My gut is telling me that you ain't handing your dragon over either... so let's call a truce."

"Don't make me laugh, Billy. How does this... Sun Wong plan on doing that? We're the ones who have Henry."

"The Chinaman has one too," Billy replied excitedly. "And it's way bigger than Henry. That's why we're here."

A silence fell as Jake looked up at Henry. The dragon let out a low rumble, though Jimmy couldn't make out quite what that meant. It wasn't as aggressive as he'd been before roasting Ira and Doc, but Jimmy's hands stayed on Agatha and Delilah nonetheless.

"With our combined manpower and Henry, hopefully we can kill that son of bitch and his dragon," Billy added.

Marshal Davenport shrugged. "It's peace I want," he said. "Your hanging too… but that can wait."

Jimmy smirked. "That all you offering me, old man?"

Davenport's gaze was level and unwavering.

"It is."

"It's rich of you all to talk of peace and making a truce," Jimmy replied, "but I can't say I believe you. Your wild beast there killed Doc Otis and Ira. What kind of justice is that?" Jimmy's fingers drummed against the holsters of his two pistols and scanned the posse members around him. "Maybe I should take two lives so we're even."

"Now you know that ain't how it played out," Jake replied at once. "Doc was fixing to kill me, and Henry struck out in self-defense. That'd be lawful in any county."

"I don't much care for laws," Jimmy said. "Justice, on the other hand—"

"Don't you blather to me about justice!" Jake continued, approaching Jimmy's horse and jabbing a finger at the bandit. Jake ignored the half dozen guns which now swiveled to face him. "You burned down our crops! You gunned down the people of Rattlefort with that infernal machine!"

"That wasn't my doing," Jimmy replied, adjusting his position in the saddle. "Well... we did burn your crops, that's true, but it was Lester who shot up the town. We knew nothing about it."

"Of course you didn't, you brainless, ball-less fool," Lester said in amusement. "You've never had what it takes to—" he grunted as Rawhide slammed a meaty fist into Lester's stomach.

Jimmy scowled. "If you want to hang him now then I'm all for it, by the way."

Marshal Davenport assessed the setting sun in the distance. "That can wait until dawn. I want the people of Rattlefort to have the chance to see justice done."

"So... you accept my peace offering?" Jimmy asked. "We can have..." he hissed, finding it difficult to get the words out. "A truce?"

"Agreed," Davenport said, raising his right hand and spitting on it. Jimmy stared at the hand for a long moment, then spat in his own palm, finally clasping the older man's hand together. They stared at each other for a long moment, squeezing down hard, then finally pulled away.

Farce though it might have been, the gesture relieved the tension around them all at once. The sounds of banging metal and crinkling leather echoed out as both sides holstered their weapons. Marshal

Davenport waved Jimmy Wolfe over, bearing an unconvincing smile for the crowd.

"Why don't you join us in the barn?" Davenport insisted as he led them over. "I hope your family doesn't mind us being here too much, Jake."

"I'm sure they want an end to all this, one way or another. The Wolfe Gang devastated our crops," Jake said. "It don't quite feel right to be working with them."

Jimmy Wolfe made no comment as the crowd of armed men and women bustled around. "Rawhide, Sam, Preacher. Keep an eye on Lester and the skies above. We won't be caught off guard by anything."

"Y-Y-Yes, Boss."

"Pray with me, Lester," Preacher said, making himself comfortable in the crowded wagon. "Seeing as this is your last night alive."

"The Demon does not pray," Lester insisted, but Jimmy ignored him as he squeezed into the barn, finding an empty keg to rest on. Someone passed over a warm, half empty flask of whiskey, and with cigar smoke filling the barn the mutual suspicions of the Outlaw Union and the posse members began to fade away.

"Sam is a good shot," Billy observed, taking a seat next to Jake. "Maybe he can down them both; dragon and rider."

"Rider, maybe," Jake replied skeptically. "If he's real lucky. But that hardly solves our problem."

Several of the more disinterested bandits and posse members began setting up a card game, and soon their taunts and chuckles began to fill the barn. Jimmy resisted the urge to either snap at them or join in. Instead he rolled the empty keg over toward Billy and took a seat beside his brother.

"I could send a telegram to San Francisco," Davenport mused. "Maybe they have information on this Sun Wong character... reports of potential dragon sightings, maybe?"

"Marshal, you know as well as I do that there ain't no way we're getting useful information within the week—and that's too late," Deputy Milton replied. "Besides, we can't rely on anyone else but ourselves, with the Civil War still raging in the East. Nobody gives a rat's ass what happens out here."

"I know," Billy broke in, spreading a map of Arizona on a stained, rickety table with three legs. He tapped at a mountain range close to the border with Mexico. "Since the Chinaman will be waiting for us to meet him in the Dragoon Mountains, we can bury explosives in strategic locations in advance," said Billy.

"Now you're using your noggin, little brother," said Jimmy, placing a hand on Billy's shoulder, a map of Arizona laid out in front of them. "We could have our guys hide on the mountainside and detonate the explosives remotely."

"Dynamite on the ground to take out something that's flying in the sky?" Gerald Swann said, his false left eye drifting around. "Am I missing something?"

"My bounty," Al scoffed.

"He's gotta land somewhere," Jake cut in as the Swann brothers bristled. "You might not know what it's like since you haven't ridden a dragon, but they can't stay in the air forever, and they'll need to land somewhere. So just get them close enough and blast explosives... that should do it." He paused, glancing back at Henry's head, craning into the overfilled barn as he watched the others plan. No doubt Jake worried about his own dragon meeting the same fate.

"It sounds like a good idea, but the plan won't be effective unless you have a lot of dynamite," said Deputy Milton.

"We got plenty, don't worry," Jimmy replied, leaning back on the empty keg he was using for a seat. "Oh, that reminds me, Marshal Davenport. I had Powaw Tom rig your office with dynamite before coming here."

"Noted... thanks for telling me," Davenport replied. "And just so you know, if we make it out of this alive, I'm still gonna take you and your Outlaw Union down. That's a promise."

"Well, a promise is a comfort to a fool," Jimmy blurted out.

"We could also use the Gatling gun from a distance, but that'll have to be a last resort," Eugene added. "It ain't built for shooting into the sky, and it burns through ammo."

"Jake, you and Henry are going to have to take that dragon head-on," Marshal Davenport mused, scratching irritably at the white stubble growing on his chin.

"Fight fire with fire," Powaw Tom commented.

A silence filled the barn, broken by a sudden guffawing as Vincent gathered up his cards, the leader of the Deadly Six having won the last hand. A bottle of whiskey popped open, Stagecoach Mary grinning as she poured herself a full measure.

"Might as well get good and toasted, boys, while we still can. If I was a bettin' woman, and I am, I'd say we won't all be here to celebrate taking down that dragon. So let's make this a night to remember!"

Chapter 28:

Justice

A gout of flames burst through the air, stunning the audience. In the center of the stage, a wooden statue began to burn, and then a dozen ropes beside it began to smolder as the flames continued toward the ends. Almost simultaneously, the fire reached the sparklers attached to every rope, and an array of sizzling fireworks cast the stage in shimmering light. The audience *oohed* and *ahhed* as Lifun Chen pulled Bailong back into his cage.

Mr. Sun Wong smiled thinly from his position at the side of the stage. The performance had gone even better than expected, judging from the audience reaction. He noted with approval that a woman had fainted in the audience and was currently being led away. Squinting through the smoky gloom, he realized that she was one of those that he'd planted in the audience to clap uproariously and lead the crowd in excited applause.

It seems she's earning her coin tonight, Sun Wong thought with approval, though he suspected it hadn't been needed. With both Xingteng and Bailong, two full-grown dragons, the performance had been as impressive as any he'd ever seen before. The audience certainly seemed to agree, though the applause was now finally dying down as the smoky air began to thin.

Sun Wong's shoes echoed as they strode along the wooden stage, and he swiveled to face the audience directly, tapping the ground with his circus baton. "Be sure to tell your friends and family, for next week…" Sun Wong paused. *Dare I say it?* "Next week, I can assure you, the performance will be even more spectacular!"

The crowd burst once more into applause and he took a deep bow as the curtains closed behind him. Sun Wong spun on his heels, setting his bowler hat back on, and weaved through the curtains. The dragons were snuffling and shifting positions as chains were draped around them to restrict their movements. Still, they had learned not to resist.

"Bring them over here," Sun Wong's cousin Jun Zhao snapped in Cantonese, waving over a crate carried by two workers. He grabbed one of the rats held within and tossed it through Xingteng's cage. The big dragon caught the dragon in the air at once, raising her head and swallowing the tiny morsel. Another crate full of rats was being hauled over toward Bailong, though Lifun left the feeding of the dragon to the workers, instead rushing over to Sun Wong.

"Quite the show, wasn't it?" his assistant said cheerily as she snatched up a cup of water. "Perhaps it's time to raise our prices. With two dragons as the main attraction people will pay more money," she said in Cantonese, handing her boss the water.

Sun Wong downed the water feverishly. These performances always drained his energy, as he had to strut about in the ostentatious clothes of a circus performer while the dragons shot out bursts of fire. He nodded after a moment.

"Agreed. Hopefully we'll make even more money when we get back Feilong!" Sun Wong added. "We will meet with Jimmy Wolfe and the farm boy Jake Mullens—the insolent fools who kidnapped Feilong—in two more days near the Dragoon mountains."

Lifun drank from a cup of her own and nodded. "Why meet them at that specific location, sir?"

"Yeah, why there?" asked Jun Zhao as he approached, wiping the sweat off his brow.

"I'm not naive enough to believe that they'll peacefully hand over Feilong," said Sun Wong, removing his bowler hat as he took a seat. "And we have a better chance at avoiding any traps they set by using those mountains as a high ground."

"Always thinking one step ahead, Boss!" Lifun said approvingly.

"Yes, one has to stay on the cutting edge if one wants to make it in San Francisco," Sun Wong observed, then switched to English, which few of his workers understood. "And with three dragons?" He grinned. "What is it they say here? 'The whole world is my oyster.'"

***

"A cigarette, cabrón," Lester called out, sauntering onto the execution stage. He looked unbothered even with his hands tied behind his back. "I think I deserve that much."

"You're already getting what you deserve," Stagecoach Mary shot back. "A hanging." Beside her, the silent Herbert was tightening the noose beside Preacher McGowan. Along with Rawhide Cooper, who was keeping a tight grip on Lester's rope and another on his knife, they were the only remaining representatives of the Outlaw Union.

The *clop-clop* of hooves echoed through Rattlefort's plaza, which was beginning to fill with angry citizens eager to see justice done that day. Deputy Milton squinted in the sun, his badge shimmering in the light. He glanced from side to side, finally bringing his mount to a halt as he approached Madam Josephine and her prostitutes, who were gathered near the foot of the execution stage. Peggy Riley glared daggers at both Rawhide and Lester alike, her eyes shifting from one to the other. Madam Josephine placed a discreet hand on Peggy's shoulder and raised an eyebrow at the approaching deputy.

"Ma'am," Deputy Milton said, inclining his hat. "I have a message for your daughter," he continued, flagging over Lucille. She looked confused even as she made her way through the crowd.

"Yes, Deputy?" she asked. "Can this wait?" Lucille gestured at the stage as Rawhide Cooper taunted Lester, hissing into the Mexican bandit's ear. The crowd murmured, full of survivors from the Gatling gun shooting, looking forward to their revenge with contemptuous stares and occasional jeering. "Jake should be here to see this with me…"

"I'm afraid that's not possible. Little lady, Jake is a bit preoccupied at the moment, helping Davenport and Jimmy. Our work goes on without pause."

"Well, I'll be damned," replied Lucille with a heavy sigh. "After that Gatling gun ripped Rattlefort to pieces I'm surprised to not see y'all here."

"Ohoh, I think they can handle one captive," Deputy Milton said with a chuckle, gesturing upward with a gloved hand. "We have more urgent concerns, and desperate times call for desperate measures. You see, some Chinese fella threatened to burn down Rattlefort if they don't return Henry, so they called a truce." Deputy Milton pulled out a rolled-up map and handed it over to Lucille. "Jake said he needs you to

Belly Through the Brush

ask Chief Sipatu for help. Tell him to be at the Dragoon Mountains in two days' time... around noon."

Lucille nodded, her golden curls bouncing. "I understand. He must be talking about the Chowilawu Indians... no doubt they'd be a big help." She bit her lip. "I wanted to see Lester hand, but I guess there's no time to lose. Enjoy the show, Ma."

Lucille embraced Madam Josephine as Deputy Milton weaved his way back through the crowd. A few of the most prominent citizens of Rattlefort were denouncing the bored-looking Lester for his cruelty and debauchery as the long minutes dragged by. Deputy Milton soon disappeared once again. Lester's eyes flicked from one person to the next but otherwise he made no motion as Preacher McGowan began droning on about godliness and purity. The prostitutes were unable to hide their smirks.

"And we are but the instruments of His will," Preacher McGowan continued. "A righteous will, that does not shirk from striking down—"

It happened in the barest flash of motion. Somehow Lester snatched Rawhide Cooper's knife with his bound hands, then jabbed him deeply in the thigh before dashing away. Before anyone could react, Lester was sprinting through the crowd, his rope bindings giving way. A shot sailed by overhead as Peggy Riley quickly drew and fired her derringer and the crowd began to scream. One broad-shouldered man stepped in front of Lester, but the Demon simply stabbed him in the gut with three lightning quick strikes, then pulled the startled, mortally wounded man to the ground and darted into the general goods store.

"Get him!" Olive shrieked, as Stagecoach Mary, Herbert, and Preacher McGowan rushed after Lester Reyes. Rawhide Cooper gasped, wobbling on his feet, then staggered forward through the quickly dissipating crowd of Rattlefort's startled citizens.

"Down on the ground!" Stagecoach Mary called out as she rushed into the general goods store. She swiveled her shotgun from side to side, but the store was empty, as even the owner had been observing the crowd. There was a blur of motion, and she fired, smashing a jar of moonshine to smithereens. Lester chuckled from his position behind the counter. After throwing the jar, he sprinted toward a window with a stolen revolver and a box of ammo. Lester leaped out just as Mary's second shotgun blast spattered the area, one of the shots landing in his shoulder.

Lester rolled on the ground outside, gamely rising to his feet to stare at the approaching Rawhide. "Here's your knife back," Lester snapped, whipping the knife up in an underhanded toss. The blade sailed through the air before landing in Rawhide Cooper's right arm. He groaned, his revolver falling to the ground.

Lester was already sprinting away, quickly snatching bullets from the box and moving erratically through the alleys of Rattlefort as the crowd either ran away or in pursuit. He pulled up short as Madam

Josephine and her prostitutes rushed up one cramped street. Madam Josephine whipped her derringer up and took a quick shot, smashing the ammunition box and scattering most of the bullets. Lester glared but simply moved down another side street, loading a few bullets and snapping the cylinder of his stolen revolver shut.

"Where'd he go?" the normally silent Herbert shouted, his deep voice echoing through the alleys beside Rattlefort's plaza.

"He's in the Allen Mining Company warehouse!" Olive called out, noticing the door still swinging.

"Hurry!" Madam Josephine shouted. "There are explosives inside!"

Preacher McGowan rushed over with a repeating rifle in hand, peeking inside. He squeezed the trigger twice. "Lord be good," he muttered. "He's headed east! Cut him off!"

"If the Demon goes, he's taking all of you with him!" Lester called out with a cackle, his voice echoing from the warehouse. He burst out the other entrance, stumbling forward with a bundle of dynamite clutched in one hand. With the other he was repeatedly striking a match on the side of his revolver. "Damn thing won't take light…"

Lester came up short right as he turned the corner, his boots skidding as he turned to face Herbert blocking his path. He jerked back just as a shotgun blast echoed out.

"End of the line," Stagecoach Mary barked out from behind him, and Lester tossed the spent match aside, turning and whipping up his stolen revolver. "Drop the gun!"

"How about I drop y—"

The shotgun blast shredded Lester's hand as well as his revolver, spattering the ground with blood and bits of metal. He gasped out, sinking to one knee and gripping his ruined right hand with his left, the dynamite falling to the ground.

"You shot me," he moaned, half in disbelief. Then he rose up abruptly as Herbert grabbed him from behind. The startled bandit rocked back and forth but couldn't tear himself free. Stagecoach Mary pumped her shotgun and rested it on her shoulder.

"Don't know what you thought was gonna happen," she muttered, then jerked a thumb back to the execution stage. "Alright, enough dilly-dallying! Let's hang this crook and go about our business."

Herbert dragged Lester back as he stared disbelievingly at his bloody hand. Several fingers now littered the alleyway. Those few who remained in the plaza gave way with soft sounds of surprise as Lester was pulled up next to the noose. He barely even felt the coarse rope being placed around his neck.

"Glory be to his name," Preacher McGowan said in a soft voice. Herbert pulled the lever, and Lester dropped, his neck snapping as he was finally hanged.

There was no applause. Instead there was simply a stunned silence, broken only by moaning. Several concerned citizens had gathered around the man Lester had killed in the center of the plaza, and another one was beside Rawhide Cooper, who had gingerly pulled out his own knife and rested himself against the general goods store.

"Hush now," one of the townsfolk was saying, kneeling beside Rawhide Cooper, who was wincing and twitching from side to side. "Some brandy on the wounds and bandages should set you right. It doesn't seem like anything's fatal—"

"We got it!" Goldie said cheerily, setting a hand on the man's shoulder.

"What?"

Peggy Riley pushed him back, a bit less than gently, and squeezed on Rawhide Cooper's bloody arm. Cooper yelped at the touch as the other prostitutes formed a circle around him. He was dragged to his feet even as he squealed, and the townsfolk formed a wary distance from Madam Josephine as she waved them away.

"Don't worry," Madam Josephine called out as the sobbing Rawhide Cooper was being taken away, pulled by Olive and Peggy Riley as Goldie cleared their route. "We'll take care of him." She gritted her teeth, nodding approvingly at Lester Reyes as the body swung from side to side. "Justice is being done this day."

Chapter 29:

Preparation and Reparation

"Whoa there," Marshal Davenport murmured as Jimmy Wolfe's wagon rocked from side to side. "Easy..."

The wagon settled down a few moments later as the wheels passed over a cluster of hard-edged rocks and boulders. It was rough going here by any measure, and with a caravan as large as this one that meant the dangers only increased. As it was, Marshal Davenport couldn't be entirely secure in the company of these bandits. He spurred his horse forward to ride astride the wagon carrying the Gatling gun as well as what supplies they could hastily procure.

Ned and Shirley looked chipper as ever, talking in soft voices as they steered the wagon through the wild lands of Southern Arizona. Ahead of the column of riders Marshal Davenport knew Powaw Tom would be scouting a path forward, with the Deadly Six acting as outriders along the flanks, watching out for enemies both on ground and in the sky.

That's more than enough threats by any means, Marshal Davenport mused to himself, *so I should put these bandits out of my mind for now. It's possible to be too paranoid.*

Still, he felt reassured to have his own crew with him—minus Stagecoach Mary and Herbert to see to Lester's execution, and Deputy Milton, who had been sent to fetch what reinforcements they could get. Henry ambled forward on foot behind Jake, though the two flew from time to time. Marshal Davenport suspected it wasn't too easy for a dragon to walk on foot, but it did help them keep a low profile.

Besides, we wouldn't want to spook one of the Deadly Six into taking a potshot at Henry.

One of the convoy's other wagons rattled past. Sam Reeves silently guided the horses forward, scratching at his black beard, while Billy Wolfe nodded at Marshal Davenport and raised a bottle of whiskey. "Thirsty, Marshal?"

Marshal Davenport tapped the canteen on his belt, the sound of partly hollow metal echoing. "Got plenty of water," he said. Over the sounds of hooves and chattering men he could make out the occasional sloshing of their water barrels, stowed on a separate wagon. That would be a godsend in the desert here, though it wouldn't be nearly enough to put out the explosives on Sam's wagon if they caught fire.

That whole damn wagon is stuffed full of dynamite and ammunition… and being driven by a drunkard.

"I'll take an-an-another schwig," Sam said with another hiccup as Billy passed the bottle over.

"I think you better take the reins, Billy," Marshal Davenport said, riding up close and glaring at Sam. "You know, I'd be well within my rights to fine you for that."

Sam rolled his eyes and tossed the reins over at Billy. The younger man caught them and nodded at the Marshal.

"I hate w-w-working with the L-L-Law," Sam muttered, taking a long swig of whiskey.

"Oh, lookie there!" Ned called out from the lead wagon. "Beautiful, ain't it?"

Marshal Davenport adjusted his hat to block out the sunlight and squinted into the distance. The rocky ground gave way now to a flat prairie of green grass and flowers. Framed by the afternoon light was Powaw Tom, riding back on his spotted horse. Even one or two of the outriders seemed to be approaching the caravan once again.

Jimmy Wolfe spurred his mount, Eugene Cook following close behind.

"Might be you should join them," Calvin Swann's deep voice broke through the Marshal's thoughts. "Don't want them plotting against us, you know?" He chuckled, but it didn't lessen the seriousness of his message. Silently, Marshal Davenport set his spurs to his horse and left the bounty hunters behind.

"As nice a country as you could hope for here," Powaw Tom continued, emotionlessly glancing over at the approaching lawman. "For about a mile, leastways." He gestured over at the towering mountain ranges to their left and right. "Good spot in the valley, I'd say."

"It's not very defensible," Jimmy replied. "We'd be better off in the mountains."

"For a thief, you need to learn a few more tricks," Marshal Davenport said with a chuckle as he joined them. "It's so defensible that it's the obvious thing to look for. Look at this nice grass here right in the center. Perfect place for a meeting, and no reason to look around for surprises. Easy to dig in too… and set our explosives."

"So you think we should plant the dynamite right in the open," Jimmy mused. He tapped his two revolvers—not threateningly, but almost as if they were giving him advice. The bandit leader nodded after a moment. "My brother says the Chinese feller was a real arrogant sort. Could see us set up right here and land in the open… yeah, I see it. Maybe an old dog like you does know a few tricks," Jimmy acknowledged. "But the Gatling gun goes in the mountains," he added, challenging Marshal Davenport with a hard stare.

The Marshal didn't take the bait.

"Of course," he said with a snort. "Where the hell else would you put it? Just make sure to keep it concealed."

A smile slowly spread on Jimmy's face as Jake and Henry approached. "It's a solid plan, I reckon. Why don't you and your boys handle the digging? We have a few shovels to go around. We can set up the Gatling gun."

That's hours of hard work after a long day of riding. Still, it's what I expected.

Marshal Davenport shrugged. "I'm not opposed."

"Keep your shovels stowed," Jake put in. The older men frowned over at him as he quickly clambered onto Henry's neck. Jake patted Henry, who rose his wings high. The men edged away cautiously even as the wagons slowed and began to form a loose defensive circle in the open plains. "We can handle the digging. Come on, Henry!"

Gusts of wind blew back those nearby, sending a few hats flying as Henry soared up in the air. Those below watched in awe and fascination as Henry weaved around, then came in low, his claws slashing downward to sink into the ground and dig deep furrows.

"Well now, I'll be!" Marshal Davenport chuckled, beaming upward as the dragon again and again dug holes into the landscape. "Might need some smoothing out," he muttered as he scratched at his gray stubble. "But that's mighty convenient."

Jimmy grinned over at the lawman, and for a few brief, shining moments they felt like comrades in the same struggle. Yet that feeling slowly slid away. Jimmy Wolfe's smile faded and he jerked his head aside.

"Ned! Get that wagon moving up there. We need to get the Gatling gun in place while there's still light."

"I'll take a look tomorrow," Marshal Davenport said before Jimmy and his gang could ride off with the wagon. "See if I can notice it from a distance… maybe Jake and his dragon can try and spot it as well. So keep it as hidden as you can."

Jimmy Wolfe snorted. "A bit of friendly competition, eh? Well, it ain't like I mind that, Marshal, but…" he tapped both of his revolvers again with a distant look in his eyes. "You fancy yourself a gunslinger, old man? I want to see if those leathery paws of yours can still squeeze a trigger. How about a target shooting competition?"

"There are a dozen outlaws just like you who could attest to my shooting skill, were they not six feet under. If you want to make an embarrassment to yourself among your crew then I will not stand in your way. I'm game, but only after you finish setting up the Gatling gun. Revolvers?"

"Yes. I prefer two, but I'll stick to one just to keep it remotely fair," Jimmy said, tapping one of the revolvers at his side. "Delilah…"

Marshal Davenport grinned. "That's the one named after your dead lover, isn't it?"

"That reminds me…" Jimmy abruptly pulled his reins away, galloping after the others. "Hey Billy, where's Rawhide? I wanted to ask him about something…"

"Oh, Cooper? Well, he said he was gonna watch over Lester and stick with Preacher until the hanging. I reckon they're riding over to join us unless he's tied up with something."

***

Rawhide Cooper was tied up with rope to an upper-story bed in Madam Josephine's cathouse, with a well-used and unwashed gag stuffed in his mouth. He gurgled, making soft sounds of distress as the prostitutes frowned down at him. Madam Josephine sighed, setting her hands on her hips.

"We can't interrogate him like this."

"What's there to interrogate?" Olive snapped. "He's a murderer through and through. Let's kill him and be done with it."

Madam Josephine shifted from foot to foot, staring down at the man. She knew it was the truth, and didn't mind spilling blood in defense of her own, but…

Ah, the hell with it. Ain't no lawman in town to sort this out. We'll deal out justice on our own.

"You killed one of my own, Rawhide, and that's entirely aside from being a sorry son of a bitch who's played havoc with Rattlefort. Still, I'll give you a chance to give me a reason why I shouldn't gun you down." She snapped her fingers. "Take that gag out."

"But—"

"Enough, Olive!"

Peggy Riley crossed her arms, which were muscular yet flabby, though she'd lost weight ever since she'd been taken in at the cathouse. Madam Josephine knew she was eager to kill the scoundrel; perhaps even more so than Olive. After all, the Wolfe Gang had gunned the Riley Gang down before her very eyes. At least she was controlling herself and kept her derringer concealed in her bosom.

Rawhide Cooper spat as the gag was removed. "I... I need Preacher McGowan here. Someone fetch him."

"You're kidding," Olive replied. Cooper's desperate eyes flicked upward to focus on Madam Josephine.

"No, he'll talk some sense into you women. You'll see that what you're doing is ungodly and—" He winced as Peggy kicked him in the balls. Cooper gasped, reeling on the ground.

"I've gotta say, Cooper," Madam Josephine said calmly, leaning down and grabbing a fistful of the man's hair. "Your argument ain't too persuasive. I see a legal career was never in your future." She hauled him up. Rather than the swaggering bully they were used to they instead saw his face reddened as he burst into tears.

"It's so unfair! You ain't even treated my wounds, wounds that I got from saving this sorry town from a criminal."

Madam Josephine chuckled despite herself. "That's better, I suppose, but the sentence for your murder is clear enough. Death."

As one, the prostitutes nodded in satisfaction. It had never really been in question, but Madam Josephine felt better for at least giving him a chance to plead his case.

"Last rites then," Cooper sobbed, snorting as streams of mucus flowed down his nose. "Since I'm dyin'."

"Oh, like the last rites you gave her?" Olive replied, spitting on Cooper. "Madam Josephine, let's be done with it."

"But how?" Goldie asked thoughtfully. "Best if it looks like an accident…"

"Oh, it was the Demon who killed him, should anyone ask," Madam Josephine replied calmly. "And with his own knife, at that. Everyone saw it."

"This knife," Peggy said quietly, tapping Rawhide Cooper's knife in her palm. At once, she lunged forward, plunging the knife deep in Cooper's gut. He roared out in agony and Goldie quickly fumbled for the gag, stuffing it in Cooper's mouth as Peggy wrenched her knife back out.

"That was loud," Goldie murmured.

"Screams ain't too peculiar, coming from here," Olive said, reaching for the bloody knife. "Give it here, Peggy."

Rawhide Cooper tried to say something, half-rising from the floor, but Goldie and Madam Josephine both grabbed his shoulders and forced him back down. With his bonds there was no hope of escape, anyway.

"Stop your squirming!" Madam Josephine said in annoyance.

"Yeah, you're a murdering outlaw," Olive observed, flipping the bloody knife in the air and snatching its handle before plunging it into Rawhide Cooper's torso. "Try to die with some dignity!"

Over the muffled panting Madam Josephine heard the distinct sounds of knocking on the door of her cathouse.

Oh, is Lucille back? She shouldn't see this...

"I'll take care of whoever that is," Madam Josephine said, gathering up her skirts and leaving the room as Olive passed the bloody knife over to Goldie, who gulped and accepted it. "You can... deal with him."

"Don't worry," Olive said to the wide-eyed Rawhide Cooper as Madam Josephine stepped away, "we won't kill you right away, Cooper. Just know that you won't be leaving this establishment alive."

Madam Josephine hurried down the stairs toward the entrance. "Wait a moment, Lu—" she trailed off as she opened it to see the grinning face of Preacher McGowan. He nodded toward her, taking a step forward, but she barred the door.

"Ah, I thought I'd check on you soiled doves before leaving town. How's Cooper doing? We planned on riding together."

"He…" Madam Josephine licked her lips. "He's taken several grievous wounds."

Preacher McGowan blinked. "So what do you think? Should I check on him?"

"Oh, Preacher…" Madam Josephine smiled, batting her eyes at him. "I think we both know why you're here. You can drop the pretense."

He chuckled. "Ah, well… I suppose you're right. So do you have time for a quick—"

"You'd best get going before dark," Madam Josephine interrupted. "Bandits like you don't do so well on your own," she added, shutting the door in his face and bolting it for good measure.

***

Marshal Davenport's gun sparked fire, glinting in the light as he nailed the target from forty yards out. Keeping a steady count, the Marshal smoothly ejected the cylinder and slid in six bullets, barely pausing to glance to his side. Jimmy was fanning his revolver, pressing back on the hammer even as he squeezed shot after shot out. It seemed absurd to fire at such a high speed while also hitting targets but somehow Jimmy managed it. Glass shattered in the distance to the wild acclaim of the outlaws gathered nearby.

The lawman felt a bead of sweat trickle down his neck as he snapped his revolver back up and squinted down the sights in the fading light. He squeezed the trigger, feeling his worn finger give out that same familiar twinge of pain. Even the shattering of a glass bottle at fifty yards out and a wave of applause wasn't enough to relieve him.

This Jimmy Wolfe is good, damn good...

Marshal Davenport bit his lips, not letting his thoughts slow him down as he moved on to the next target.

And this truce is not going to last forever.

Chapter 30:
One Chance

"You must be about my age, Marshal," Preacher McGowan said the next morning, smacking his lips contentedly as he forced more chewing tobacco into his mouth. Marshal Davenport tried to ignore the man with about as much success as he'd been having over the last hour. It wasn't much. "You ever think about hanging up your spurs? Being a lawman seems like a young man's game."

"Trying to talk me out of hunting you down, Preacher?" Marshal Davenport replied. "You might as well try to talk the sun out of rising. Besides, most criminals are half your age. Or younger. Shouldn't you know better than to continue a life of villainy and perdition?"

"Don't speak to me of that," Preacher McGowan replied, looking almost offended. "Look, taking a few things here or there is no great sin. We are all of us imperfect beings, Marshal, but at least I have the decency to spread the word of the Lord. I like to think that more than evens my own sins out, Marshal, and I pray each day that the Lord above takes mercy on me and welcomes me in once it's my time."

"I bet you like to think that," Marshal Davenport grumbled. He looked away, spotting Eugene Cook delicately adjusting the Gatling gun. They'd dug it in partly into the ground and placed logs below it to allow the repeating gun to swivel much further upward than seemed natural. Still, it was a silly thing to look at, seeing a Gatling gun pointed up into the sky.

I suppose this will be the only time something like this exists, Davenport mused, striding over to where Eugene Cook was squinting down the sights. *It ain't like we'll ever be in a fight with dragons again; not unless there are a good deal more hiding around the world.*

"How's it handle?" Davenport prompted.

"Like a dream. From side to side, anyway," Eugene said, still closing one eye as he looked down the sights. "If we have to adjust it up and down, well, that's another issue. Think you and the Preacher can help me when it comes time?"

"Help you?" Marshal Davenport mused for a moment. "You saw my marksmanship last night, didn't you? Chances are we'll only get one shot at this. Let me handle this contraption, sonny."

"Well... alright," Eugene allowed. "You sure you can see a dragon from that distance, though?"

"You can be my spotter," Marshal Davenport said, wedging himself into position behind the Gatling gun. "Anyway, we might be waiting a while. Hmm... let's see, what time is it..."

***

"High noon," Jimmy commented.

Jake Mullens shifted uncomfortably. It had been the first thing the bandit leader had said to him for the better part of an hour. Jimmy sat astride his horse as he perpetually scoured the skies and distant horizon. Beside him, Henry craned his long neck over. The three of them stood there alone in the mountain valley, clearly visible. The Dragoon Mountains overlooked them, and Jake knew that they'd be bristling with deputies and the Outlaw Union, all lying low. The ambush was set; the bait was ready.

Jake squinted up, shielding his eyes with his wide-brimmed hat. A black spot emerged in the distance. For a moment it looked like a flight of geese. Then it grew larger and larger. Henry made a strange grunting noise as his wings spread partway out, only to settle back in place behind him.

"Easy, boy," Jake whispered.

"Right on time," Jimmy muttered.

Together they watched as the dot grew and grew, until the large outspread wings were recognizable. It was still some distance away when a few differences became apparent. Even this far from the valley Jake could see that it was brown. Before he could comment on it, however, the massive dragon swooped down for a sudden, graceful landing. Its talons clutched the ground as it came to an immediate stop.

Seated atop the brown dragon was a man Jake didn't recognize. He didn't wear the bowler hat that Sun Wong favored. In fact, he wore an elegant silk robe, and sat atop an ornate custom-designed saddle. The brown dragon tilted its head toward Henry, letting out a low rumble as smoke drifted out from its nostrils.

"Feilong," the stranger said with a smile, looking over at Henry. "My cousin will be pleased to see that you are cooperative," he continued in accented English. "My name is Jun Zhao. Release Feilong and your lives will be spared."

"Hold on," Jimmy cut in. "I thought we'd be talking to a Mr. Sun Wong. Where is he?" Jimmy asked, glaring at the sky above. "He was riding a green dragon, wasn't he? Who's this brown one?"

"Ah, this is Bailong," Jun Zhao said, still grinning avidly at Henry. "Feilong's father."

Henry made another peculiar snuffling noise, his head weaving from side to side as the two dragons hesitantly sniffed at each other. "Easy there, Henry," Jake said, hopping over and clambering up into his saddle. Bailong's rumble turned more heated, and Henry rumbled back, the two twitching their wings upward as if squaring off to fight.

"Just let Feilong go," Jun Zhao said, with a touch of fear now.

"Wait just a minute now, where's our reward?" Jimmy asked, glancing back at Jake. "Seven thousand gold dollars, wasn't it?"

Jun Zhao sputtered. "My cousin made no such arrangement."

Jake nodded silently in agreement. He'd talked it over with Jimmy Wolfe and decided on the use of numbers as signals when it came down to bargaining with Sun Wong—and seven meant the battle was on. The man had decided not to show, and they hadn't anticipated this turn of events... but, in the end, the plan would just have to go on.

This was never going to end peacefully.

All at once they sprang into action. Even as Jun Zhao was making another demand, Jimmy drew Delilah in a smooth, lightning-fast motion. He squeezed the trigger and shot Jun Zhao straight through the man's left eye. At the same time, Jimmy spurred his horse away, galloping along the line of discreetly placed empty glass bottles that marked a safe route out of the minefield.

Bailong roared in surprise as Henry flapped his powerful wings up high, quickly ascending. Jake grabbed his wide-brimmed hat tightly as the gusts of wind threatened to blow it off. The younger dragon was lighter and faster, and he was soon soaring up into the air.

"Now, Billy, now!" Jimmy roared.

At his signal, Billy Wolfe plunged the lever attached to the long fuse weaving through the bushes. The mountain valley rocked with the sounds of detonating explosives. Jake shouted and hollered as loud as he could, his ears ringing as the explosions slowly fell away. Henry had been buffeted from below, but the dragon quickly recovered.

Bailong had not been as lucky.

The great dragon had been caught in the explosion, and even its thick scales hadn't been enough to fend off the blasting powder. Bailong lay collapsed on the field, shattered and torn, with clods of dirt and grass falling like rain all around.

"Are you alright, Henry?" Jake asked, clapping a hand to his ringing ear. The dragon made no response. Jake gritted his teeth, not knowing quite what to say. He simply patted the side of Henry's neck.

With a rumble, Bailong twitched on the ground. Jake watched with a mixture of concern and compassion as Henry flew in a low circle around the older dragon. Bailong pulled himself partway up from the cavity that had been bored into the ground and adjusted its wings. The dragon didn't seem to be in any particular urge to fight. Jake gritted his teeth.

"We can deal with him later... but it looks like it all worked out. Just take us to the edge of the mountain there," Jake said, pointing forward.

Below them, Jimmy's horse was still a dark blur as it galloped away. The kegs of black powder they'd spent hours installing had been expended in a single shot. Just how they'd take down Sun Wong and his dragon was unclear.

But perhaps he's not even here. Maybe we have time to plan another trap.

Standing beside the plunger was Billy Wolfe, grinning up at them. To his surprise, Jake smiled back at the bandit as he passed overhead. Sam Reeves grabbed Billy in a full embrace, hooting and hollering enthusiastically. Stagecoach Mary and Herbert emerged from the trees nearby with wide smiles as they came into the open. The odd bunch began clapping and laughing loudly in their victory. In the center, Billy paused, shading his eyes as he looked up at Henry, who was making a tight turn to descend.

"Dragon!" Billy called out in shock. Sam laughed and clapped him on the back.

"That's j-just H-H-Henry."

Jake stared at the ground, looking for an open spot to land, but felt his blood rushing cold. He glanced upward to see a dark blur partly blocking out the sun. Then he made it out—a full grown dragon streaming downward, talons extended. The great beast slammed into Henry in a sudden rush, almost knocking Jake out of his saddle, and Henry roared in a mixture of pain and surprise as the two dragons hurtled downward. The last thing Jake saw was the ground approaching much too fast—and then his vision went black.

***

"It's too far," Eugene hissed.

"Shush," Marshal Davenport muttered, adjusting the Gatling gun. The arrival of the third dragon had taken them all by surprise, and the creature's steep dive had been too much for Davenport to risk a shot. Now the full-grown dragon spread its wings wide as it clutched onto Henry. Davenport let out a low breath and held it, noting the gentle breeze and pulling the barrel up a hair. A dull, rumbling noise echoed in the distance, sounding like hundreds of hooves. But Davenport put it all out of his mind.

He cranked the Gatling gun, stopping abruptly, sending a handful of bullets streaming outward into the distance. Pausing, Davenport watched as three sailed just overhead, a few slapping into the left wing of the dragon. It twitched around in shock. A shotgun blast echoed out from below, along with a few rifle and pistol shots as the dragon abruptly swung its massive wings down. It soared into the air just as Davenport's bullets streamed past, barely missing. The dragon twisted in the air, sending a burst of flames into the trees where Stagecoach Mary and Herbert had been stationed alongside Sam Reeves and Billy Wolfe.

From this distance, Davenport couldn't make them out. Henry lay smashed on the ground in the mountain valley below, where the rumble of hooves was now crystal clear.

"The Chowilawu Indians," Davenport mused in wonder as Sun Wong and the dragon sailed into the sky. "I hoped they might show up in time…"

"Praise the Lord!" Preacher McGowan cackled, but fell silent as the dragon circled around, now clearly heading to their position. Marshal Davenport gritted his teeth even as he aimed the Gatling gun once again, leading the target as he went.

"Well, here's my one chance," Davenport murmured quietly, then began rapidly cranking the Gatling gun. Bullets streamed out and upward. They were low at first, but Davenport quickly adjusted, and several slammed into the center of the approaching dragon. The dragon slowed, agony seeming to ripple through it, but the amulet on the distant figure of its rider glowed red. Spurred on by Sun Wong's commands, Xingteng flapped its wings again and again, picking up speed on a charge that circled around, dodging and weaving as it tried to evade Davenport's steady fire. More and more rounds slammed into the center of the dragon, or tore shreds in its wings, but still the dragon approached.

Brass cartridges fell to his side as Davenport cranked the Gatling gun, again and again, staring down the sights into the growing orange flames in

325

Xingteng's upraised mouth. He gritted his teeth, tasting coppery blood, staring unblinking as he cranked away.

"Save yourself, lads," Davenport grated out. "Guess you're getting away after all, Jimmy W—"

A rush of flames soared outward from the dragon as it swooped down, engulfing the Gatling gun and those around it in fire.

Chapter 31:

The Three Dragons

Jake groaned in agony, blinking rapidly and touching his head. He had a throbbing headache and when he pulled his hand away it was daubed with blood. Dimly, he felt his left leg in absolute agony, and heard distant whooping and galloping.

"Henry," Jake gasped out, and the dragon rumbled as he pulled himself up, freeing Jake's trapped leg. The young dragon seemed as dazed and confused as Jake had been. "They got us," Jake admitted, trying to drag himself free. He screamed in pain as he tried to clamber onto his feet. "Broken," he whispered, clenching and unclenching his fists. "Leg's... broken."

Jake stared outward, only now seeing the distant spray of Gatling gun bullets. He hauled himself partway up, blinking as he saw Xingteng diving toward the forested mountain slope where they'd concealed the Gatlin gun, seeing the great beast getting pelted with bullets. "No," Jake whispered, as the dragon launched a great gout of flames that set the whole mountainside on fire. The Gatling gun fell silent now, then suddenly exploded as the unspent rounds cooked off. But Xingteng was wobbly in the air, twisting from side to wide, and nearly slammed into a tall pine tree as the dragon approached them once more.

"I'm sorry, Henry!" Jake called out, squeezing his eyes shut with pain. "I tried to do right for ya. I tried to protect ya. But my leg's broke, and I can't—" he fell silent as Henry leaned in, licking the side of Jake's face. Henry rumbled, turning to shield Jake from the approaching dragon and rider.

Xingteng fell as much as landed, coming to a shuddering halt some paces away from the wounded Henry and Jake. Sun Wong was glaring atop it, one hand clutched to his ear, where a lucky shot from the Gatling gun had ripped half of it away. He pulled his bloody hand away and glared at it. "Ai yah!" he grumbled, smearing the blood on his trouser leg. "Why do you have to make this difficult? You steal my dragon and kill my cousin…" Sun Wong grimaced.

Xingteng rumbled as her snout smoldered. Jake realized that the dragon's eyes glowed an unnatural red, just like Bailong's had. The amulet on Sun Wong's chest glowed the same, growing brighter as he clasped it with his bloody hand. Then Henry rushed forward, blasting out a wave of hot fire that engulfed the bigger dragon. Then it stopped at once, Henry yelping in pain and fright as Xingteng viciously bit Henry in the neck. The fire dissipated at once, turning to smoke. As it cleared, Jake could just make out the glaring Sun Wong, waving away smoke with his tattered bowler hat. He let out a string of Cantonese curses as he swatted out a few smoldering fires on his clothing and saddle with his ruined hat before tossing it aside.

Henry let out a low, mewling sound of pain, and Jake tried to shamble to his feet. "Stop hurting Henry!" he cried out. "He's your child!"

Xingteng faltered, pulling her fangs out of Henry's neck. The brilliant red in her eyes faded into a duller color as Xingteng made a peculiar, strained sound.

"No!" Sun Wong shrieked, tightly squeezing his amulet with his bloodied hand. "I command you, Xingteng. And you, Feilong!" Henry stiffened, even as blood trailed down his long neck. "I want you to kill for me," Sun Wong said.

At once, Xingteng took to the sky. Henry half-turned his head to reveal a glowing red eye.

"No," Jake murmured, squeezing his broken leg. "Henry... Henry!"

The dragon flapped his wings, then rose upward into the skies after his mother. Dimly, Jake became aware of the chaos in the distance as Sun Wong's wounded dragon flew low to the ground, wobbling precariously. The Chowilawu Indians were charging through the valley now, whooping as they loosed arrow after arrow upward, a few firing rifles and pistols as they rode. But a blast from Xingteng burned scores of riders in seconds flat—and then Henry followed his mother's example. Jake gritted his teeth, pulling himself atop a boulder, and watched in shock at the horror that followed.

Shrieking outlaws, deputies, and Chowilawu Indians were writhing on the ground and smoldering while the two dragons passed by overhead. Already Henry sprouted a few fresh arrows and thrown lances, his wings torn in parts by gunfire.

"No, no, Henry, no," Jake mumbled, blinking away his tears. The Swann Brothers had shot upward from behind a boulder, firing rapidly as Henry went past, but now nothing was left besides a couple charred corpses and a scorched black boulder.

"Can you command your dragon?"

Jake turned at the words. Riding hard for him, then pulling his reins up short, was Jimmy Wolfe. Behind him the landscape was hellish, a mix of gray and orange, already turning the sunny day in the Dragoon Mountains into a vision of damnation. Yet if it bothered him, Jimmy made no visible reaction, sitting tall in his saddle like a horseman of the Apocalypse. He raised an eyebrow.

"Well? If you can ride Henry then we still have a chance."

"Leg's broke."

"He's still your dragon," Jimmy insisted. "We can work with that. Ah... they're coming around now."

"Not my dragon anymore," Jake mumbled through the pain as Xingteng and Henry streamed toward him. The dragons slammed into the ground, and this time Sun Wong was laughing, looking scorched and bloodied but victorious. "He used that amulet on him, and... oh it hurts," Jake said, wincing.

Jimmy made no comment, though he spurred his horse forward, moving to shield Jake.

"Feilong, kill Jake Mullens," Sun Wong called out, then fixed a hard stare on Jimmy Wolfe as Henry's mouth widened, flames growing within. "And just who are you?"

"The man who killed your cousin," Jimmy said, drawing his twin revolvers. Sun Wong reacted at once, ducking down below Xingteng's head, his amulet rising high in the air. Two shots shattered the amulet just as a wave of flames smashed into Jimmy. The horse whinnied, trying to dart away, but it burned to ash along with the bandit even as Jake held his breath and kept low to the ground. He twisted around, batting away the fires spreading around him, trying not to look at the smoldering remnants of the bandit who'd taken the brunt of Henry's flames.

"A priceless heirloom," Sun Wong muttered, just as a shotgun blast tore through the air above him, a couple pellets slamming into the side of his face. He collapsed in an undignified heap beside Xingteng as several figures approached. Gerald Swann, his false eye gleaming orange from the fires around him, and his clothes bloodied and burned almost to shreds. Stagecoach Mary and Henry, limping over to join him, just as Billy and Al Crosby came near.

Galloping hard, a dozen Chowilawu Indians encircled the area, along with Deputy Milton, Ned and Shirley, and a few survivors of the Deadly Six. Powaw Tom approached, a revolver in one hand and a hatchet in the other, with a severely burned Eugene Cook wavering on his feet, limping his way over.

But Sun Wong ignored them all as he crawled along the ground. "Bailong," he called out, smiling in agony as the heavily wounded brown dragon hauled itself up and staggered near. "Help me… kill them… all…"

"Henry," Jake grated out as the dragons all sniffed each other, this time in frank curiosity rather than hostility. "They're your family…"

Henry made a snort, as if to express that it was obvious, then mewled in a mixture of sadness and joy as he spread his wings wide. All at once, the dragons wrapped their wings alongside each other, rumbling together as one. In the very center, Sun Wong stopped crawling, twisting over to stare upward at the dragons.

"Obey me," he whispered. "Together you will win me my thro—"

In one synchronized burst, the dragons immolated Sun Wong, sending a few of the cautious survivors stumbling back.

"Jake Mullens," Chief Sipatu said, breaking the silence as he urged his pony forward. He sat proudly on his mount at the head of the Chowilawu Indian contingent beside the stern-faced Atohi. "The sky lizards seem calmer now. Is it done?"

Jake licked his lips, adjusting himself and taking a deep breath. "Jimmy Wolfe destroyed the amulet that was controlling them," he declared, for the benefit of all those gathering near. "He gave his life so that the dragons would finally be free. Yes, Chief, it's over... I thank you for coming."

"Many of my braves lost their lives this day," Chief Sipatu said mournfully, as the dragons continued rumbling to each other. "I hope it was worth it. I must see to my wounded," he announced, slapping Atohi on the back and wheeling away.

"Henry," Atohi said, staying in place while the others left. "Several of those arrows in your chest are from me. I didn't want to, but—"

At once, Henry twisted his neck around. A few of those nearby bristled as Henry moved near—and licked Atohi's neck, letting out a low, compassionate rumble.

"I know," Atohi said with a sigh, patting the dragon's cheek. "It's been a tragic day. But at least you are now free, my friend, and with your family."

"We've lost so many," Stagecoach Mary broke in, half in disbelief.

"My brothers," Gerald muttered, tears streaming down his right cheek.

"Where was Billy?" Al Crosby asked Mary and Henry. "And Sam? They was with you, weren't they?"

"Billy said we needed to get free; that he and Sam would cover us. I didn't... I don't know what..."

"Sam got it in the back," Billy grunted, emerging from the nearby woods. A stained bandage covered half his face, which was flushed red. "Couldn't save him. And my brother..." he sighed heavily as he approached the fallen Jimmy Wolfe. "That's him, ain't it?"

"Saved my life," Jake croaked.

"That's something, anyway." Billy gritted his teeth. "I don't see the Marshal here."

"Burned," Eugene said, pausing to cough. "He and Preacher. Stayed there cranking the Gatling gun to the very end. Told me to run for it."

Deputy Milton let out a long sigh. "Never did see as devoted a lawman as Marshal Davenport," he admitted. Before he could say anything else, the dragons turned as one, spreading their wings upward. The survivors backed away, giving them a respectful space.

"Henry, you're leaving?" Jake licked his lips, feeling a catch in his throat. "I... I thought... well." He cleared his throat. "It's been a pleasure knowing you, Henry, but I reckon maybe that's for the best. You're welcome back any time."

Henry let out a soft, strained sound as Bailong flapped into the air. Henry's father strained upward, his wounds clearly taking a toll, but eventually began gaining elevation. Xingteng licked Henry's neck wounds, then beat her wings, sending gusts of wind in all directions. The big dragon soared upward, quickly approaching Bailong and forming a close formation as they circled over the mountain valley.

For a long time Henry stood there, motionless, braced and ready to fly. Then his wings unfurled. The dragon turned, ducking his head down at Jake, and licked the young man's neck until Jake couldn't help but laugh. He grinned through the tears, grabbing Henry's cheeks.

"Alright, buddy, have it your way. But there are two things you need to promise me." Henry stared at him, unblinking, as Jake rubbed his hand along the smooth, scaly surface of Henry's snout. "One: you need to lay low and keep your belly through the brush. I won't keep you in a barn or nothing, and you can fly around in the desert, but I don't want nobody seeing you. I couldn't bear something like this happening again." Henry's head ducked down in agreement. "And two..." Jake licked his lips. "Should she do me the honor… and I reckon she will…" Jake grinned. "Never mind that you're a dragon. I want you to be the best man at my wedding."

Henry nodded, pushing his snout into Jake's face and snuffling in excitement.

Epilogue:

Rattlefort, AZ
Summer 1865

"You know you have my congratulations, Sheriff, but it wouldn't be proper for a man like me to attend," Billy explained, tipping a hand to his white hat. He turned his head, revealing the reddened welt that had still failed to heal even after all this time. Jake suspected it would be a reminder of the fight down in the Dragoon Mountains to the very end of Billy Wolfe's days.

"I'm no Sheriff," Jake protested, "and there's already been a lot of changes this year. Lincoln dead, the Civil War over…" he shook his head as if in disbelief. "It's a time of forgiveness and reconciliation. I said as much to Marshal Milton when he asked me to stay in the posse."

"Yuma's new Marshal still wants to see us hang, eh?" Billy Wolfe replied. "Well, that's why I say you'll be appointed Rattlefort's Sheriff soon enough. You have friends in high places, Jake Mullens. And low ones, if you include myself."

"I'll count you as a friend. Gladly."

Jake watched as the remnants of the Wolfe Gang passed on by, murmuring their congratulations. Al Crosby sitting proud on a black stallion, Ned and Shirley riding along together in a wagon, and the burned Eugene Cook trailing on his own palomino. Bound for parts unknown—as Jake had thought it best not to press the issue.

Maybe I really will run for Sheriff, Jake mused as another band of outlaws approached. *I don't know that I could go back to farming, and my grandfather was the last lawman in town aside from that Secessionist scoundrel who left us, after all.*

Powaw Tom nodded as he rode past. "Thought to extend my congratulations," he said, his words curt and simple. "We were on opposite sides for a time, but we fought together in the end. Besides, there's nothing quite like love," he added, with a distant look in his eyes. The gunslinger nodded and rode on past. Three others followed him: the survivors of the gang formerly known as the Deadly Six. One of them, a man with a pince-nez, offered Jake an elegant bow even as they rode past.

"Are you ready, son?"

Jake turned to see his father Lawrence approached, looking a bit haggard. Decorations were set out all along the farmstead, and the pleasant sounds of violin music echoed out from their house. A spitted pig was slowly roasting away and providing a mouthwatering aroma as conversation and laughter emanated from the invited guests. Lawrence frowned at the riders galloping out of town.

"Those fellas look like trouble."

"Well, trouble's leaving me with wishes for a better future," Jake pointed out. "Is everyone ready?"

"Just waiting on you," Lawrence said, turning around. "Play on!"

The music continued with gusto as the former owner of the Silver Springs Saloon passed out celebratory champagne to the guests. The preacher they'd hired from Yuma was already smiling benevolently as Jake and Lawrence stood up straight.

"Come along then," the preacher said, turning to the side. "All of you."

Jake's heart pounded as he finally saw Lucille emerge in a shimmering white gown. She was a vision of beauty, with her mother looking elegant and refined right beside her. It was hard for Jake to even remember the words as the ceremony continued. He did, however, glance to the barn where he'd carved out a hole. Henry's shadowed face gazed at him with a toothy smile.

"You may kiss the bride," the preacher concluded. Jake pulled Lucille close and pressed his mouth firmly against hers as the audience burst into applause. They stayed together for a long moment, longer than perhaps was necessary, but with half the guests being prostitutes Jake figured there'd be some allowances. He thought he heard a distant, appreciative rumble from the barn.

Then the violin music continued as the assembled guests broke out into dancing and tucked into their meals. Even the stern-looking Gerald Swann smiled, raising a cup in delight. He'd gotten permission to attend from Marshal Milton, who'd extended his own compliments and apologies for his absence. With the Outlaw Union all but dissolved, the remaining posse members had been forced to round up bands of Confederate deserters drifting into the Arizona Territory.

Jake approached the barn, ostentatiously chewing on a big hunk of pork meat, then "accidentally" dropped it inside. "Glad you could be here, buddy," he murmured as Henry rumbled excitedly from within. He turned, to see Lucille blushing as Olive was whispering into her ear.

"Trust me on this," Olive said with a grin, winking at Jake as he approached.

"What was that all about?"

"You'll thank me for it later."

Jake raised his eyebrows. Lucille shrugged, her blush fading away, and pointed over his shoulder. "Oh... more guests?"

"A good afternoon to you, Jake Mullens!"

Jake looked over in surprise at the boisterous words. Stagecoach Mary approached, her shotgun slung over her back, and accepted a glass of champagne even as she gestured to a slender Chinese woman beside her.

"Had to ride hell for leather to get here in my stagecoach, but someone's here to see you. Oh, you know I would have accepted the invitation, but Marshal Milton has us combing the desert and delivering justice to all sorts of bandits and ex-Confederates. I've never seen Herbert so happy in all his life."

"Pleasure to have you," Jake replied. "Sit and stay a while. But..." he blinked at the new arrival. "Do I know you?"

"My name is Lifun Chen," she said in perfect English. "I worked for Mr. Sun Wong in San Francisco."

Jake felt a chill in his bones. "Ah... that was..."

"Sorry, to be clear, I do not mourn his passing. He was a carnival barker with insane dreams of ruling a country. But with his circus gone, there's no need for this any longer, and I cannot bear the responsibility..." she hesitated, holding a trunk between her arms. "I think it's best that you have it. Consider it a wedding gift."

Jake licked his lips. He placed a hand on the trunk, his heart beating heavily. Then he pulled the top open and stared in surprise.

A single golden dragon egg lay within.

Made in United States
Orlando, FL
17 March 2023